ase
)wn

/w.l

ﬧnev
·xtpﬃ
)eec

ﬧ2

Without his will, his hand cupped Thessa's cheek, pulling her to face him.

'I am baiting the trap,' he said, and knew the words were merely appeasement for what he was going to do.

The feel of her cheek against his palm took him from being a captain to being a man looking into the eyes of his beloved. Every time he gazed into her face he saw something that made him forget how a man was supposed to act and start thinking of those treacle-laden words that made a woman smile.

Touching her, he realised he'd completely erred in thinking Thessa had any resemblance to the stone statue. She was far more appealing.

She watched him just as intently as he looked at her.

His lips closed over hers, tasting, letting her femininity caress every part of him. The kiss fired up his spirit. Erased the memory of what she'd forgotten to tell him. The touch of her lips cloaked him in armour and told him such beautiful things.

AUTHOR NOTE

Captain Benjamin Forrester first appeared in my novel SAFE IN THE EARL'S ARMS, and almost instantly I knew I wanted to tell his story. I saw him as a man without a care in the world except for a love of the sea and a deep fascination with mermaid lore. For months I looked forward to writing the first scene in this book.

But Captain Forrester's personal story didn't unfold in the way I expected.

During my research I read about some of the hardships a Regency sea captain would have experienced. Voyagers could take several years before returning to their home port, and every day at sea was much the same—except for when something happened to make things worse. If tempers flared no one could immediately leave or be let go.

To live in such conditions, and to be able to return to them, would take a very strong man—particularly if he had a privileged life that would have welcomed him back.

The day after I'd finished the story of this captain I missed writing about him—much in the same way you'd miss a good friend who'd moved out of your life.

I hope you see Benjamin Forrester the same way I do.

A CAPTAIN
AND A ROGUE

Liz Tyner

First published in Great Britain 2014
by Mills & Boon, an imprint of Harlequin (UK) Limited,
Large Print edition 2015
Harlequin (UK) Limited, Eton House, 18-24 Paradise Road,
Richmond, Surrey TW9 1SR

© 2014 Elizabeth Tyner

ISBN: 978-0-263-25541-6

Harlequin (UK) Limited's policy is to use papers that are natural, renewable and recyclable products and made from wood grown in sustainable forests. The logging and manufacturing processes conform to the legal environmental regulations of the country of origin.

Printed and bound in Great Britain
by CPI Antony Rowe, Chippenham, Wiltshire

Liz Tyner began creating her own stories even before she decided on the lofty goal of reading every fiction book in her high school library. When the school gave her a career assessment they came up blank—they double-checked and still came up blank. Liz took it in her stride, because she knew that on the questionnaire she'd ticked an interest in everything but scuba diving. *She* believed the assessment proved she was perfect for becoming a novelist.

Now she and her husband live on a small acreage, where she enjoys strolling her walking trails and wishes the animals she shares the trails with wouldn't visit her garden and fruit trees. She imagines the wooded areas as similar to the ones in the children's book *Where the Wild Things Are*. Her lifestyle is a blend of old and new, and in some ways comparable to how people lived long ago.

Liz is a member of various writing groups, and has worn down the edges of a few keys on her keyboard while working on manuscripts—none of which feature scuba divers.

A CAPTAIN AND A ROGUE
features characters you will have met
in Liz Tyner's debut novel
for Mills & Boon® Historical Romance
SAFE IN THE EARL'S ARMS

Look out for the final book in the trilogy!
Coming soon

DEDICATION

To my mother, who is making heaven
an even better place for the angels to be.

Chapter One

'Capt'n. There's yer mermaid.'

At his first mate's words, Benjamin's head snapped around and his eyes locked on the form slicing through the Aegean Sea.

Benjamin took two steps closer to the edge of the craggy rocks overlooking the water. The sea air took some of the rotted-egg smell of the island from his lungs and the shape reaching the shoreline took all thoughts from his head.

He reached to his side and took the spyglass from the hanging sheath, and peered. His movements must have caught her attention, because as soon as her head appeared in his eyepiece— she treaded water. Her eyes locked on his, capturing him.

Then she turned, long arms finishing the swim

quickly. Everything else in the world disappeared but the vision in his spyglass. His breath caught. He'd truly found a mermaid.

'Ah, she saw us,' Gidley grumbled. 'Now she'll go and turn into a reg'lar woman. Blast the luck. Once a mermaid sees a man, she sprouts legs. Happens every time.'

The woman stepped on to the sand. Benjamin grunted in disappointment, realising he'd been lost in a fantasy.

He tipped the end of the glass downward to ascertain she did have legs. She wore a chemise, but the thin, wet garment viewed through a strong imagination left little covered. He braced himself, keeping his knees from giving way, while he leaned forward, trapped in his thoughts.

Gidley nudged Benjamin. 'Lend me that glass, Capt'n. Want to see if she be sportin' a tail.'

Ben pulled air into his lungs, giving himself time to relearn to speak. 'No,' he said. And then he murmured. 'No fins.' *Breasts, yes.*

'Bet she's the one we're looking for,' Gidley said.

'I hope so,' Benjamin spoke softly. 'She's…'

'Mermaid like or reg'lar woman like?'

Benjamin paused. He'd not really studied her face. He raised the view of the glass, taking in the sculpted lines of her jaw and moving up to the graceful cheekbones. 'I would say—better than either.'

Then he saw her pulling clothing on and he lowered the spyglass. He turned and slapped Gidley on the arm. 'Turn your back. We're gentlemen.'

Gidley grimaced, shuffling around until he faced the opposite direction. 'Speak for yourself. I be an able-bodied seaman. And that's a mermaid. Had to look and so did yer. Would be wrong not to appreciate, like spittin' out good ale. Don't let her get close enough to spit at yer, though. They've venom in their mouths.'

Benjamin shook his head. 'She's not a mermaid. She's a woman. And if she's Melina's sister, then she's not someone to dally with.'

'Then I need to find the little treasure that I left behind last time. Bouboulina or Alenakous or something like that. Would 'uv remembered if I'd known we was returning. I brought more coin this time—so I'm expectin' true love.' He dropped the canvas bag of gifts they'd brought to give Melina's sisters. Gidley tugged up his trouser waistband, puffed out his chest and straightened the rag of a cap that stuck to his head even in the roughest squalls.

The island breeze blew across them and Benjamin waited on the woman to scramble upwards through the rocks.

'This ol' island's not a bad place, if yer don't mind breathing in the whiffs of an old volcano demon's breath.' Gidley peered around the area. 'But we need us a real voyage under our legs—not bouncin' around to make yer brother happy. Just seems wasteful.'

'Not if I make good on the deal,' Benjamin muttered half to himself. He wanted to leave as badly as Gidley. Sailing was his life—not running errands for his brother, the earl, who just happened to share ownership in *Ascalon* with Benjamin.

But the earl had made a solemn promise. If Benjamin returned with Melina's treasure—some artefact that neither of the men truly gave a whistle about—Benjamin could own the *Ascalon* from port to stern.

Marriage. His brother was so besotted with his wife that he was willing to trade away half a ship just to make a woman happy.

'Yer snarlin'.' Gidley's words broke Benjamin's reverie, while the first mate scratched his head and made his hat wiggle. 'Thought seeing a real live mermaid would put a smile on yer face.'

'I'm thinking of my brother losing his mind.'

'Some women are worth losing a mind for. Just never seen one myself, 'cept that mermaid climbin' this way.'

'Don't be daft, Gid. She's just another island lightskirt.'

And at that moment, Benjamin heard her scrambling footsteps bounding up the rocks beside him, turned to her and lost his grip on the spyglass.

Even Gidley didn't comment on the glass dropping, tumbling to rocks far below them.

Ben saw the resemblance to his brother's wife—but this woman caught his eyes in a way no one ever had before. She might not be a mermaid, but Benjamin wouldn't rule out her being descended from Aphrodite.

* * *

Thessa pushed back the dripping tendril of hair she'd not managed to capture in her bun and let her eyes linger over the *agklikos* who'd had that looking piece trained on her.

She waited for him to speak. She'd heard his last words. He was English. Like her father, a man who believed lies would feed his family.

'I'm Benjamin, the captain of the *Ascalon*. I took your sister to England.' This from the one who had weak fingers and too-strong eyes.

So many questions pounded into her mind at once that she couldn't speak. She couldn't put the words into the English she'd learned at her father's knee. She couldn't ask what she wanted to know most—her sister's fate. If the ship had returned and her sister wasn't with them, then she must be dead. Thessa shoved the thoughts from her mind and stared at the man in front of her. He had taken Melina to her death.

He lifted the bag at his feet and moved towards her. She didn't take the offering. She knew not to accept anything from one of the sailors. Gifts were not without cost. And never would she take something from a man who'd caused hurt to Melina. She'd die first.

'Captain. Vessel. Melina. Away.' He spoke carefully, snaking his other hand up and down in a bobbing motion to indicate a ship sailing.

'We.' He touched his friend's arm and then his own chest. 'Are here.' He pointed to the ground. 'Searching.' She thought he mimicked digging. 'Melina sent…for treasure.' He touched the gold ring and she noticed both his smallest fingers had rings.

She shook her head. But he'd mentioned her sister. And he spoke as if she were still alive. The thoughts darkening her vision vanished. The world around her reappeared and she stared at the two men.

'Try French, Capt'n,' the straggly one said. ''Cause of all the French ships that dock here, whores has to learn it early.'

'Whores?' Thessa snapped out the word.

'See, Capt'n…' The silver haired one smiled so big she thought his face would burst. 'Just have to find the right words. Melina told me both her sisters can speak King's English better'n me. '

'I did not learn it by choice,' Thessa said. 'My father forced us.'

'I must be grateful,' the younger man said. 'To see a woman swimming and then to be able to speak with her is indeed a treat. Women in London do not prefer to swim.'

She searched his face. He didn't have the thrashed-around look she'd seen on many men. In truth, his eyes had the colour of sky and sea combined.

'It's true,' he added. 'A few of my men still cannot swim. The ones who have been with me longest, when we're in warm ports that are not well populated, I have commanded them to learn. But near people, the water carries away the waste. You'd not willingly immerse yourself.'

She looked the tall one over carefully. An officer's coat contrasted with the seaman's duck trousers, the legs tucked into scuffed knee boots. Wind whipped hair with strands of lightness, possibly put there by some spirit running her fingers through while he slept. Small whiskers at the sides, but trimmed, near his ears.

He did look pleasing to the eyes. Better than the usual men she saw.

His nose wasn't broken. He had teeth. Both ears. No scarring. A bit odd, that, but then he was from a country where the men rode horses instead of using their own legs, worked with ledgers and wore flounces around their necks. But this one left off his lace. Near the string tying the neck of his shirt closed she saw darkened skin, almost like a man from her own country.

Even though she couldn't fault the man his appearance, he needed to leave Melos. The men who docked on the island were refuse tossed out by their own countries. If they'd been worth anything, someone would have kept them at home.

'If yer mermaid had a tail when she was afloat, might 'uv been a bit sharp at the end—pointy like,' the older one said quietly, one brow twitching aslant.

'With such perfection of face and form, one can't be too upset that there's a flaw somewhere,' the captain answered. Then he gave her a smile which she was certain would help any woman overlook his heritage.

She realised her sister could be sitting in their home at that very moment. Just because she wasn't with the men didn't mean she hadn't returned with them. 'Did you bring Melina?' The words rushed from her lips and her eyes locked on him. She moved two steps towards the trail to the house before he answered.

'No,' the captain stated. 'She married my brother and we feared the trip for her as she could be adding to the nursery. Her first trip did not do her well, and since she is already having seasickness on dry ground, she couldn't manage another sail.'

'She's gonna drop a babe on the ground real soon. Doing herself proud,' the older one said. He looked too bland and spoke too sweetly. 'Knows a woman's place.'

'Nothos.' She bit out the word. They had let her sister stay behind—or forced her. Surely Melina had been forbidden passage if she did not return. And the child. That meant Melina had sold herself to a man. Her sister had sacrificed for family.

Gidley leaned his head to Benjamin and spoke from the side of his mouth. 'I don't think that was praisin' me on either one of my parents bein' wed. Maybe if we toss her into the sea she'll turn back into a mermaid and swim away.'

'But then we would lose this charming creature,' Benjamin said and tilted his head in acknowledgement.

Thessa looked at the man, then let her eyes move skyward to dismiss his flattery.

The captain's lips quirked up. 'It takes more than two sea ravaged men to impress a mermaid.'

She waved an arm, indicating the gnarled olive trees and scrubby grasses behind her, and then pointed to the cragged rocks rising majestically from the edge of the perfect sea and the water itself. 'I live with this every day. I am not easily impressed.'

'I wouldn't prefer a woman who was,' the captain said, and in that moment, he looked away from her.

But just before his head turned, something sparked behind his eyes, watching her in such a way her breath caught and warmth tickled in her body. She took half a step back and squared her shoulders.

'What do you want?' Thessa asked.

'Melina said you could show us to the artefacts. The stones.'

She raised her brows. 'Artefacts. For an English-man? The island is covered with rocks. Take your pick. They are all valuable to me.'

They were, but only as places to put her feet. She was more concerned for her *stomachi*. The rocks couldn't save her now.

Marriage to Stephanos would not be so bad. She would have the home he was building. She would have a friendship with his mother. She would have food to eat. And she would learn not to breathe the spoiled air when Stephanos stood near.

Chapter Two

Benjamin imagined his plans for ownership in the *Ascalon* sinking and he felt his resolve harden. His fingers tightened on the bag he'd brought. This woman had to help him. And Gid was right. She did have a pointy-tailed look on her face, more like Boadicea ready to eviscerate her enemy than any water creature. He liked her much better when she was in the sea.

'I'm sure all the rocks are quite precious at one's birthplace,' he said. 'But this particular rock has the likeness of a woman's face on it and Melina uncovered it near your home. She wasn't able to take it with her on her voyage to England and I've returned with funds to purchase it from the man who owns the land.'

Thessa gave a shrug. 'You did not let my sister

return. I will not help you.' She nodded towards the sea. 'And you should be on your way. Because I have no intention of giving the treasure to you. I do not know if Melina requested the rock or if you have locked her away somewhere. She could be a prisoner on your ship.'

Benjamin didn't say a word. This was why he liked his imagined mermaids. They never spoke. They never argued. And they were always gone when his dream ended.

'Didn't think of that, now, did ye, Capt'n?' Gidley's cheeks puffed with humour.

Her dark eyes challenged Benjamin. But even if she pointed a flintlock at his heart, he was not moving.

Without the stones Melina claimed to have found buried just below the land's surface, it would be a decade or more before he could hope to buy his brother's share of the ship. By then the *Ascalon*'s hull would be ravaged by sea worms.

And his sister-by-law desperately wanted the stones—claimed the face resembled her mother and believed, in some long-ago time, a member of her family had posed for it.

He didn't care who'd posed for the rocks—they

were stone. Colourless. Lifeless. Bland. But if collecting mouse whiskers from the island would get him his ship, he'd be hunting mice. He would take on the whole island if he had to in order to get his *Ascalon*.

He'd been told by Gidley many times that fortune had favoured Benjamin his looks and kicked Gid in the teeth. Benjamin had hardly passed his sixteenth year when Gid had suggested Ben give a tavern wench a most indelicate proposition and a smile, and see what happened. Ben had assured Gidley that no woman would accept such a brash offer. He delivered the words and was half in love by morning when Gid had thumped on the wench's door to awaken Ben. For the whole of the next voyage, Gid had ducked his eyes, shook his head and grumbled about the fates. Ben had grinned back at him each time.

Benjamin watched Thessa, then he smiled.

Her eyes narrowed and she took a step back.

Gidley's snigger did not hide well under the cough.

Ben changed tactics and then clasped Gidley's shoulder. 'My first mate is superstitious. And he believes, if he casts his eyes on this stone woman, our vessel will be protected from storms.'

She looked as if they'd just suggested she collect all the mice whiskers in the world.

'Wouldn't hurt,' Gid said. He patted the decades-old waistcoat he'd worn in anticipation of impressing the females on the island and lifted the hem and pulled a handkerchief from his waistband. The handkerchief probably hadn't started out as the colour of wet sand. 'Thought if I could wipe her face with this, I'd have a protection from all them evil spirits been chasin' us here.'

Gid waved the cloth with a flourish and Ben jerked his head back, dodging a not-so-innocent snap of the fabric. The rag smelled as if Gidley had been washing his feet with it although Ben knew that wasn't possible.

Ben turned to Gidley and glared, before softening his stance and appraising the woman again. She would not slow him down. He had a cargo waiting to be loaded in England and needed to leave Melos quickly. Though his ship was not one of the gilded East Indiamen, if returned to the docks in time, he'd been promised a voyage for the company. Two years he'd be at sea, but he'd wanted this since before his first sailing. To be a captain, and to sail for the East India Company—nothing meant more.

'Miss. Think of your sister. In her…' he paused '…family condition.' He blinked and put a look on his face he thought a vicar might use when comforting. 'Wanting a precious memory from her homeland, probably to show her own little one what their grandmother looked like—how can you keep that from her?'

'She left us and she didn't come back with you. If her *stomachi* was already fighting her, then it could have fought her at sea and she could have returned to us. Why did you not bring her to say these words herself?'

'My brother worried for her safety.'

The woman touched the sash at her waist. Her eyes narrowed. '*Fidi*. Snake. That is Englishmen.' Her eyes challenged him. 'You have kept my sister and refused to let her return home, and now you want the treasure.'

He kept his eyes on her hand, watching for the hilt of a knife. Disarming her didn't concern him, but it would be harder to convince a woman who'd just tried to slash his throat to show him to the stones.

The *Ascalon* was in his grasp. The voyage of a lifetime was waiting and the ship was still young enough to have at least two more good trips in her before the sea took her hull. She was made of good English oak, but even that didn't last long in the oceans.

Benjamin could not go back and admit failure to his eldest brother. He took in the sandy soil and the shallow-rooted trees. Surely he could find the rocks on his own. Surely. But he couldn't bring all the men from the ship. If anyone knew he must have the rock, he wouldn't be able to bargain. He needed a strategy and he did not want this woman to think him defeated.

He firmed his jaw and let his eyes linger on Thessa's face, but he spoke to Gidley. 'Melina said it was near her home. We'll start searching in the morning. I'll bring the crew and we'll look at every rock.'

Gidley nodded to Benjamin, the first mate's voice a scholarly tone. 'I'll find it if'n it's here. Have eyes like a ferret and I can sniff out treasure better'n any ten pirates.'

But they could find the stones a lot faster with the woman's help and Ben didn't have time to dig up the island, no matter how small it was.

He picked up the bag Gidley had dropped, aware of its weight, and put it on the ground in front of the woman. 'We did bring some things, and if you look closely I think you'll agree they're things a sister would select for another sister. Not anyone else. She couldn't send this if she'd been a captive. She'd want you to help us.'

Benjamin had no idea what kind of fripperies were inside the canvas, but Melina had had tears in her eyes when she'd asked him to give it to her sisters.

Thessa didn't move. He strode forward and put it gently at her feet. 'She sends her love.'

She bent, reached in, pulled out a parcel and unwrapped it, unveiling a thick woollen shawl. She retained her wariness and trapped the clothing and its wrapping under her arm.

Then she pulled out another parcel, but before she examined it, she looked into the bag and laughed. The sound of joy from her lips moved through him quicker than a dive into a warm freshwater pool and he had to wait to come up for air.

She dropped the canvas sides of the bag and reached inside. He expected some jewel or house folderol. Instead she pulled out a kettle and held it by its bail.

Looking at Benjamin, she said, 'My sister. She claimed we could never heat enough warm water because by the time we heated the pot again, the first was cold.'

Her face softened even more and she put the kettle down. She took the shawl under her arm and hugged it close, letting the soft wool touch her cheek.

He watched. A kettle and a shawl, and the woman sniffled.

Ben looked at Gid. Gid opened his eyes wide and shrugged, then showed a bit of his teeth and nodded to Benjamin. Ben refused to try the smile. Besides, it wouldn't work. The woman was too caught up in the wool, stroking it and rubbing it against her cheek.

His body's reaction irritated him. This was a business endeavour—nothing else. His brother was the one trapped by skirts—not him. He never neared a woman who truly tempted him. Never approached a woman who might net him. He was the sea creature. The water was his breath and the oceans his home.

'We've missed her so.' She kept her eyes on the fabric. 'I thought when she didn't come back, that a storm had taken her, or the sea. Or she'd been killed by the Englishmen.'

'Your sister wants those stones.' He heard the grit in his words.

Her eyes rose to his. And he saw the face of the nymph who'd risen from the sea. Her image outshone every painting he'd seen of mermaids, even the ones he'd commissioned to his specifications.

Her eyes rose to his. 'So she is well?'

Benjamin nodded. 'She married my eldest brother.'

She sighed. 'I cannot believe my sister would marry a man not of our own island.' Her lip trembled. 'She would sacrifice so much for us.'

Benjamin tilted his head to one side, turned his body slightly away, putting her from his vision while he collected his thoughts. 'He's an earl.' He glanced sideways, gauging her reaction to his words.

This time her shrug was almost invisible. 'I'm sure you think as much of him as I think of Melina.'

'I'd agree with the miss,' Gidley said, wobbling his head. 'Wouldn't want my sister to marry an Englishman neither.' He smiled at Benjamin. 'We be a foul lot.'

Benjamin glared.

Gidley grinned. 'I like bein' part of a foul lot myself. Saves on washin' and makin' pretty words with the widows.'

'The treasure?' Benjamin turned his words to Thessa.

'Malista.' She nodded while she folded the shawl carefully and put it atop the other things she'd not examined in the bag. Raising her eyes, she said, 'It's no treasure. Just broken carvings. When the man from the French museum came, he said we should look for such things. That people would buy shaped rock. Father was excited and had us hunt because he wanted to have a discovery. We found nothing at first. The Frenchman left and Father...left.'

'I've promised Melina I'd get the carving for her.' Benjamin watched Thessa's face. The change in her eyes and her voice when she mentioned her father leaving told him she had no more love for the man than her sister had. He couldn't blame them. He'd met the man.

She looked at the sky. 'This is not a good time for it. The light will be gone soon and the stones—my sister left them under the dirt. I'm not certain I know…where they are.'

Ben's breath caught. 'You don't…remember?'

She frowned. 'I remember… It's somewhere on Yorgos's land.' She squinted. 'And there are other rocks scattered about. Pieces of an arch. I didn't notice much. Melina was the one who was excited. I just did not wish to tell her no one wants broken rocks.'

Gidley kicked at the ground. 'Just my blasted luck. We sail a near lifetime to get some whittled rock on a stinkin' island smellin' of brimstone and the stones is broke and no one knows where the pieces is buried.'

'We'll dig up the whole island if we have to.' Ben wasn't letting the ship get away.

She looked at Benjamin. 'I would not do that if I wanted the stones and I wanted to live.'

Her lashes swooped down into a long blink. 'The island is small and, since the English ship took my sister, Stephanos has not been pleased. He had noticed my sister and to him all the women of the island are more his than anyone else's.' She shrugged. 'We thought it best to tell him she was taken against her will. He planned to go for her, but I told him…I told him I did not want him to leave for her. I told him he should think of me instead.' Her face turned in the direction of the sea. 'I thought I could give her time to return to us.'

'Then I need the stones before I have to fight someone. I'll dig tonight.' He had to get the rocks back on the ship. If the winds changed, they needed to take advantage of it. Waiting around for months in a harbour with an angry man on the island wanting to stir up trouble wouldn't be good for anyone.

'I'll carry the bag to your house.' Benjamin reached to take the gifts. 'It's heavier than it looks. And then Gid and I can start searching.

You know how much the sculpture means to your sister. Let me give it to her.'

She stepped from his reach and pulled the canvas close. 'My other sister is in the house. I'll tell her Melina is safe and be back.' She glanced at the trail they'd followed. 'When Stephanos discovers you are here, I might need to soothe him.'

He saw a shadow pass behind her eyes, something she wouldn't speak of. Then she turned away, scurrying up the path.

Even though her slippers looked to be no more durable than a few strips of leather, she moved as easily over the pebbles and stones as if she walked a hay meadow. He followed, unaware of where he put his own feet.

When she reached the steps which led up the side of her house, she put a foot on the lowest plank. He thought the whole house swayed with each movement and she had no railing to hold, but she made it to the top and darted inside, as nimble on land as she was in the sea.

'Close yer mouth, Capt'n. And be glad yer brother's not here to see you lookin' at his wife's sister that way.' Gidley swallowed a chuckle, shaking his head. 'The ship'd be needin' a new capt'n.'

'*Ascalon* needs a new first mate now.'

Gidley grumbled while he scratched under his arm. 'Yer wouldn't give me the spyglass to look at her and then yer dropped it when your fingers fell open like yer mouth. Ain't no way it survived a tumble down the rocks like that. Reminds me of the time we seen them lightskirts and I had to pay full cost and yer services was requested by the bawd. Yer could have bedded her and she promised yer afterwards yer could have one of the others at no cost.'

'She was jesting.'

Gidley snorted. 'She'd 'a been bumpin' yer head into the bed frame 'fore you finished sayin' yer agreement. And me standing there and she didn't even note my manly form.'

'You overwhelmed her. She took one look at you and saw your experience showing through—'

Gidley interrupted, waving a hand. 'Save yer perfume-y words for them that wears such. I know better'n believin' any yer treacle.' Then he paused and squinted at Ben. 'Well, in this case, yer might be right.' He puffed himself taller. 'Probably shows right from my eyes what I can do to make a woman beg for my attentions. Just takes once and they be talkin' about ol' Gidley for the rest of their lives…assumin' they survive the pleasure.' He turned to Ben. 'I ever tell yer about that woman who fainted dead away at the sight of my manhood?'

'Yes.'

'Well it won't hurt yer to hear it one more time…'

He let Gidley's words fade from his hearing. He watched the fading sky, wanting so much to step foot on *Ascalon* and know he finally owned all of her—not just part.

Gidley's talk penetrated Benjamin's thoughts when he heard the woman's name mentioned. 'Too bad that Thessa one sprouted legs.'

Benjamin thought of Thessa in the sea. He couldn't get the image of her stepping on to the sand out of his mind.

'Capt'n, I can see what thoughts is in yer eyes. A sailor doesn't need a woman to drag him down. 'Specially not for nothin' permanent. Married man goes to sea—he drowns. You know it as well as I. Weight of leavin' a family behind pulls him under.'

'Nonsense. But a man can't expect a woman to remember him when he's been gone two years.'

'Bet yer my braces it be bad luck to marry.' He looped his thumbs under the leather straps holding up his trousers. 'No. I don't bet yer my braces. They's my lucky ones. But I'm wantin' to keep yer around, Capt'n. So just yer remember—yer can look. Yer can touch. Yer can promise. But yer can't say no vows. Not even them short marriages a seaman can give a woman on an island he'll never see again and her only knowin' his first name and no other.'

'I don't want a woman. I want a ship. You know how I feel about *Ascalon*. Best ship I've ever sailed and better than gold. Even if that treasure's only broken rocks—Warrington promised me a ship for them. And I'm taking the stones to him—with a ribbon 'round them. He'll make good on the promise.'

'Fine talkin'. But a mermaid flash a little tail at you and you be forgettin'.' Gidley laughed at his own joke. 'Wouldn't mind staying on this rock pile, if I had me a mermaid. Long as I didn't get finned in my man parts. No. I'm thinkin' wrong. A mermaid would pull the life right out o' me.'

'There's no such thing as mermaids.' His mind flashed to Thessa stepping from the water.

Gidley snorted. 'I seen her and so did yer. She just sprouted legs. I know my history, Capt'n. On a moonlit night, don't get in no water with her— she'll turn back fish, drown yer and swallow yer just like yer a minnow.' He raised a brow. 'Yer has to promise me, Capt'n. No swimmin' in the moonlight with the woman. All we'd have left o' yer is yer boots. She may look tasty on the outside, but on the inside she's all scales, bones and slimy parts.'

'Don't be ridiculous.'

'Ain't a man alive now what's coupled with a mermaid in the water. On land they be fine, but get 'em in the sea and they's all bite.' His eyes narrowed. 'I bet that other sister sports whiskers longer'n my own.'

'She has big eyes and gills. Smells like bilge water. So get your mind off the women.'

'Yer seen her last time?'

Benjamin shook his head. 'Just seeing if you'd believe my fables as well as you do your own.

If you mention one more word of that superstitious muck you'll be tied to the mast, heels up,
singing hymns.'

Gidley stopped for a moment. He mused,
'Wonder if that one swimmin' has one of them
marks like her sister has.' He touched above his
breast. 'Kind of draws a man's eyes.'

Instantly, Benjamin's thoughts jerked back to
Thessa's body. The sight of her stepping on to
land. His imagination searched her skin, though
the shift hadn't allowed him to see close enough
for a birthmark. His brother had said all the sisters had a small skin discoloration of some sort.
The earl claimed it a longing mark. A remnant
of something a mother wished for before a child
was born.

Benjamin had no longing mark visible but
when he looked at Thessa, he felt one deep inside his body coiling and bumping against his
skin. He had no belief in mermaids or goddesses,
but when he looked at her, he wished he did.

Chapter Three

Even before she left her house to return outside, Thessa thought of the captain standing at the base of her stairway, waiting for her to take him to the stones. She remembered his eyes, surprised at how she hadn't wanted to turn away from him. He had lightness in his gaze which reminded her of the way the early morning sun shimmered across the blue of the sea—when the golden glow of the morning made her feel she'd awoken into a world fresh and new.

Stephanos would remember the name of the ship that took her sister. He would be angry to see it in the harbour. She would have to talk to him, otherwise the captain would be in danger. Even if the captain worked all night getting the stones, Stephanos would gather the men of

the island and attack before the ship could sail.
She would have to speak with Stephanos very
soon—before the captain lingered on the island
digging in the earth.

Thessa opened the door and moved to the top
of the stairway. The older man stood away from
the house, his eyes on the landscape, but the captain waited for her. When the captain stepped
aside so she could descend, she noted the width
of his shoulders and the firm line of his lips. He
looked no happier to be on the island than her
father had been the last time—no man should
disdain the island so. But she did want to help
her sister and the captain had no knowledge of
what could happen to him on the island.

'You should take care.' She studied the paths.
'Do you have weapons on your ship?'

He didn't answer and took his time turning
back to her. His voice was soft. 'Whatever would
I need weapons for?' He stood as still as the
fallen columns at the top of the island.

She let the wind ruffle her hair before she answered, 'Sea serpents.'

'Ah, yes.' His lips turned up the barest amount.
'Sea serpents. I've dealt with them.'

'They have deadly teeth.'

'Mine are just as sharp.' His chuckle both warmed and chilled her at the same time.

To men spilling blood hardly seemed to matter. But she hated the quick death. The suddenness where light went to dark.

Her mother's brother had been celebrating the birth of a child and everyone had been merry. But someone had said something about the child not favouring the father and, before she even realised anyone was truly angry, a knife had slashed through her uncle's belly. Everything had changed in less time than it took to scream. Her uncle bled to death almost before her aunt could kneel beside him.

She had learned how a world could be wiped away with a moment that happened in the space of a few heartbeats.

Even when Thessa's sister left, this sea captain did not know how carefully Thessa had chosen her words to Stephanos. She had pretended her sister had said she was visiting their aunt and that it had been days before they realised she'd left the island. She'd even begged Stephanos not to search out the ship, flattering him and hint-ing that her sister was marred—in case Melina returned. Thessa didn't think the Greek could have found the ship in the vast seas, but she'd not wanted him to try.

Melina had been trying to provide for them all and Thessa knew her elder sister had wanted to search out their father. Melina couldn't have survived marriage to the Greek, but she insisted Thessa not go near him. Melina believed in art and beauty. Thessa wished every painting on the earth destroyed. They only caused grief.

If she thought and spoke carefully, she hoped to put off marriage to Stephanos long enough for him to notice someone else.

She became aware of the captain examining her face. Straightening her sash, she said, 'I wanted to be certain you take care. One bite from a sea serpent and a man can sleep for ever.'

'I realise life can be deadly.' He looked at her and had the look of secret humour in his up-turned lips, but his eyes had blandness behind them, as if he wouldn't even let himself look back at his own memories. 'Creatures of the sea...or land...they are nothing compared to the storms the heavens can send and I don't fear them either. If I wished for a different life, I would be with my second brother, watching flowers grow while I sipped wine and swirled it on my tongue, wearing unscuffed Hoby boots. I take your words carefully, but they are not necessary.'

'Don't try to outlive your welcome.' Thessa's voice lowered to a whisper. She needed to be careful of what she said. Voices could carry on the wind, or the sailor with the captain could be a fool who spoke to the wrong person.

The captain moved close. 'I've outlived my welcome before.' His words were soft, but she didn't think he tried to hide them from someone, only that he wanted to convince her of the truth of what he said. 'No fables of mermaids or serpents will change one furling of the sails on my ship or cause me to change one step of my well-travelled boots.'

She glanced at his boots. They were marred with lighter worn spots and darkened places on the leather. 'Are those bloodstains?'

He didn't answer and yet he did—with that same blank look.

'Then I will not be concerned for you,' she said.

He turned away. 'Waste of your time.'

* * *

Benjamin had to put some distance between him and Thessa. She'd had care for him in her gaze. He didn't like that.

He wished he'd never seen her swimming. Just because she'd been so at home in the water, his thoughts had lodged on her more strongly than they should have.

Thessa didn't have the flowery scent of the few women he'd danced with at soirées in Warrington's home, nor did she have the sometimes jarring perfume of the tavern wenches he'd enjoyed. She smelled of warmth and a different kind of soap than he was used to. Something which seemed exotic to him, perhaps a blend from island herbs or plants he didn't know of.

The first hues of the sunset fell on her face. She wore the new shawl and her hair was pinned, but still, she didn't look like any woman he remembered. Just like when she swam.

'We should search out the stone in the morning,' she said.

'No. Absolutely not. I may not fear a sea serpent on the island, but I don't wish to stir up any nests of them.'

'You would listen to me and wait if you knew what was good for you.'

'Really, Mermaid? Tell me more.'

Thessa shrugged his words away and moved past him, walking inside the bottom part of the structure and returning with a crude wooden spade. 'It's your neck.' She moved away from them.

Tendrils of hair bobbed freely at the back of her collar, drawing his gaze to her skin.

'Stay here, near the woods, Gid,' Ben said, turning to Gidley. 'Watch the path. If someone is approaching, then catch up with me and let me know.'

'Right, Capt'n,' Gidley said, and as Thessa moved away, Gidley mouthed the word *smile* and pointed to his own uneven teeth.

Ben did the opposite, then travelled along the white-sand pathway edged by stones removed from the trail possibly a thousand years before. Clusters of spindly vegetation dotted among the white stones, like rounded-over bonnets. Only a few scattered bits of green interrupted the burnt red and brown plants dried by salted wind.

The beauty contrasted the island's harshness.

He knew from the last trip that black glass-like shards could be found in places on the island, probably left from a centuries-old volcanic eruption.

His men had told him of the catacombs they'd found and his own eyes had amazed at the sharp white cliffs sticking from the sea, their bold colors contrasting against the blue water. One rock jutted from the sea, its top shaped like the scowl of a raging bear. If he sailed deeper into the islands around, the rocks could be like stone fingers reaching to rip the *Ascalon*'s hull.

As they walked the paths, the trees filtered what was left of the sunlight. But nothing softened the edges of the rock. Staring at the land around, he almost missed seeing Thessa step forward to move an olive branch aside. When it slapped back, he dodged and it grazed his cheek.

This could never be his home and he marvelled that Thessa seemed so enamoured of it. Except, she did have her sea to swim in—her own endless sea.

In one stride he'd caught up with her and walked at her elbow on the narrow path. He thought of Gid's advice. Smiling couldn't help if a woman kept her eyes averted from him.

Ben touched her arm to give her assistance when she stepped around a huge rock at the side of the path.

Her eyes flicked to his hand and then to him. 'You should not show notice for me. It will not do you well.'

'I would not be a true man if I did not show concern for a woman.'

She puffed out a grumble. 'Englishman. Full of pretty speech.'

His hand dropped and he met her eyes. 'I've never seen so much beauty on an island.'

If she wanted out of his grasp, she had only to take a step. She didn't move.

'Why have you not already married this Stephanos?' he asked.

She gave a shrug. 'I am waiting for the house to be finished.'

'If we find the stone, then will you take me to Stephanos so I can purchase it tonight and leave straight away?'

She laughed and he instantly tensed.

'It's not the kind of thing you can put in a small place. Did you not see the marble Melina took?'

He shook his head. 'I saw the wrapped parcel. Not inside it. My brother said it was a carved stone. That was enough for me.'

'It was part of an arm.' She moved her hand from fingers to elbow. 'Not much, and yet bigger than my own. The rest is part of a woman's shape, but I would wager it would take two men to carry each half of her.' She looked at him, her eyes telling him she questioned his wisdom.

Thessa turned and began moving up the path. 'The rocks are on the highest part of the island. You can still see walls from long ago which have crumbled to the ground. And I warn you, Stephanos will not let you take them from Melos easily. If someone else wants a thing, it becomes valuable. You will have to pay twice. Stephanos holds the land, and Melos, in his palm.'

He took her arm and stopped her steps. Watching her expression, he asked, 'You're sure the statue Melina wants is broken?'

She nodded.

Warrington had sent him on a voyage for some

damaged statue? His brother's nursery maid must have bounced him on his head thrice a day.

But his brother was besotted. Warrington did have a tendency to choose a wife who was a bit cracked. His first wife Cassandra had been full cracked and on the jagged side. Melina was only normal-woman daft.

'Your sister knew this?' he asked.

Thessa nodded. 'Yes. She insisted I view it when she first found it. We helped her dig and we covered it back afterwards. And we all talked about the look of her.'

'What was it about her appearance?' He released her arm.

'She looks like our mother did. And that made us sad because the statue was so destroyed.'

'Destroyed?' He heard his voice rise. For the cost it had taken to get his crew to the island a second time, an Italian sculptor could easily have been commissioned to do a statue of Melina and probably both the other sisters.

Thessa sighed. 'She saw our mother's face in the woman, so to her, this was a treasure. She is not like me. She thinks with her heart.' Her lips turned up, but her eyes didn't smile. 'She's insensible that way.'

Benjamin shook his head. 'I understand…quite well.' His brother Warrington hardly thought at all when he was around his wife though, unless it was of her. The only thing he'd been firm about was in not letting her take another voyage. But from the look of relief on Melina's face, she'd not minded. The woman had been fish-belly white on most of the trip to England.

Thessa stopped and stared at him. 'Did she describe the stones to you?'

'No. She assured my brother you would know exactly what it was and where to find it.'

'It is a woman. Both arms are broken. My sister left with one of them. The other we did not find, but parts of it.'

He stopped moving. 'Are you sure this is the statue Melina wants?'

Thessa nodded. 'You would have to understand my sister. She thinks leaves and feathers are beautiful.'

He grimaced. 'I do not think my brother knows what he sent me to retrieve. And I hate to say what he will think when he realises he is trading his share of my ship for a long-buried statue of a woman with no arms…'

Chapter Four

Thessa looked at the captain as he turned to examine their surroundings.

Fading light touched a lengthwise section of column splintered long ago. Mounds of near-barren dirt pressed against the forgotten rock, with only occasional vegetation grasping for life among the harsh environs.

She could forgive him for gazing at her with such intensity, if he would keep his eyes from her for a bit longer so she could examine him. He reminded her of the rocks that jutted from the sea. Majestic. Feet staying in water. Daring the world to try to move them. Commanding. But he wasn't a rock and he would not treat her as another wave to be brushed aside.

She tapped the tip of her spade against the

ground. 'I don't remember just where the statue is buried. I helped my sister dig so many places and there were so many bits of chipped rock. It didn't seem possible we'd need to dig up such rubble again.'

'What do you think was once here?' Benjamin asked.

Thessa turned a half circle, examining the area as if she tried to see through his eyes. 'A site to speak to the heavens?' Laughter bubbled in her voice. 'A place to hide from your mother who wishes you to weave when you do not wish to?'

When he saw her humour, he watched her again, eyes speculative. His mouth opened, then he chuckled. 'I would have thought you would hide at the shore or in the water.'

She frowned and shrugged. 'It would be the first place she looked... I think she was half spirit herself sometimes, always knowing where to find us.'

'Just a mother's way.'

She studied him. 'Do you not believe in things you cannot touch? On voyages, you do not think some unseen spirit creates the wind?'

He shook his head. 'I think there are things

unexplained, but that doesn't make them magical. It just makes them not understood. Men used to say a ship could sail off the end of the earth. But I think that was a tale started by seafaring men to make them appear brave. A man gets a little ale in him, a woman sitting on his knee and he's likely to spout nonsense just to watch her eyes widen or hear her gasp.'

'And she's likely to pretend her awe just to see if she can convince him she believes his nonsense.'

'So, do you believe in mermaids?'

She pressed her lips together before shaking her head. 'Mermaids all died out because they couldn't find a mate worthy of their esteem.'

He looked at her and then laughed. 'We have to be thankful women are not so particular.'

'True. We aren't.'

He looked around. 'So where is the treasure?'

She knelt, using the spade for balance, and picked up a shard of marble. 'As a child I heard the stories of spirits roaming here.' She turned the rock in her hands over, examining. 'My mother must have said that to keep us from roaming too far. When the sun is overhead, I

do not believe in the spirits, but in the dark...'
she met his gaze, and smiled—almost laughing
at her next words '...I would not want to trip
over one and discover myself wrong.'

'Any bones ever found?' he asked.

She shuddered. 'No. We would not disturb a
final sleep. But this is not a burial ground.'

'Why do you not think so?' He walked beside
her.

She turned, tucking a lock of hair behind her
ear. 'I would know. Burial grounds are remembered.' She handed him the rock. 'This wasn't a
place to bury, but perhaps a chance to gather and
be merry. Boats float easily in our harbour now.
I think it could have been the same years ago.'

She took the stone from his hand, brushing her
fingers against his, feeling the roughened skin,
his touch jolting her as if he had some magic
about him. He examined the rock she gave him,
running his fingers along the straight side. One
of his ringed fingers, and the one next, didn't
bend with the others. So the man and his boots
were marred. She wondered if it happened in
the same fray, but she didn't want to think about
death.

She looked around. 'If I were a spirit, I would be at the shore, my toes in warm water and the sun on my face. Not rumbling around sharp-edged stones.'

'Swimming?' he asked, his eyes intense.

She nodded. 'The water cleanses my mind.' She looked off in the distance. 'If there was another life before this one, I lived it in the sea.'

When she turned to him, he stood immobile. Immersed in something in his mind. 'Captain?' she asked.

He breathed in, dragging air inside himself, and then he barely smiled, tilting his head to one side. 'My pardon. I think one of your imaginary spirits is standing too close to me.' He put a hand to the back of his neck. 'Breathing against my skin.' He turned. 'I have to get the stone and leave.'

He walked to her and took the spade from her hand and tapped the ground with the tip of the tool. 'Where should I begin?' He gave a testing thrust of the tool into the dirt, jammed his foot on to it and a twinge of pain flashed across his face. 'Blasted knee,' he mumbled.

He was just as ravaged as the men on her island, only it was covered better.

'How did you hurt your knee?'

'Just fell into a spar on the last voyage. It's still healing.' He stopped digging. 'But I don't want to start sounding like I should be sitting at a hearth, wearing a cap on my head and a nightshirt.'

'I imagine you'd not mind that if you had someone sitting on your knee who you could tell stories of bravery.'

A lock of hair fell over his forehead when he looked down, but he hadn't moved fast enough to cover the smile in his eyes. 'I'd only tell the truth.'

'And I'm a mermaid.'

He raised his gaze and she saw the tiniest crinkles at his eyes, but he wasn't smiling. 'You're better than a sea goddess. They evaporate in the early morning light when a man wakes.'

Thessa shook away the thoughts his words conjured and pointed to an area at the centre of the clearing.

'There. That is the first place to dig.'

He moved and began scraping the earth from

the stones—the rasps quickly disturbing the straggly vegetation, but hardly marring the surface. When he finally pushed aside a bit of the earth, a breeze passed over her, the scent of mouldering dust hitting her nostrils and she tasted the dirt.

She brushed at the shawl, not wanting the fabric soiled. 'My sister was so excited when she found the statue. She pretended to nudge us with the arm when she brought it home. And then she brought us to help her dig again, but we refused to help for long. A person cannot eat rocks.'

She gave a small shake of her head and clenched her fists at her side. 'I did not yet ask. Did Melina find our father?'

He nodded. He again took the shovel and ground it against the earth.

'Is he dead?' she asked. That would be the only reason she could forgive him for not returning.

'No.'

'Married?'

The captain watched the ground. 'He has a wife.'

Thessa's teeth clamped together. She had suspected as much. The only true fight she'd ever seen her parents have was when her father had suggested a man must have a woman to be inspired to paint. And they all knew he painted wherever he went.

'What did my sister think of the woman?'

He moved earth as he talked—and used the tip of the shovel to pry loose other stones. 'My brother told me Melina has nice thoughts of her. I am not certain when Melina met her, but it was before the ship was ready to sail back to Melos. I was to make the trip to return your sister to Melos earlier, but I delayed it after she decided to wed.'

'She chose…' her words were choked with disbelief '…marriage to your brother when she didn't have to wed?' *Traitor. Melina was a traitor.*

How many times had they sat in the night and said how mistaken their mother had been to marry a foreign man? If Melina was to do such a foolish thing as marry, why had she not stayed on Melos with them and simply married Stephanos? At least the sisters would be together then, and only one would have had to be trapped.

Thessa turned away from the man, not wanting him to be able to read her thoughts. She would have to go through with the marriage to Stephanos. She'd at least be able to provide for her younger sister and Bellona wouldn't have to marry anyone she didn't wish to. One of them would be saved.

'I cannot believe she married willingly,' Thessa said.

His hands paused. He looked at her. 'My brother has the title. He's not poverty-stricken. His house is near as big as this whole island. And woe to anyone who might stand in the way of a breeze of air that would cool Melina if the day is warm.' He lowered his voice, speaking more to himself than her. 'He is whipped by her skirts.'

'I don't understand what you mean. Men are not…like that.'

'No. Well, most aren't. But he's always had a weakness of sorts. I've never understood it.' He shrugged, but then grinned at her. 'Sometimes, it is humorous to watch, though.'

'And she is fond of him?'

'Doesn't matter much if she is, or isn't. He's at her feet.'

Her brow furrowed. 'I cannot think that is true.'

'If you say so.' He lowered his chin. 'And you? Are you fond of this Stephanos?'

'I don't have to be. He is of my home. He is a sturdy Greek. He will have fine children. They will eat well. His mother and I speak pleasantly.'

He turned his head from her. 'So you're not particularly fond of this man?'

She tried not to think of what she really thought of Stephanos and hoped she never found out what he did when he was away from the island.

'I didn't say I am not fond of him. I will grow close to him after we are wed.' She hoped to teach him to bathe.

'Yes.' His words were overly innocent. 'That's how I've heard it works.'

She gripped the shawl. Her voice rose. 'You know nothing of this island. Of the world I live in.'

'No.' He stared at her. 'In truth, I know very little of England either. My world is the sea. My home the ship. My family the crew.'

'In England, did you meet my father?' she asked.

'Once. Only briefly, years ago. I looked at his

art. We talked concerning a painting I thought he might create for me. I'd seen his seafaring land-scapes and portraits from his travels and liked them.'

'He did not wish to finish something for you. Did he?'

Benjamin shook his head.

She tugged the ends of her shawl into a thick knot. 'My father only paints what he is directed to paint from within himself. Otherwise he be-lieves it is not truly inspired work. He believes no one can see the world as he does. And it is true. He did not see our mother cry each time he left for his home—he called London his home—and when she sickened, he did not see her die. He sees *only* himself in his world.'

She looked at the rubble they'd moved. 'After the death, Melina wrote him many times. She sent letters with the ships leaving. He never an-swered. Only what is at the end of a paintbrush has meaning to him. Our mother's dying meant nothing.'

He turned his gaze from the dislodged earth, watching her, and spoke softly. 'By the time he found out about your mother's death, it would have been too late to do anything for her.'

Her face changed, eyes narrowing.

'It was not too late when he left.' Her words were quick. 'He'd only been here days. When he saw she was not well, he began to look for a vessel to take him away. He left on the first one that would carry him and it wasn't to England. I asked at the harbour to see where the ship went.'

'Sometimes…a man does things he should regret, whether he does or not.' His movements stopped. He watched the end of the shovel. 'My father died. I was there. But had my cargo been ready earlier…I don't know.'

Benjamin sailed every voyage with the knowledge that when he returned home—*if* he returned—he would visit a different family than the one he left behind. And if he died at sea, he would be buried in the deep. His final resting place would be alone. Fitting.

He'd never truly thought he saw the world the same as his brothers, and after the first voyage he knew he did not. In two years, or more, at sea, much more changed than the people living their lives on shore realised. He'd never told anyone how unsettling it could be to walk back into the family estate and see the different fabrics and furniture moved in a room so much that it was almost unrecognisable. They thought they'd made no changes. But the world he'd left behind never was the same one he returned to.

Only the shades of the sea never changed.

Thessa turned away. She found a bit of the broken structure to sit on.

'You do not have to marry Stephanos.' He glanced away, planning to tell her of the dowry his ship carried for her. 'Thessa, in England many men thinking of taking a wife would only have to look at you and would want to marry you. And with my brother's help, you could find many suitable men to choose from. And if your younger sister is only half as comely as you, she would have no trouble finding a man who would wish to wed her. And then, there is also—'

She interrupted before he could get the words out about the funds.

'Words so sweet.' She laughed, moving her head back and tilting her chin to the sky. When she lowered her head, her voice became soft.

'But Stephanos will do for me. He is of my country. I do not want to make the same mistake my mother did. Stephanos will stay here. His family is here and he loves Melos. I will have a home that I know.'

He let out a breath and turned to look at the island, so different from his birthplace. The trees weren't even the same—more like aged fingers reaching up to the leaves. The ground was hard to till. Even when the air didn't have the taint of sulphur, it didn't smell the same as the English countryside.

'Think hard about what you want.' He looked at the horizon, wishing he could see the *Ascalon*. 'Your sister, Melina, chose a different path.'

And then she stood and stepped beside him. She shut her eyes and shook her head gently before she viewed his face. 'She thinks English.' Thessa smiled apologetically. 'She has the tainted blood.'

He forced a glare into his eyes and she chuckled in response.

'Our father made her learn to write,' she said. 'She is like him—art fascinates her—or what she thinks is art. I am different. Even my bones know what I must have. This land, where I can speak my mother's language and see my mother's people, and know every one of my true family. To me, painting is a lie. It is beauty that someone imagined.'

Then she turned and, with the grace of an empress, picked up one of the small stones he'd tossed aside and threw it against one of the broken archways jutting from the earth. 'I will wed Stephanos. Then when Melina is forgotten by the Englishman, I will have a home for her.'

When she mentioned marriage to Stephanos the image of her in another man's bed stopped him. This was not an English society woman with constant chaperones. Her sister had given her body to his brother, Warrington, for ship passage.

He turned, anger gripping him as the knowledge of how likely it was that this Stephanos was already rutting with her. Benjamin knew if he were betrothed to Thessa, in a remote location, not a night would go by without her in his arms. And he'd swim with her and they would be like two sea creatures floating in the waves. He'd throw out every piece of nautical artwork he'd left in London if she'd just shed her clothes and bathe in a warm sea with him.

'Your face is angry. Why?' she asked.

'I told you. My knee. It pains me.'

Her face tilted to the side, studying him, and her mouth opened slightly. Her eyes didn't leave his and she nodded. 'My father said that castor oil was medicine for his complaints. He left some. We can return to my house for it.'

He frowned. 'No need for any bitter mixtures. I have a bad enough taste in my mouth from being on land.'

Thessa took a step back to escape the dirt from the shovel. The captain's coat pulled across his shoulders, and his hair curled different directions at the ends. Never before had a man's movements interested her so, but she supposed she'd never really watched a man work—unless she counted watching her father paint and she would have called that torture. This was not.

She spoke, afraid if she didn't, he'd somehow be able to sense her watching him. 'When the man from the museum in France visited, he asked if anyone had seen anything of value. Anything of history? After the man left Melina began secret trips to the highest part of the island, searching. *Mana* was sick, but Melina would not stop hunting the island.'

She'd dug and discovered the woman. 'She didn't want Stephanos to know we'd found something which might be worth coins, so we covered the marble—deeper.' She tossed the rock to the ground. Thessa had been as certain that statue was worthless as Melina had been certain it was valuable.

But the one time Thessa had looked into the stone face, she'd refused to look at it again. Stone and cold and beneath the ground and resembling her sick mother.

And when she'd returned home and looked at her mother, shivers took over her body. She'd had to leave the room so her mother would not see her tears.

'My mother always welcomed my father home,' she said. 'She was like the statue…waiting. Not complaining.'

Thessa tried to push her memories away. She'd wanted her mother to tell him never to come back. And then, when her mother was dying, her wish happened, but then her mother needed him more than ever. She was dying and he didn't care as long as he could escape. How could he have not wanted to spend every moment with someone as wondrous as *Mana*? Thessa kicked some of the dirt in the direction of the shovel.

Her mother was buried, just as alone, on another part of the island. Deserted in life and death.

The captain never looked her way, intent on the mixture of dirt and broken bits of an archway.

The movement of his shoulders kept her attention and took her mind from the past, and she watched him, reminded of the water currents just before they broke into waves.

In a fair fight with Stephanos, she could not guess who would best the other. Their bodies were similar in size, but Stephanos… Everyone on the island knew of his temper and he did not fight fair. No one would have expected it of him.

Grumbling, the captain used the end of the tool to scrape dirt from the white mound he uncovered—a rock.

He put the shovel on the ground and dropped

to his knees, pushing aside the dirt with his hands. Rough hands, comfortable with the soil now sticking to them. He pulled aside a section of the wall which had been trapped under stones, unearthing in moments what would have taken her half a day to uncover.

'Nothing,' he rasped out and stood, his left hand briefly massaging his shoulder. Then he looked at her and his face stilled. 'But, then, you knew that, didn't you?'

'You come here to take her and leave. My father took my mother's heart and left. You took my sister.' She shrugged. 'I cannot help you. I want to help my sister, but I cannot help you.'

He threw down the shovel. 'I don't want the artefact. Your sister does. You have to know that. Yes, the stone will help me secure my ship, but I am here because of your sister's whim—and my besotted brother and his wish to put in front of her whatever your sister asks for. This is for Melina.'

'My mother is gone. You've taken my sister. Now you want the one thing left that has the image of my mother's face.'

'Yes. And if she looks like your mother, and

you can rescue her from the earth, why wouldn't you? Wouldn't your mother wish to have her likeness freed?'

'Wait until morning,' she said, fighting to keep her face unmoved. Digging in the earth had brought back the memories of her mother's burial. 'The light is going and you will be able to talk with Stephanos then. It is worthless to dig her up if he will not let you leave the island with her.'

'I suppose.' His chest moved as he inhaled. 'You're right. I can't risk destroying already worthless rocks. If you wish it, I will return in the morning and I'll buy her before I dig.' He looked at the earth and then snatched the shovel from the ground. 'You will tell me tomorrow, won't you?'

Her heart thudded. 'I suppose I've no choice.' When his ship left, she would truly be losing her connection to Melina. She'd never see her again. Not if a man had her who valued her. The earl would never let her sail away from him into seas that could turn angry. And the statue would be gone, too, just like *Mana*.

She crossed her arms. Turning, she held her chin high, back straight and moved to the trail.

His footsteps scrambled behind her and he grasped her arm. He stopped in front of her, still touching her. 'I have funds...'

'But what I want is my sister. Can you return her?'

He let out a breath. 'I can't give her to you. And truly, she is happy where she is. I am sure she misses you, but she'll not be coming back. Women tend not to leave their children, and from the looks of things, she'll be having many of them.'

'Oh.' Thessa thought of the nieces and nephews she would never see. Never. She jerked her arm free. The captain stilled.

'You stole her,' she said. 'You took her from me for ever.'

'She chose to go. Willingly.'

She lowered her eyes. 'My sister would have died for us. That is why I do not...I have trouble believing she didn't return.'

'She sent me and I have brought you—'

'Do not tell me,' she interrupted. 'I do not want to hear any reasons she didn't come back to us.

We will manage. I am to marry.' She shrugged. 'You must not let Stephanos know how badly you want the woman,' she said. 'The price will rise.'

He turned so he faced her directly and now intensity flared from his eyes. 'You think he will not guess? A man doesn't sail this far for no reason. He might think I returned for you.'

'You'd not met me before.'

He looked at her and gave a little grunt of agreement, but something else was in the sound.

If the captain had met her on the first voyage, all three sisters might have gathered up the bits of the woman and taken her to England. But then they would have been stranded in the same country as their father. She wished never to see him again. Even when he told the truth, he added something or left out something. To him, deceit was merely a better form of the truth. If he was caught in a tale where he'd misled the listener, his eyes would gleam. To have this pointed out to him was to have his craftiness rewarded— an admission by the listener that he'd been outwitted.

'You are sure my father is alive?' she asked.

He nodded. 'He was when I left England.'

'I am not like my sister,' she told the captain, speaking more easily in the shadowed world of the nightfall. 'Either sister. Bellona does not worry. She knows we will care for her. We told her so over and over when she cried after our mother died. And Melina thought if she just searched enough she would find a way to keep our father. I…'

He waited.

She shrugged. 'I am not sure what I am like.'

He examined her. 'You don't have to tell me you're nothing like your sisters. Or any other woman. I knew that from the first moment I saw you.'

She darted her eyes back to his to see if he jested. His watched her and his lips parted. He looked at her the same way Stephanos did, but it didn't make her uneasy. But instead of taking a step towards her, the captain moved the distance back.

Her teeth tightened against each other.

He turned, watching the skies. He studied the heavens, but she supposed captains did that often. And then he looked at the trees and the barren ground around them. Before his gaze finally returned to her, he put one hand on the back of his neck, then his arm fell and he looked to the sky again. 'Will you swim with me?'

She studied his face. He spoke the words with more intensity than Stephanos used when he told her he wished to marry her. 'It is either to be you or Bellona,' the Greek had said. 'I want you. Her, I do not like so much. But she will do.'

Thessa had challenged Stephanos that such threats would not sway either sister, but still, inside, she'd worried and known she had no choice but to agree to marriage.

She shook the memories away.

His vision locked on her and the muscles of his face hardened.

'Swim?' She leaned her head forward.

'You cannot imagine how much it would mean to me.'

'I cannot.' Oh, but she knew what it would mean in her life. If she shed her clothing and moved into the water with him, she could have no recourse if he took her body. Stephanos would be enraged if he discovered it and the sea captain and his entire ship would be at risk—not that she cared at this moment. 'You ask an improper thing.'

'I know. But you are like the art on the walls of my London home, yet you are alive. I've never seen a woman such as you. Your sister doesn't even come close. When I look at you, I see something I never saw before. When you swam it was as if you were free of the restraints of the earth, much like I feel when *Ascalon* is moving in a brisk breeze.'

She laughed. 'A Frenchman told me I was an angel on earth and I didn't take his offer either.'

'He wasn't wrong.'

'You've been away from a woman too long.'

He paused, words low. 'I always think that.' She noted a faint apology in his eyes. 'But this is not the same thing.'

She stood and pointed to the trail. 'Go back the way you came. Take the second path in the direction of your right, and then—' she waved her hand in the direction '—and then again right. You'll see two houses close. The smaller one is the one you want. The woman there will swim with you, for as long as you wish if you have enough coin.'

'No.' He shook his head. 'You're the only one.'

She clasped her hands in front of herself. 'I think not.'

'I'll be proper. You have my word as a…a sea captain.'

She touched her chest. 'I have always thought the word of a sea captain quite…quite like the word of my father, a man who could forget his promises as soon as they left his lips.'

'I only wish to swim with you.'

She raised a brow. 'And nothing else.'

He snorted. 'I'd have to be dead not to think of *something else* with you, but, no, I will expect nothing more.'

'No.'

'You can return with me. I'll take you to England. Your sister, too. My brother will make a home for you both. We have a town house in London we hardly ever use. You could stay there.'

'No. Never.' She turned her head and, to show her distaste at his words, spat on the ground. 'My father left us for England. A painter who valued paintings more than the people in them.'

Even in the darkness, when she turned back

to him, she could see his lowered jaw. 'You…
Women don't…'

She reached down, grasped the sides of her
skirt and lifted. His eyes locked on her legs.
She took two large steps to close the distance
between him. His gaze never left her calves and
he stared.

She kicked his shin hard and then let her hem
flutter down.

He jumped back, raising his eyes to her face.

She asked, 'Women don't spit and they don't
kick. Are you cured of wanting to swim with
me now?'

He half frowned, and half smiled. 'I doubt I
will ever be cured of that. But you can kick me
again if the next time you raise your skirt another inch.'

Storm-like currents of air exploded inside her
body, but the air pressing into her touched nothing else on the island. She wondered if his gaze
had somehow brought spirits alive and they
danced around her. He wasn't the only one with
senseless thoughts. Now he was making them
explode in her head. She had to make him hate
her and to make herself dislike him. That would

be the only way she could have a haven from his presence and make sure she didn't do something foolish.

'You senseless man,' she said.

He raised his shoulders and held a palm up. 'My pardon, Sweet. I wasn't made to be a vicar.'

She raised her chin and stared at him. He truly didn't seem offended by her actions. 'I would say you chose well.'

'I agree.'

The smile he gave her near took her legs out from under her. Her jaw lowered.

'Are you certain you won't just step into the water with me?' he asked.

Something inside her screamed to say yes. 'No.'

'Uncertain?' he asked and his eyes widened for a heartbeat with too much innocence, but then they changed again and he seemed to look into her. And his gaze promised her something she could not name.

Thunder that only she could hear pounded in her ears. She could even feel the lightning flashes burning into her skin from the inside out. She knew the lore of mermaids being able to create weather. But he was the unsafe one. He was the one who could call up storms.

Chapter Five

Thessa turned and started on the trail back to her home, leaving him to dig or not. It didn't matter to her. She had to leave his presence and return to her home so she could shut the door behind her.

The captain unsettled her.

In the night, she kept dreaming of storms, full of violence and thunder, and waking into a world of silence.

She dressed, not wanting to be alone, and went into the other room of the house where her sister slept. Thessa lit the lamp and began to sew, trying to forget that they'd never see their eldest sister again.

As morning closed in, someone rapped three precise times on the door. Bellona didn't wake, but Thessa rose. The captain would be outside. No one of Melos would rap so gently and with such purpose.

'You didn't bring more men?' she asked, opening the doorway.

He nodded. 'They're at the longboat. I can get them if I need them. I've asked them to wait.'

Lips shut, she let out a long breath, then spoke. 'It will go faster with more men.'

'I can get them later,' he said, turning, taking a quick step down the stairway. 'We can't sail anyway until the tide is right and there is wind.' He spoke over his shoulder. 'And I don't want you having them dig up half the island because you don't want to part with a statue that you've let stay under the ground.'

He grabbed the shovel at the base of the house and moved towards the trail.

She followed him. 'You will need help.'

He stopped and let the tip of the shovel clunk against the ground. He leaned on the shovel. 'You can stay here if you wish. At least if I start digging on my own, I'll know there's a *chance* I might find it.' He trudged along, in front of her, ducking olive branches.

'*Englishman,*' she muttered to his back and her feet made rushed sounds on the earth behind him.

'*Woman,*' he responded in kind.

'Thank you for the kind word.' She kept her voice overly sweet.

He pushed aside a small limb and couldn't let it go quickly because it might slap her, so he settled it back into place, but he didn't turn to her. Instead he kept his eyes forward.

'Only an Englishman would sail so far for a few broken rocks,' she said.

'Only a Greek woman would not take him straight to the place, show it to him and not go back to her home to leave him to dig in peace.'

'I am Greek and I am woman.'

'So, are you going to show me where the statue lies?' he asked as they stepped into the clearing.

She sighed. 'Of course. I know my sister wants her. I suppose I was angry and not wanting to give the statue away because I wanted to punish my sister for not returning to us.'

His eyebrows slanted to a V and he shook his head. 'If the rocks are as you say they are, I think the most punishment would be to give them to her. I wouldn't like to receive a crate of broken rocks. By the time I get them to her, she might realise her mistake.'

She shook her head. 'Not Melina. These rocks… She whispered of them day and night.'

Thessa walked the rubble, looking, kicking aside smaller stones. Finally she stopped. 'I really am not certain, but I think it is under where I stand now.' She pointed to a boulder. 'The three of us rolled that as her headstone.'

Stepping so close he could scent the spiced air that flowed around her, he thrust the shovel into the dirt.

'Careful,' she said, her hand shooting out, resting on his arm. Even through the coarse cloth of his shirt, she could feel the muscles. Quickly, she pulled her hand away. 'She's near the surface.'

He used the shovel more to push earth aside than to dig and in seconds he revealed a torso.

'She's…not wearing a dress?'

'No.'

He turned to her, tilting up one side of his lips. 'She might be worth more than I thought.'

'Dig,' she said.

The shovel slipped. He gave a shake of his

head and looked up at her, apology in his eyes. 'I broke off a sliver of nose.'

'I would not care at all, except she does look like our mother.' Thessa knelt beside him and used her hand to clean more dirt from the face. She pulled her hand away and stared. 'I know *Mana* was beyond others in good appearance. Father loves beauty. He would never, ever marry a woman who didn't appeal to an artist's eyes. Art. Not one piece of it is worth one moment of my mother's sadness.' She looked at Benjamin. 'If the stone in the ground did not have my mother's face, I would take a chisel to it myself if I thought my father wanted it. But I cannot destroy my mother's face.' She looked at him and her voice faded into the wind. 'And you broke her nose.'

'I did not mean to, Thessa.' He stepped closer to her. 'It was an accident. There are men who can restore these statues.'

'I understand. But it is rock. Hard on the inside as well as outside. Do not worry that you hurt her. Men made her and then they let her fall to the ground alone.' As her father had done to her mother, quoting poetry and speaking of devotion, and then ignoring her for days while he painted. And finally leaving, with sadness in his words, but his eyes looking to the ship and his steps quick. It was better not to love than to live with a man who didn't care enough to stay. Statues could be restored. Hearts could not.

Benjamin crouched, one hand moving the dirt, then he brushed back a lock of his hair and left a smudge high on his cheek. His shoulder brushed hers. His coat held a scent she recognised from when she'd walked on board a vessel to tell her father goodbye. Pine, from the material they used to waterproof the boat.

He studied the carving, then her face, and she stilled. She knew he compared the two and rose to increase the distance between them. He stood, wiped his hand across the duck trousers he wore and carefully put a finger beneath her chin, tilting her face up to his. 'You are many times the loveliness of her.'

His eyes moved, tightening as he studied her face.

Wind danced around them, as if spirits caressed them with their breaths, and the air caused shivers on her arms.

He released her face, but the breezes kept tousling his hair.

'No one could compare the two of you, though. You've the dark gift of the islands and skin as flawless as perfectly crafted marble. The statue should be of you.'

'No.' She shook her head, shuddering. 'I want nothing to do with art. It lies.'

'Perhaps.' He didn't smile. Silenced lengthened. 'But a statue of you would be no lie.'

She wanted to brush away the smudge on his face, but to touch his skin could be dangerous and she must remain true to Stephanos in all ways. She was betrothed to him—a man of her own heritage. One who shared the same soil she had always walked on. Even though Stephanos made his own sea voyages, he never stayed long, and called the same land home that she did. His relatives lived on Melos. He would never desert his children.

'You must wipe the dirt from your face,' she instructed, stepping back, pulling herself from his captivation.

He brushed at his face, not taking away the smudge at all. Completely missing it.

She firmed her lips, but her fingertips softened. She wanted to touch him, but could not be so bold. His hand reached out to move the spot away again, but still he did not dislodge it.

'Stop,' she said and grasped the sleeve of his coat, enclosing his wrist under her hand, but keeping the barrier of the fabric between them. She guided him to smooth the dirt away. He stilled, as if she had him in some kind of spell, and when his eyes changed, something in them tumbled into her. He no longer looked like a man, but had the innocence of a boy in his eyes.

He turned his face away, and pulled his arm free. He studied the ground with the half-exposed bloodless face looking up at him.

'I must have the treasure.' He spoke softly. 'The treasure.' He took a breath. 'That is what I am here for.'

She shivered at the intensity in his voice. 'You will have the statue if you bargain for her,' she said. 'No one here wants her or they could have taken her long ago.' Thessa leaned forward. 'She's rock. Broken and marked with scars. Worthless.'

His smile only tilted at one corner. 'Perhaps.

Perhaps not. To me she is priceless. She is the coin I need to buy my…world. My world of the sea. I'll have my dreams if I get her. My brothers will know I am not the infant they remember.'

She turned and knelt at the stone face, trailing her fingertips over the marble, feeling the indentation at the chin, the jagged part of the nose.

He closed the distance between them.

She could feel him every time he stood beside her just as if he touched her, and yet he didn't.

'I know you are curious of England,' he said. 'I know you wonder what is so good about it that your sister doesn't leave. That she sends gifts instead of returning.'

'I am curious of death, too. But I've no wish to die.' And her mother's grave was on the island. Who would tend it if not her and Bellona, and if they went to England, they would be deserting her as their father did.

'You must meet Stephanos.' She put the slightest emphasis on her betrothed's name and the captain's eyes flickered in acknowledgement.

'I would like nothing more,' he said. Then he looked away and she could hear a smile she could not see. 'Perhaps I should have said, there are few things I would like more.'

'You must watch what you say around him.'

He turned so she could see his face again. 'I suppose. I suppose I should take care, especially if I want the woman.'

Her chest heated when he said woman and even though he looked completely away from her, she could feel him watching.

Chapter Six

Stephanos's home looked little different than the others he'd seen, two stories with the lower one used as a barn. Chickens pecking and a goat chasing another.

He heard a hammer, and when he scanned the area, saw the bare wood of an unfinished structure that Thessa would some day live in. Windowpanes had not been added.

The new house wasn't as large as the town house Benjamin owned with his brothers, but in the setting of the gnarled trees and dusty earth it would have a grandness when finished.

'That is the home Stephanos is building for me. He will be there,' Thessa said, then lowered her voice. 'And do not think, because he does not speak your language, that he does not understand. He talks as he wishes. His father supplied goods to the vessels in the harbour, and now Stephanos does the same, and sometimes they sail for what they need. When it is festival time, he tells such tales of what he's seen and heard, but says no place lives in his heart like Melos.'

A man stepped out of the new doorway, his form lessening the size of the opening by comparison.

He wore a turban head covering, which flowed down to wrap loosely around his neck. His clothing was rough woven and worn to slide with his body. His boots, high to the knees, could have been made by the same man who cobbled Benjamin's. No waistcoat, just a colourful sash looped twice around his waist. Benjamin instantly noted the handle sticking from the band of fabric. Both men carried their knife in a similar fashion, only Ben's was in a sheath.

Stephanos took long strides towards Thessa, unhurried, but full of purpose.

The Greek's eyes stayed on Thessa, but Benjamin had no illusions that the man didn't see him. Stephanos didn't stop until he stood close enough to reach out a hand, touching Thessa's shoulder.

'*Oraios.*' Stephanos's lips turned up and his eyes rested on Thessa, and lingered.

Benjamin didn't know what feelings Thessa had for the Greek, but the man's stance near her reminded him of a rooster preening around a hen. Ben couldn't blame Stephanos; he was fortunate indeed to be born in Thessa's world and be the one rooster to catch her eye.

'I bring this ship captain to you.' Thessa spoke in English to her betrothed. 'My sister has sent him back for the things she left behind. She misses our home, but cannot return because she is to have a child.'

Stephanos answered, his words splattering into air. Benjamin didn't understand more than a few Greek phrases, but he understood the underlying hint of derision. Thessa spoke again. This time her voice soothed in the native language. Calm words. Gentle. Direct.

Then the Grecian turned to Benjamin, his words more fluid than the sea. His tone remained companionable, but his eyes narrowed, and Benjamin knew no friendship was offered.

Benjamin refused to say he didn't understand, but instead turned to Thessa and flicked his brows upwards.

'He offers you hospitality, hopes to help you with your needs so you can be on your way quickly,' Thessa translated, rushing the sentence.

All those words could not have been quite the same neat package Thessa presented him with, but they would do.

'I too wish to leave soon, though the beauty of the harbour is rare.' He thought of Thessa's face. But he didn't want to lose the cargo waiting in Blackwall and wanted the feeling of owning his own bed, his own world. Staying long on Melos would not do him well.

A hint of redness touched her cheeks. Stephanos said something else and she grimaced, but the frown was the result Stephanos desired because his laugh bellowed out.

White-hot sparks burst into Benjamin's thoughts. He'd never felt this kind of jealousy. He knew the emotion. On his first voyage, he'd been jealous of the seamen who knew everything there was to know about sailing. He'd been envious when he'd seen a particularly handsome sailing vessel—before *Ascalon.* But jealousy concerning a woman—an unthinkable emotion for weak minded men.

The stirrings of the unfamiliar feeling hit him in the stomach and anger flared towards Stephanos. The man was a dandy. Granted, not a Brummell version, but all the same, a dandy.

And he had a slashing scar which began above his eyebrow and moved into his hairline. Completely unbecoming and likely from some drink-sodden frivolity gone awry which he turned into a tale of bravery to impress Thessa.

Stephanos waved a hand towards a stone wall, uncompleted, and with stacks of rocks near each side of it, gesturing Benjamin to follow.

Just inside the low wall that would surround the new house, Benjamin saw a rough table, with planked boards for seating. Trees, not big enough for true shade, gave the illusion of coolness.

'*Poto.*' Stephanos raised his hand. His words, while not loud, carried to someone Benjamin couldn't see until a head darted from the doorway of the smaller house.

Stephanos took Thessa's hand, leading her, and guided her to a seat.

Thessa spoke to Stephanos in Greek, reproof in her tone. He laughed and his eyes crinkled at the edges. His head leaned towards her and he said a few soft words, and a blush spread on her cheeks.

Then he turned to Benjamin and perused him. Stephanos's cheeks puffed, probably because of the thin line of his lips.

Thessa spoke again and the man's eyes met her face, though his attention had never really left her. She gestured, her arm going towards the harbour.

Stephanos shook his head.

Thessa's eyes narrowed and the speed of her speech increased. Her voice became more intent. While she talked, rapidly, the man placed his fingertips at Thessa's arm and the fingers tightened.

'Polyagapimenos.' He looked into Thessa's eyes and spoke the word as if they were alone—an endearment.

Benjamin could feel a grinding in his stomach,

and a sudden need for movement, but he forced himself to sit silent and appear unconcerned.

Stephanos spoke again, words quiet and effectively shutting Benjamin out of conversation. Even if the words had been shouted Benjamin couldn't have understood, but Stephanos knew that well. Then he reached out and brushed back a tendril of hair from Thessa's brow, one wisp so small the invisible lock could not have distressed her. And his hand lingered, then fell away.

Benjamin felt something crack within him and anger began to war with the good sense in his body.

Thessa was going to be married to the man. But the display of possession was not necessary.

Stephanos's gaze locked on Benjamin's and he spoke, but the words were more measured, slow drops in a pail, not the rapid spraying to confuse.

Thessa took a moment before translating. 'He wishes you to spend the night here. He wants you to have his hospitality, though you will soon be leaving. And discuss the transaction of the stone.'

Her eyes didn't match her words. And Benjamin had heard tales of the area. And not just the myths or the legends of the women, but of men who could fight until the last drop of blood had been drained. Looking into Stephanos's eyes, he decided the stories he'd heard had not been yarns. Enjoying the Greek's hospitality would not be healthy or wise. Ben knew he would stay on *Ascalon.*

Benjamin felt his chest expand with his breath. 'I need to discuss the purchase, so my men can begin digging.'

Stephanos spoke, his dark eyes never leaving Benjamin's face. Benjamin had observed more pleasant looks on the faces of men who'd tried to gut him with a blade. He knew, though, that the man wasn't thinking of violence. Instead, he was fluffing his feathers for Thessa and doing a little blustering dance.

'He feels a guest should not have to dig and he wishes to see what is so important to you that you would sail so far to collect,' Thessa translated.

Benjamin put his forearm on the table, aware of the strain to the sleeve fabric of his coat that stretching his muscles could bring. He would wager his feathers were as bright as Stephanos's.

Benjamin answered Thessa, but his eyes met Stephanos. 'It is an old stone with a woman's face and women can be so sentimental. My brother is besotted with Melina, who wants the stone as a memory of her homeland. My brother's mind is not clear, so he thinks the folly of my retrieving it will endear him to his new wife. A quest of the heart, if you will.'

Benjamin might—might—have thought Stephanos didn't understand him, but at the mention of the heart quest, Stephanos's pupils ascended upwards in a quick dart to show his feelings of such a journey.

'My brother,' Benjamin continued, 'near puts rose petals at his wife's feet. Sings of his love to her standing under her window at night. Composes poetry for her at all hours of the day. It is the way a true man of my country treats his beloved.'

Well, Warrington had married Melina and he surely had time for the Byron-and-flowers nonsense since a man's eyes didn't always close when his head hit the pillow.

Thessa watched Benjamin. She opened her

mouth to translate. He continued before she could speak.

'In fact, she has complained of her fingertips being tired of his kisses. It is such a sincere love. Made all the sweeter by the flavour of her culture that Melina brings to the household. Having a mix of the two worlds makes her all the more fascinating. Even I would never have imagined how the English and Greek could blend to bring the best of each to life. A woman with such a history is a rare discovery, a treasure for an Englishman.' Benjamin's gaze flicked to Thessa and back to her Stephanos.

Benjamin knew diplomacy was more important than challenge, but something else had controlled him in that half second, and the primitive urge to taunt Stephanos kept rising up.

Stephanos's eyes narrowed. Then he spoke slowly to Thessa, each word a sentence in meaning from the way he bit down on it.

She turned to Benjamin, her words slow. 'The price on the statue just increased since it is so valuable to the English.'

Benjamin kept his tone soft. 'It is of little consequence to me if I decide not to purchase it. I don't need a basket of rocks.' That wasn't entirely true. But from watching Stephanos's face, he had no doubt that the man could understand English quite well. 'Rocks are nothing compared to the beauty of heaven-sent treasures around us.' Benjamin had no trouble letting his gaze rest on Thessa when he said the words.

'Since I will not leave quickly with the rocks,' he continued, 'I will stay longer and enjoy the natural beauty of the island.' And no matter if he'd be surrounded by blades on all sides, Thessa did capture his eyes.

Stephanos stood and shouted out two names, and men from inside the new structure stepped outside.

Movement ignited around him.

One man stood no bigger than Benjamin's shoulder and Benjamin estimated him to be all wiry muscle. The slighter ones could be asp-like in their movements and hard to grasp. His clothes, well patched, paired well with his face, which also had been mended a few times. The young one stood taller and wider, and he dressed more with the bloom of youthful pomp.

Benjamin would gauge the older one the most dangerous.

Stephanos stood and spoke to Thessa, and even before she translated Benjamin knew what the man had said because she rose and they looked to the path. Stephanos wanted to see the stones.

A silvery-haired woman descended the stairs of the older house, her gait favouring one leg. She brought wine and mugs to the table. Stephanos spoke to her and she looked up at him, her eyes sparkling, and chattered back. She cast a glance at Thessa and spoke softly to her. Thessa responded in kind.

The old woman's eyes appraised Benjamin, then she turned to Stephanos. Her voice sharpened and she pointed to the wine, and then stepped forward to pour. Stephanos's answer was little more than a grunt.

'We should drink before the walk to the stones,' Thessa translated, sitting.

Stephanos and Benjamin returned to their places and the old woman continued talking. She gestured to the two men and they strode into the unfinished house and returned with their own cups and put another bottle on the table.

She walked over, splashing liquid into the containers, never stopping her chatter.

Then she returned to the table with the empty bottle and her eyes included them all while she talked, and Benjamin nodded to her as if he understood. And she smiled, rattled on more quickly, and reminded Benjamin of how a favored aunt might treat a nephew.

Benjamin tasted the wine and smiled at the aged woman. She beamed and moved back into the house, her words falling away.

The wine wasn't particularly to his taste, but it quenched his thirst and was better than most ale.

Stephanos poured more for them all, without asking, before they even finished the first mug. When he reached Thessa's drink, he added a few soft comments—and her smile at him didn't reach her eyes. Benjamin's fingers squeezed the mug. He'd known a man who liked to inflict pain once—he had broken Ben's fingers—and Stephanos reminded him of that heathen.

Benjamin looked at the new house and imagined Stephanos taking her through it, showing her this room and that, and she would be planning where the children would sleep. This house wouldn't have straw bedding, but real furniture and mattresses. She would be the reigning queen of the island, but at what cost to her?

'Captain?' She spoke the word quietly and stood. 'We are ready to leave now.'

He turned his head to them. Stephanos watched him with the look of a man about to trounce a rival in a duel taken beyond first blood. Benjamin saw Stephanos signal the men nearby—the older scarred one and the young one. With a tilt of his head, Stephanos told them to follow.

Benjamin noted that Thessa's fingers twisted in one end of the sash at her waist, absently pulling it tighter, but watching the men.

Benjamin only had the one weapon in his waistband and instantly plotted out a strategy, knowing the biggest one's body would work best as a shield, and the knife in the brute's sash would be quicker to reach, and larger, than the one in his own boot should he need a second weapon.

'Are we ready to see the stones?' Benjamin raised his left hand, palm out, and then as he lowered it he unbuttoned his coat.

Stephanos turned without waiting for a translation and walked beside Thessa.

The Greek wanted Benjamin to know he understood his words, Benjamin realised. A game to Stephanos—pretending ignorance while admitting he knew the language.

Benjamin kept his right hand resting at the opening of his coat and his ears listening to the movements behind him. He didn't like such games, but he understood them.

Chapter Seven

Arriving at the site, Stephanos gave a brief shake of his head. Thessa moved to the ground where the figure lay. Bits of freshly unearthed stone mixed with the dirt the captain had moved. No one could walk into the area now and not see the small mounds of freshly scattered rocks and earth. The opened ground was no deeper than a man's hand and might have been long enough for him to lie in. Several blocks Benjamin had uncovered were part of a circular arch and he supposed the figure of the woman had once stood inside the arch.

Stephanos stood over it, one hand at his hip, looking down.

Benjamin stopped beside him. The woman's features were visible. He could see where he'd slivered away a piece of her nose and she had a chip on her right brow. She even had a pock scar on her chin—though he supposed it was from an errant chisel, or her fall on to the ground. But the mark made her more real. Her eyes stared up, but they weren't lifeless. The poor woman had seen a lot and now her final resting place was being disturbed.

An urge to sail without her hit him—to leave her in her own world. He thought of his ship, filled with idle men who, even though they were of good enough character, were not ones to be ignored for long. They were intelligent enough to think of their own ways to amuse themselves and rarely did these amusements endear everyone. Often, they were preludes to disciplinary measures.

But he needed the rock to trade for *Ascalon*.

Thessa's face came to mind even though he looked at the rigid carving. That was the countenance the artist should have put on the rocks. He wished to have a painting of Thessa—in the water.

He kept his eyes down, but he imagined the work he could have commissioned if she posed, shoulders just above the waves. Perhaps the painting would be horizontal, with her swimming on her back and just the tiniest tip of her toes sticking from the blue.

Shutting his eyes, he took a breath. A woman should not be as alluring as Thessa. It was not fair to mankind. Particularly sea captains.

He'd fallen in love a score of times and the sea always washed the object of desire from his thoughts, but none of the women had flashed through the water—and risen from the waves.

He must leave the island. He had to get Thessa from his head. Looking again at the pale rock, he thought of the *Ascalon.* He needed his ship. She was his life and his future. The statue was his gold to support the mistress of his heart.

Stephanos moved to one knee and with his sun-browned fingers scrubbed away the dirt from the rock's face. He dug a bit longer, using his hands, and hefted one way and then the other to pull out a ball of ridged stone. He held it out for Thessa to see.

'The bun of her hair.' Thessa examined it, moving it in a circular fashion.

Her fingers traced the rock ridges, thoughts

hidden, and she used her nail to dislodge the caked dirt, bringing the carved locks of hair into full view.

Stephanos stared at Thessa. *'Melina thelo aftos?'* His brows wrinkled.

Thessa let out a deep breath, shut her eyes briefly and nodded. Benjamin felt certain the other man could hardly believe Melina wanted the stone.

Stephanos stood, turned to Benjamin and spoke a few more sentences.

Thessa frowned. 'He says she is a goddess. Worth much. Very much coin.'

Stephanos gave a hard toss, hurling the rock to Benjamin's midsection.

Benjamin caught the thrust. He tossed it upwards with one hand, catching it. 'Maybe if one needs something to break out a window glass.'

Stephanos's lips quirked up. His words flowed quickly and Benjamin recognised one word quite well. *Musée.* The French, not Greek, word for *museum.*

'Over two years ago,' Thessa translated, 'when the man from the French museum visited, he told everyone he would be interested in seeing any carvings we might find. To have two men, you and a man from a museum, interested in stones convinces Stephanos she should be guarded carefully. Perhaps the lady is worth many coins.'

Benjamin nodded. 'Perhaps. Or a rubbish heap.' He frowned while rolling the stone ball of hair around in his hands, seeing every side. 'Except for this bun, of course. I see its value in many ways. It would look quite attractive sitting on a desk to hold down papers when the breeze flows—in a dimly lit room.' He pitched it to Stephanos, and the man caught it. 'How much for just the hair?'

Stephanos tossed the bun back on to the ground, barely missing Benjamin's boots. The Greek's words quickened.

'He does not want to bargain for her piece by piece. The hair you can have. The rest of her— he is not sure you are a man to take anything from his land.'

So the bargaining began. Benjamin hid a smile inside himself. He turned his back to the excavation and let his eyes roam over the faces of the two guards Stephanos had brought along. Then he turned to Thessa. 'I'm a ship captain. I have spent much feeding the crew to bring them here, I have so little left. I have no time to haggle for a broken rock. When I heard of it, I didn't know it was in so many pieces. He should pay me many coins to take the rubble from here.'

She didn't speak to translate, but when Benjamin faced Stephanos again, the Grecian's blink was a bit too long and his lips too still.

'But you may tell him,' Benjamin continued, 'out of my extremely generous spirit, I can offer him twenty piasters.'

Stephanos didn't move a muscle and Benjamin wondered the Greek didn't tire of hearing the same thing twice, having to wait while she translated between them. A damned annoyance. Both the waiting and the man.

But perhaps Stephanos used the words of translation to test his own knowledge of English and to discover if Thessa spoke the exact words or softened things.

Stephanos didn't shake his head, but instead, stepped to the hole. He put one of his boots against a mound of whitish dirt and raked the dirt back over the opening.

He looked at Thessa and spoke as he stepped from the excavation.

'He says she doesn't want to leave and that is well with him. He will think about the price overnight, but you must have a higher offer or he will send notice to the museum in France. He says it is sad that it costs you to let the ship sit idle and he does not want to make you linger. But, he cannot decide. So you wait.'

Benjamin had his true initial bargaining price planned and had left himself room to double it. His first offer had been a jab, a first foray into the process, nothing more.

'It could take some days, many days,' Benjamin continued, 'to have a response from the French museum. And the more knowledge of a transaction, the more people who will have a hand out for a share. If Stephanos takes the funds from me he can take his share and tell the leaders of the island he sold it for whatever price he wishes. I make him an offer of...' He paused, knowing this one was more in line with what he might expect an old statue to cost. A broken one could not be worth much, especially in the pieces he saw. Thessa's sister had taken an arm, which now rested in Poseidon's world. The worthless hunk of stone could never be put back together properly without an arm. Never. And he was certain the remaining one had been broken. He'd been a bit careless, and, while he'd certainly not meant to hurt the face, he'd not been particularly careful with the piece.

It would be less costly to have a whole statue commissioned than to put this one together and have new arms reconstructed. His sister-by-law was daft.

The stone woman's hair wasn't even attached to the head.

The bun now sat, askew, on the cheeks, near the poor nose. He couldn't help himself. He bent down and moved the hair from the face. The woman wasn't looking too pleased.

He stared down and then across to Thessa. He could see her likeness in the statue. But maybe it was all his imagination.

He looked across into Thessa's face. Nothing out of alignment. Eyes dark and rimmed better than any kohl marking could ever accomplish. Face powder, and whatever else women used to enhance their appearance, would be wasted on her. She was crafted better than the woman at his feet. But if he looked closely, the resemblance to the statue was there.

But the bland stone could resemble many other women. And perhaps that was why she'd been created. A woman to have no features of her own, except maybe a nose too much in the way. She'd have a connection with all the others who might peer upon her.

He realised he'd been staring at Thessa, but she watched Stephanos.

'One hundred piasters,' he offered, but when he looked to Stephanos the man's eyes had changed. He'd watched Benjamin's perusal of Thessa's face. The dark glitter in Stephanos's glare wasn't greed. His fist clenched and he spoke quickly, until he paused with force. His next words chopped the air.

'Bariemai ta Agklika.'

Thessa spoke. 'He is sick of English. He has no intention of parting with the statue.' Thessa's eyes darted from Stephanos to Benjamin and then back to Stephanos.

Benjamin gave Thessa a smile—a smile Stephanos could see. Benjamin controlled his temper. 'As you wish.'

Benjamin took a step to the side and looked at the disturbed earth. He crouched down a moment, examining the stone profile, trying to imagine her in a museum. He shook his head. She couldn't be worth much. Some men did get all lathered over broken pottery shards though, so he could be wrong. He stood.

The statue stared up, blankly. He moved to examine her from other angles—noting the not open and yet not closed mouth. When he squinted, he could imagine challenge in her face.

But perhaps he imagined it because he felt the challenge in himself. He wasn't certain his older brother hadn't concocted the journey and involved *Ascalon* as a test to see if their *infant* brother could finally follow through on a task they felt worthy of their family.

Benjamin had not been very old when the tutor suggested to their father that education would be wasted on the boy. The man had left his post, saying he couldn't teach such a child. Benjamin knew everyone in the family agreed. Even he agreed. He couldn't keep his mind on anything in a book.

His next tutor had been given instruction not to spare the rod and the tutor took it as a boon. From daybreak until well into the night, Benjamin was forced to keep his face in a book. So he determined to forget everything the man taught him and sometimes he swore at the man because he knew the punishment was coming anyway and he wanted to get it over with.

University had loomed and he'd heard the stories Warrington and Dane brought home from Oxford. He'd thought he would die to be confined with all the tutors. So he'd done the sensible thing and had run away from home. The first time hadn't been well planned and he'd been brought back. The second time had not been so simple, but he'd been twice as determined.

His father had slapped Benjamin so hard when they'd found him that Benjamin had crashed into the wall and broken a lamp. He still had a mark on his shoulder from the glass. He'd been relieved the light hadn't been lit because oil had dripped from his hair. As far as Benjamin knew, their father had never touched War or Dane in anger.

They almost didn't find Ben the third time he escaped—and looking back, Ben was surprised his father had even looked after the words they'd had—but the older man paid well and coins spoke. His father hadn't brought Benjamin home, though. Ben had been sent to live with Gidley's father, his punishment to work at the docks. His father had said his youngest child had to learn what it was like to toil without coins.

He'd worked in a dank, dark warehouse, moving out everything from whale oil to dried animal skins. He'd learned to live with the scent of death around him.

And now, when Stephanos moved behind him, the whiff of death touched Benjamin's nostrils and he listened for the slightest shift, and he watched the two sentries, knowing he'd be able to tell by their expression if Stephanos moved to attack from behind.

He needed to get off the island—and take this mocking statue with him. And soon. Not only for his ship, but also to stop the feeling of dis-

turbed things better left alone. And some of
those things were inside him.

He should leave the stone woman. He should
go back to Warrington and say he'd failed. He
could keep his ship and still sail under the aus-
pices of the East India Company. He wouldn't
own *Ascalon*, but he wouldn't lose it. If he lost
both the contract and the offer from Warrington,
he'd be unable to pay the men and would have
to sell his share of his vessel just to fund another voyage. He damned sure wasn't going to
say he'd failed.

Stephanos spoke again, to Thessa, and Benjamin wished he'd at least paid attention to the
tutor during the Greek language lessons.

'My sister,' Thessa said to Stephanos, 'wants
the rocks. As a gift to me, a wedding gift, give
them to her.'

Stephanos's response was guttural—sharp,
erupting with the force of Vesuvius.

Thessa answered. Her right palm went out,
fluttering towards the disturbed earth, her voice
choking with her emotion. Her eyes darkened.
Benjamin could not understand the words, but

he could understand the raised tones and pleading hands.

Stephanos had made a tactical error. He had refused to give his beloved's sister something the former viewed as waste.

Stephanos took a deep breath and planted his feet firm. Thessa closed the distance, stopping less than an arm's length in front of the Greek. Melina's name was mentioned several times. Thessa pointed to the stone and to her own chest.

The Greek's words were short, terse, to Thessa. His eyes moved to Benjamin, obsidian-black. He stared at Benjamin, muttering under his breath.

Like pebbles bouncing down against the side of a rock outcropping, Benjamin's thoughts banged against his skull. Stephanos shouted so strongly his words spat into Thessa's face.

Flames of anger scorched Benjamin's gut. He wasn't aware of his movements. They were no more planned than his heartbeats and he had his knife in his hand before he knew it, and he tugged Thessa behind him as he stepped towards Stephanos.

Thessa screamed.

She tried to wedge her body between them, but

Benjamin's shoulder kept her back. Stephanos's blade now pointed towards Benjamin's stomach.

The sharp tip didn't concern Benjamin. He fully intended to leave the blade in Stephanos's hand. That would be a safe place for the weapon after Benjamin had removed the man's arm.

Benjamin shouted, warning Stephanos from Thessa, but he wasn't sure what he'd called out.

The other two men, Stephanos's guards, only now snapped to awareness.

'He wasn't hurting me,' Thessa gasped out to Benjamin.

Benjamin stood ready to resume his task. 'His words… His hand on the knife…'

'He said no harmful speech.' Her hands were clasped on Benjamin's arm, trying to hold him back.

Stephanos spoke again, words low, direct and to Benjamin, but without translation. Thessa turned to her betrothed, speaking rapidly, soothing. Stephanos shook his head, but stepped sideways, not to increase the distance, but to keep Thessa from between them. She moved, not letting the manoeuvre work.

Benjamin turned, keeping her at the edge of

the fray, but he knew he could not do well with one arm secured by her and against three men. 'Back away, Thessa,' he hissed, pulling himself free.

Her eyes were wide, pleading. 'Stephanos believes you are not to be trusted with me and he thinks you are going to take me when you leave, as you did my sister.'

'Warrington took her. I didn't.' He watched the Greek and the two others who now surrounded him.

'Your ship.'

Her skin must have paled because her eyelashes and hair looked darker. Her face lighter. Hair escaped her bun and draped around her face.

And if Stephanos was concerned with the possibility of her leaving on *Ascalon*, then Thessa could be considering it. Benjamin waited a heartbeat before answering. 'You could.'

Her eyes widened. '*Leave* with you?'

She didn't have to sound as if she'd bitten into a biscuit weevil.

Stephanos's response bit into the air, but the Greek didn't move.

Benjamin stopped. 'Thessa.' And when he heard the tone of his voice, the breathless way he'd said her name, he felt a shard of fear go into his heart. He'd never heard himself speak so. But his voice stilled everyone more quickly than a command.

Sable eyes stared at him. She brushed back the hair which didn't want to stay restrained.

'You should come to England with me,' he said. 'Your sister, too.'

Stephanos slipped the blade higher. His minions waited for a command.

She shook her head. 'That soil is tainted. Full of men who leave their families in search of nothing. The land is far from my true sea.' Her eyes followed the path towards her house. 'This land is my spirit. My mother's grandmother was born here. My ancestor's bodies made the soil of this land. Their blood has been turned back into the sea. Better to die here than live any place else.'

'Your sister, Melina, is happy in England.'

Lips closed, she murmured disagreement. 'She may be. She rarely swam and was our father's daughter. I am different. I am of this land.' She shrugged.

'You could return here if you didn't like England.'

She tilted her head sideways, eyes challenging. She shook her head. 'Stephanos…he understands.'

The Greek swaggered while standing still.

Benjamin realised his error had been much larger than Stephanos's.

Stephanos's mouth darted up into a victory smirk. He spoke, and his accent was heavy, but Benjamin needed no interpreter. 'You have the rocks, English. From me. I will take your sad price. Tomorrow bring the coin and I let you dig.' He looked at Thessa, his eyes bright. 'But I have the woman.'

Ben remembered how he'd seen her clothed the first time he spotted her. Breasts pressing against the garment slicked to her skin. Clothing shimmering down, outlining the swell of her bottom. The juncture so hard to take his eyes from, and then, the disappointment. Legs. Legs, graceful, trim and perfect. And not what he'd imagined. At first. Then he'd been relieved. A man couldn't bed a mermaid. But a woman with legs—oh, that could work out.

Especially if the woman had risen from the sea with the grace of a goddess. Her legs would wrap around his hips quite well.

And now he would have to leave her. And someone else who didn't deserve her would touch her. But then, he doubted he deserved her either.

When he stepped on to the planked deck of the *Ascalon*, Benjamin felt the comfort of being home, but also a sense he was losing as much as he gained. But the men on board were his true family. He kept them alive. They kept him alive. Every day at sea they saw the same sights, ate the same food, lived the same lives. And the sailors respected him. He'd never felt this close to his blood family.

Gid leaned against a mast and stared back at the island.

Benjamin couldn't help it. His eyes darted to Melos.

'I figured you'd be cozenin' up to Thessa tonight.' Gidley stepped beside Benjamin. 'Wonder if she changes form in moonlight? Not every day a man gets to look so close at a mermaid.'

The cabin boy ran up, footsteps thumping the deck and his reddish, dark hair flaring out behind him—at least the part of it not falling across his eyes. He stopped short, in a way that only a lad who has no meat on his bones can halt. 'Capt'n? You seen a mermaid? A real one? One with fish guts and everything? Did you save her for me to see? Or did you let her go back to the sea? What colour fins—'

'No mermaid, Stub. Just a woman.'

'Awwww.' Stubby's shoulders dropped. 'I been wantin' my whole life to see a fish woman. I'm the only one on this ship not never, ever seen one.'

'They are fables, Stub. Yarns,' Benjamin said.

'You never seen a mermaid neither?' Stubby asked. 'For real and true? Old as you are and you never seen one? Not in all your years?'

Benjamin eyed the boy. 'I'm twenty-seven. Not a grandfather. I've not seen everything in the world.'

'Twenty-seven...' Stubby muttered. 'I can

count that high, but that number be too long for me to put on paper.'

Benjamin changed the subject. 'Gid. You were to teach him numbers and cut his hair.'

'I couldn't find the scissors,' Gidley answered.

'Go,' Benjamin commanded to Stubby. 'Get the scissors from wherever you hid them.'

'I suppose I can hunt 'em down.' Stubby left, and his feet would have lagged behind him if he'd left any more slowly.

Benjamin looked at Gidley. 'You know the tricks he pulls…'

'But the little whelp didn't—'

'We are the only true parents he has.'

'I know. But he be squirmin' like a weasel and sayin' how his momma liked his hair long and…'

'You will cut his hair and keep it from his eyes and teach him to use a flannel to at least clean his face.' Benjamin's voice thundered. 'And his ears.'

'Yes.' Gidley's head dropped just as Stubby's had.

Benjamin turned back to the sea. He clenched his fists and beat the railing like a drum. 'You have to be a good example for the boy.' He waited. 'You must tell him the difference between truth and yarns.'

'Yes.'

'And I don't care if you never see a clean face in your mirror the rest of your life, he needs to have some proper ways. We have to teach him. He has no one else.'

'Yes.'

'And if you give me any grief on this, you understand—Cook will be teaching you to read the Bible and every Lord's day you will lead the men in prayer.'

'Cap'n. Men don't like to be forced to pray.'

'I will tell them it is your idea.' He smiled.

'Yer would. I'd ruther yer whipped me in front of all the men 'afore I had to learn readin'. And it's hard to say writin' is the devil's work when the Good Book is filled with it. But all it looks like is little worms moving around on paper to me.'

'I assure you. Reading can be learned even when the words are mangled. If it means putting your fingers over the letters and hiding them so you can make the others disappear while you figure out the one, it can be done.'

'A lot of work just to read the Good Book when I already figured out which rules I'll follow and which I won't.'

'Do not be teaching the boy the same commandments you taught me.'

Gid's voice plumped into a self-satisfied rumble. 'You admit though, Capt'n, mine's a lot more pleasurable.'

Ben grunted.

'And speakin' of pleasurable,' Gid said, 'we havin' any females with us on the trip back?'

'No. I gave Melina's sister a chance to sail with us and she refused.' The words scalded his insides.

'Well, they both be gettin' a fine dowry, 'cept I noticed I didn't see you leave with it.'

'I had other things on my mind.' He glared at Gid. It was hard to put fear into a man who'd been like a father to him. Gid had taught Ben everything he knew about sailing. 'I don't want any of the men on the island taking the funds from the women. And they appear to have no one to watch over them.'

'That's the idea of dowry. The woman marries and the man gets the funds and the apple dumplin's,' Gid said. 'Don't see as how you can change that.'

Ben did not like the idea of Stephanos getting the dowry. Or anything else.

'I'll give them the funds in the morning, before I get the stones. I'll tell Thessa the details of it and make sure she knows she does not have to marry the Greek toad just because he is constructing a home. She can use the funds as she wishes.'

'She not be real likely to turn down a man buildin' her a house, 'specially if he tells the chickens which way to scratch on this island. You be best just givin' it straight to him so no one be takin' it from her.'

Benjamin unclenched his fists, slowly. 'That man she foolishly thinks to wed won't know I'm speaking with her. And I'll not tell the women it's a dowry. They can choose how to spend it. I'd get the rocks now but even with lanterns it'd be too hard to dig in the dark and too easy to break them—'

'Yer just wants to see the woman in the daylight one more time,' Gid interrupted.

Ben ignored him. 'It'll take a bit to pull the marble out of the hard dirt without destroying it. The wind won't hold for ever and if we get becalmed then I'll lose even more time and money before I sail on a real voyage again.'

Benjamin bowed his head for a moment and shut his eyes, trying to blink away Thessa and her world. He could not get the image of her in the water to leave his mind. And the gnawing in his belly at the thought of leaving her. 'I have no care for Thessa, other than my concern for a woman without someone to keep the evils of the world away from her.' He said the words aloud so he could hear them.

'Can't blame yer for wantin' to look a little more,' Gid continued as if Ben didn't speak. 'Niver seen a sight like that woman slippin' through the waves myself and I be older 'n' water. Yer dropped a spyglass and yer swore not one word. A right good spyglass. Not one word. Yer couldn't speak.'

'A lady was standing there,' Benjamin snapped. 'I was being a gentleman.'

Gidley's eyes widened in argument.

'You look like one of those bulging-faced blenny fish,' Benjamin muttered, 'and you better brush up on your prayers because you're going to be needing them or saying them.'

'I already been sayin' my own. I'll be pleased to see the back o' this land. It's peaceable lookin', but there's much more'n a few rocks buried here. This here place is full of spirits. Why, that smell in the air, I'm thinkin' it be caused by demons. They leave an odor behind. Yer walk in a room and it smell funny—half the time a demon been there.'

'Gid. This is a ship. Not your personal Drury Lanc.'

Gidley tapped his nose. 'I can scent out a demon better'n anybody I ever seen. And this place...' He gave a sniff to the air. 'It's startin' to stink grand.'

Thessa and Bellona watched the single lamp flickering on the table in front of them. Both she and Bellona had already changed into their night clothing, the same garments their mother had always insisted they wear when swimming.

Their father had brought them the first ones, chemises, from London, and said all ladies wore them under their clothing.

Bellona put her hand near the globe on the small lamp, letting her fingers shadow the walls. 'You are to wed Stephanos. I do not even want him as a member of my family.'

She waved her hand back and forth through the glow of the light and both of them stared towards the shadows on the wall. The little room still contained the small figurine their father had once brought. His easel was gone. They'd burned it on a night their mother was shivering.

'If…' Thessa couldn't finish the sentence. If. *If* meant nothing. She crossed her arms. 'I said I would never marry a man who would leave his children like our father did. A man who told us how much he loved us when he left…and never looked back. A man who said the word love… and it meant less to him than a hole in his boots.'

'Forget the boots, Thessa.'

'He was planning to stay longer that time. You know he was, then he realised his boots were worn through. He had to return to London for the new ones he wanted. He did not say that, but you know it's true.'

'Now you will be wed to Stephanos and wanting your husband to leave.' Bellona made a soft fist, but left her two fingers out like little legs, letting them make running shadows on the wall.

'I thought about asking his mother if she could speak with him concerning his ways, but she hardly has a thought in her head.' Thessa put her palms flat on the table and imagined a ring on her finger. She didn't wish to wear an ornament Stephanos gave her. 'I might not marry him.'

'You can't stay on the island if you say no.'

'Nor can you.' She looked at the shapes Bellona made and put her own hand up into a fist, except for her index finger, and her shadowed image jabbed Bellona's.

'That ship in the harbour…' Bellona let her hands rest on the table. 'It took Melina. We can get them to take us. I know we can. Melina did. They're men. They're sailors. We'd have passage…just like Melina did. She did it. We can, too. It is not much different than doing what you must when you marry Stephanos.'

'This talk is why we kept such close watch

over you. *Mana* made us promise to take care of you and keep you from the men. You will not watch your ways around them.'

'I am…I am not scared of them. I want to marry some day, but I will not change when I do. I will learn to fight just as men do.'

Thessa shook her head. 'You don't understand how harsh they can be. Stephanos is only one man. One man is better than a ship full of them. We know Melina sent us the kettle and shawls, but we don't know if she's even alive now…truly. I cannot believe that she didn't return—if she is free to. The captain said she is married. It makes no sense a man would send his brother this far for nothing.'

Thessa remembered the captain's lean fingers when he touched the stone. He'd held the statue's hair and looked at her face. He'd had sadness in his eyes. Perhaps he'd not liked that she'd been broken. 'I wonder if the stone is worth something?'

'Melina promised to find Father. She said she'd send back something for us to live on. We were to just wait for her.' Bellona shook her head. 'But

I am not like you. A husband who leaves is better than one who stays.'

'Stephanos will not let me change my mind now. He would be just as hard to convince to let me go as it was for *Mana* to convince our father to stay.'

The memories of her mother crying rushed into her mind. Thessa still could not keep the anger away. Her father had left and her mother had cried. *Mana* had cared too much and sometimes Thessa had been angriest at her mother. She should have thrown his things after him and told him never to return, that she'd find someone else she loved more.

Bellona reached back to pull her pins from her hair and braided it as she spoke. 'I don't care if our father is alive or dead. You know what he is like. I know what he is like. Only *Mana* and Melina believed any good in him.'

'Perhaps *his* mother should have...' Thessa mocked her father's voice '...tossed him into the sea when he was born and seen if Neptune would send back a son.'

'He was just angry when he said that to you.

He didn't mean it. You just wouldn't sit still enough when you posed.'

'I am his *daughter*. He should know what I look like.'

Bellona laughed. 'It is not that easy. Painting is difficult.'

'Not as difficult as *Mana's* life. Father put everything else in his life before us. At least Stephanos will not leave me. I know the house he is building is as much for himself as for me. I do not care. He will be there when the children are sick and I will not be alone to care for them. I will have a home and my children will have a home. And the roof will not leak.'

Thessa looked at the bucket in the corner— the one they always left out because the water always ran into the spot there. They'd had to move the bed. Bellona slept in the first room. Thessa now slept in the one their parents had shared.

Bellona shrugged. 'Just because you marry Stephanos, do not expect your roof not to leak. All of them do.' She reached across the table and patted her sister's hand. 'I wish you and Stephanos much happiness. Better you than me.'

Thessa flicked her sister's hand away. 'Remember you will be living with his mother in the old house beside us and caring for her.'

'I will let you visit. And perhaps we can find out her secret for loving him. Because without one I do not think you can.'

Chapter Eight

In the room closest to the outer door, Bellona screamed. Thessa jerked herself awake, sitting up, covers falling to her waist. Her door burst open and a hulking form stood there.

It couldn't be true, Thessa thought, but it was. Stephanos was right. The sea captain was kidnapping her to take her from the island.

'No,' she shouted.

'Skase.' Stephanos's voice?

Lantern light shone through the open doorway. She heard rustling and realised several men were talking in the other room, all in the island language. Bellona called one a pig.

'Leave,' she shouted, forcing her mind into alertness.

'No.' Stephanos spoke as he walked into the

room. 'We are here to take you to safety. Get clothing. Now.'

'We are safe,' Thessa said. 'Leave.'

'No,' Stephanos repeated, stepping to the bed. His fingers pinching her arm, he jerked her to her feet. 'The English took your sister. I will not let them take you.'

'Stephanos. I do not see them here. Only you.' She righted her feet under herself and pushed at his body, but he didn't release her.

'The captain.' He leaned towards her, his wine-soaked breath blasting into her face. 'He will come for you. He is waiting until the moment the ship is sailing, then he will put you in the boat and take you. I cannot risk letting you leave. I lost your sister. I will keep you.'

Again she tried to push him away. 'He won't. He only wants Melina's treasure.'

'Foolish woman. A man does not sail from England for rocks. Your sister sent him for her family. When his ship leaves, he plans for you to be on it. I cannot take the chance of losing you. We will marry tonight and you will be in my home. Safe.'

'No.'

He gave her a swift jerk towards him, holding her shoulders. 'You do not tell me no—I will be your husband.'

The bed was at the back of her legs and he was at her front. She could not pull free.

'Has he touched you?' Stephanos's voice shook with rage. 'If he did, I will kill him.'

Stephanos's guttural growl became louder and his hands clamped her arms immobile.

'Stephanos. He did not touch me. He is here for the marble. They think it is something important because Melina told them of the French Museum's interest. The captain has been all that is kind.'

'You *champion* him? A man who would steal you?'

She kicked at his leg. 'Stop, Stephanos. You are breaking my arms.'

He released her. 'I do not wish to hurt you, Thessa, but I will not let an Englishman steal what is mine. We are to be married. Our house is almost complete.'

He turned to the men at the door. 'Leave.'

They backed out slowly.

'Thessa.' Stephanos's voice was calm in a way she'd never heard it before.

She wrapped her arms around herself, rubbing the burning places on her arms where he'd grasped her.

This time, his hands were gentle, and he reached one finger to trace over her cheek, the trail of his finger feeling cold and rough. 'Thessa. I love you. You know that I do.'

'Yes. I am aware.'

He whispered, 'Can you not say you love me?'

'Stephanos…' Thessa forced her voice to be light. 'We have discussed it. I am not a woman who loves easily.'

'No,' his voice rumbled. 'You do not. You wish for the house I give you. The children. But me. Me. I am nothing to you.'

Bellona's scream jarred the air.

Thessa bolted to run to her sister, but Stephanos's arm shot out, blocking her.

'I will see to her.' He scowled. 'It is what I do for you. Your wishes.' Then he gripped her hand, his touch unyielding. He pulled her out the door, shouting to his men to take their hands from Bellona.

Thessa was pulled along, just in time to hear Bellona gasp and Mikis's laughter.

Stephanos swung his free arm towards the door. 'Mikis, bring Bellona.'

Mikis lunged for Bellona, trapping her against the wall and then pulling her close to him.

'All is well, Bellona,' Thessa said, trying to calm her sister and to convince herself.

'No. It is not.' She spoke English.

Thessa pulled away from Stephanos, but he would not release her. 'Stephanos, let Bellona light a lamp and gather our things.'

Stephanos pulled Thessa to the door. 'My men will get them.'

'Stephanos.' She stopped. 'I am in my night-clothes and so is Bellona. We must dress. The men…'

'Very well. I give you a short while, but if you are not swift, we will go—dressed or not. In the darkness it matters little.'

'It matters enough,' she said, pointing to the lantern. 'Outside.' She waved him away.

She noted he didn't pull the door shut behind him.

She heard the footsteps go down the stairs and

then her mind focused on another sound. Bellona's breath was in short rasps.

'Get dressed. Quickly. Put your clothing on over the shift.'

Bellona answered again in English. 'You cannot.'

'Quiet. Get dressed.'

Both women pulled their white blouses over their heads and pulled on the gathered skirts, before twisting their sashes around their waist.

Before they left the doorway, Bellona whispered, again in English, 'We cannot do this. Convince him to wait a little longer. I will find a way to get us weapons and we can protect ourselves. Make him wait. If we had weapons, we could be as strong as the men. They would listen to us then.'

'You know as well as I that it will not work.' Thessa moved down the stairs. 'He would rather see me dead than let me go. He has already said it. And I believe him.'

Thessa's blood rushed faster with each step towards Stephanos's house. Several men walked behind her and Stephanos beside. Bellona walked in front with Mikis guarding her. Mikis put his hand between Bellona's shoulder blades and shoved her along.

Stephanos saw the push. 'Do not do that again, Mikis—or I'll think you do not like her and will call off your wedding to her.'

'Marriage?' Bellona's shriek jarred Thessa's ears.

Stephanos laughed. 'I think to have two marriages tonight. Thessa and me. Mikis and Bellona. Mikis has asked for marriage and I have given him permission.' Stephanos leaned so close his whisper tickled Thessa's ear and made the hair on her neck rise. 'Two weddings tonight.'

'Ochi,' she disagreed. 'I will not share my day.' Her sister would never survive marriage to Mikis. Mikis had broken his sister's arm and it had not been an accident.

Stephanos's hand went around her waist and he pulled her into step beside him. 'We wed first. I cannot wait any longer to have you in my bed.'

She only remained standing because he held her. She'd not thought it to really happen. She wasn't ready now. It was too soon. She couldn't marry him. Especially not if it wouldn't even save Bellona. Both of them would be trapped. Her mind cleared in a way she'd never felt before. She turned to Stephanos, leaning in to him, softening her stance. 'You should want a big celebration.'

'Do not worry. We will have your festival. We can let others dance and sing the whole night through. But we will be having our own celebration.'

'Stephanos…' She forced his name through her lips and past her frozen smile. 'You are hasty. Just because of the ship in the harbour. We were to wed after the house is complete.'

'Thessa…' He took her hand as they walked and pulled her fisted fingers to his lips and kissed them. '…I look forward to hearing you praise me to our children, telling them of this night when I rescued you from the English sea captain and claimed you as my own.'

'He is leaving the island, Stephanos. He wants the treasure.'

'He would also take you, Thessa. But you are to be mine.' He released her hand. 'Now I have a house. A wife to care for it and give me children. And the foolish captain—he can have the rocks and be on his way.'

He switched to English. Thessa knew it was so his men could not understand him. 'You will learn to love me soon.'

'What if it can never be in my heart?' She spoke softly, hoping kind words would go beyond his ears and into his mind.

He shook his head. 'I do not believe that. How could you not love me? I will have the biggest home on Melos. I am the heartiest man on the island. I can give you children. You will be so joyous to be with me you will make me happy. I give you the best man you could ever have. The other women will be jealous you have me. They tell me so now.'

'Taking me from my home in the night is not the way to begin.'

'My wife. You have much to learn about me. But I will show you all.'

He grabbed her, pulled her to him, pressed his lips to hers. Stephanos rammed his tongue into her mouth. She felt waves of revulsion. Could smell dirty hair and dried spit. She clenched her hands into fists and forced herself not to push him away. The effort caused tears to form in her eyes.

The men behind laughed.

Stephanos pulled back. 'That is just the beginning.'

'Oh…' She could think of no words to say. He'd left behind the taste of tobacco and soured milk. She already wanted to bathe.

He resumed walking, catching up with Mikis and Bellona.

'Two weddings,' he shouted out, raising his fist in a victory punch. 'What you say, Mikis?'

Mikis reached out, put an arm at Bellona's neck and pulled her into him. Her feet stumbled and her hands pushed against him, but he kept walking, pulling her along 'Only one.' He let her rise enough to keep walking. 'This one is too pale for a wife. But we will see how she is for *erotiki ormi*. If she cooks well, and you pay me enough, then maybe later we wed. But I do not marry until I know if she can be trained.'

The men in the back laughed again.

Thessa saw Bellona's hand clench.

'*Adelfi*,' she called out and took a quick step,

grasping her sister's hand. 'Later. Now you must celebrate my marriage with me.'

Bellona didn't speak.

Stephanos pulled Thessa back to his side.

'Let them court. Now you are only to think of me.'

'Stephanos,' she answered, making the word pleasant, 'I think of nothing else.'

His mother's house loomed in front of them.

Stephanos turned to look over his shoulder. 'Go for everyone. Wake them.' He moved forward again. 'Tell them it is a matter of life and death. Theirs, if they do not drink with me. My lovely Thessa and I will wed when the sun is rising over the water. We will have wine. I have much drink ready for my wedding. Mikis—have enough and you may be happy to marry, as well.' He laughed. 'Because, my friend Mikis, you will marry whether you wish it or not. I wish my friend to be as happy as I am.'

Bellona screeched and Mikis pulled her tighter.

'If I have to marry her, I will,' he said. 'She looks like she wants a man who can give her many babies. I am good with making the babies.'

The other men laughed and Stephanos turned

to him. 'You must thank the captain in the morning, Mikis, for if he had not seen our women, we would not have had so many nights with them as we will have now. The babies will be sooner.'

As his mother's house appeared in the moonlight, Stephanos turned to one of the other men and waved an arm. 'Go. Get everyone awake. Tell them it is the wedding they have been waiting for.' Then he took Thessa's hand and forced her arm into the air with his own. 'We are to be wed and everyone is to be happy.'

They filed up the stairs and into the small main room of the older home. The house was much like Thessa's, but did not have a pail in the corner. The curtains were not so faded and a broom leaned in the corner with a shawl draped over it.

The smell of cooked goat filled the air. Stephanos's mother stood at the stove, stirring a pot. She turned to Thessa and gave her a warm smile before returning her thoughts to her cooking. The table held a collection of wine bottles, all full. Preparations for the wedding were underway.

Thessa let all resistance fade from her body. She gently put her free hand on Stephanos's chest. 'Let Bellona fix my hair. I cannot marry with it looking like this. I must look to every-one as if I am happy with this, Stephanos. They must know how happy your bride is.' She pulled her fingers free from his and pulled the braid around to show him.

Stephanos reached to grab the back of her neck and pulled her forehead to bump against his. 'You are perfect as you are.' He released her. 'But I know how women are.' He waved her to the other room with a flick of his wrist. 'But you go care for yourself and Mikis and I will find something else to do.' He reached for two wine bottles and gave one to Mikis. 'This is to start with, my friend.'

Mikis released Bellona and slapped her bot-tom. 'You go, too.'

Moving to the corner, Thessa took a straw from the broom and caught it afire enough to light a lamp and take it to the room he indicated.

Bellona followed and Thessa clasped her sis-ter's arm when she moved towards the sword propped against the wall.

The bed was small, but it had covers on it. Thessa pulled the one from the top. She saw marks at the foot of it and wondered if he slept in his boots. With the sword, she slit the cloth into two large halves. 'We can't fight them all. We would only lose. We are going out the window. We'll go to the harbour. To the captain.'

Bellona nodded. 'But how do we know they will not toss us back to Stephanos?'

Thessa thought of the captain's eyes while she tied the two pieces into a knot, knowing they would not need much to lower themselves from the second floor to the ground, but she knew they couldn't run with a twisted ankle. 'He won't,' she said.

Together, they pulled the small bed to the window and she put the end of the cloth firmly around one leg of the bed.

Thessa went first, finding the descent easier than she expected.

She'd barely landed when Bellona scrambled beside her and they both took off running into the darkness towards the sea where the English ship docked.

When they reached the shoreline, Thessa bared herself down to the chemise she'd left on and

bundled her clothes. As she tossed them behind rocks, she realised hiding them would do
no good. Stephanos would go to the ship first,
knowing it was the only way they could truly
escape him.

She ran into the water. She heard Bellona behind her and together they swam towards the
dark shape floating in front of them.

She gauged them only a third of the way to
the ship when she heard men's voices shouting
on the shore.

She felt certain they'd travelled enough distance so their heads couldn't be visible in the
water. But she had no illusion Stephanos would
not believe them swimming to the ship. On an
island—there was no place to hide. Their only
other choice had been the English ship and she
could not be sure they would take any risk on
her behalf.

But the captain…he would. She knew it.

Sounds travelled well across the waves. She
heard Stephanos shouting for a boat and knew
Bellona heard, too.

All her strength was going into her arms
and legs.

Chapter Nine

Benjamin was lying on his bunk, fully dressed, unable to let himself sleep. He wanted to be awake on this night. Every minute of it. Because never again would he be so close to Thessa. He thought of undoing her hair and watching her swim with it fanning behind her in the water. Of very human legs, bared to the sea. Of the way her lips had tasted, sweet, spiced and alive.

Tomorrow he would give her the dowries for the two women, sealing their fates.

He tried to think of the ship—his true home. He reminded himself of the reason he'd docked at Melos. But his mind returned to Thessa. He would think of her for many years to come. Perhaps for ever, and if a storm wave caught him and pulled him down, pushing breath from his body, his last thoughts would be of a woman who could frolic in the water like a mermaid—Thessa.

She was a woman. Just one more woman in a world of handsome women. Just a woman who happened to have the look of a goddess and the grace of a mermaid. A simple woman routinely created—every thousand or so years.

He looked at the planks above him and told himself not to let such insensible thoughts enter his head. He was foolish to believe she would stay in his thoughts. He was thinking more like an old man who'd spent his days in a bottle and had let his memories become sotted.

He had to leave the island. He would make sure to get all the marble in the morning, have it loaded and sail at darkness when the tide changed—if they had enough wind. He hoped for the winds and wanted to hear the luffing of the sails as the air shook them.

Ascalon needed him. The men needed his leadership. And to have a woman like her, and to leave her behind when he went on a two-to-three-year voyage… It would be just as Gid said. A family pulled a man under the waves.

He could not sail with his heart dragging the ship down.

The palm slapping against the outer wood of his door alerted him that Gidley knocked.

'Enter,' he called out.

'Capt'n.' Gidley opened the door, leaning inside. 'Lantern shining on the shoreline. Somethin's happenin'.'

Energy flared into Benjamin's limbs. He followed Gid to the railing, barely keeping off the mate's heels. He needed his spyglass. All he could see was two bobbing lights. The shore hadn't had night activity before. But now, shouts reached his ears.

He watched the boats skimming in his direction. It didn't make sense. If someone wanted to board them secretly in the night, they wouldn't have the lanterns. If they wanted to talk, daylight would be a better alternative.

With both hands clamped on the railing, he saw another small boat leaving the island. Perhaps two. He didn't take his eyes away.

'Quietly. Assign weapons. Then bring me mine.' Benjamin preferred to err on the side of caution and sometimes caution included an explosive and rabid attack.

Gid whispered orders to the men. Sharpened swords waited in a barrel to be passed out. Flint-locks in a crate and then powder and balls.

Benjamin stared at the boats, watching them get closer. Gid nudged Benjamin's personal pistol against the captain's hand and he took it without a word. The weapon would be primed and ready.

'Captain Benjamin.' A breathless female voice called, barely loud enough to reach their ears. Both he and Gidley stilled, locating where the sound came from.

He heard his name repeated and leaned over the side. Two dark shapes were in the water.

Benjamin shouted an order to the seaman on his left. 'Throw down ropes with a loop on the end. That's the quickest way to get them aboard.'

Gidley stood at Benjamin's right, also staring into the depths. The first mate's voice trembled. 'They truly is mermaids. And they've gone back to their fish forms in the night.' His voice quivered.

Benjamin turned to Gidley. 'What did you say?' he barked out the words.

Gidley stepped closer and whispered, 'Them's mermaids. We can't have mermaids on board. They can call up a storm in an eye blink. They's worse than...than...than...anything.'

'They're women.' He watched, making sure his order to retrieve the women was followed without hesitation.

Gid's voice was a trembling whisper. 'We be in the land where mermaids is most potent and their powers started. Any man know's anything about sailin' will tell you mermaids is worse than—than—fevers and boils together. They'll eat our gizzards in our sleep.'

'Then you'll have to stay awake.'

'Capt'n.' Gidley's shrill whisper almost cracked Benjamin's ears. In the darkness, Benjamin couldn't truly see Gidley's eyes, but his head shook.

Benjamin squinted, seeing two shapes in the water and maybe three boats following.

'Yer makin' a blunder the size of the ocean,' Gid said, voice breaking. 'And blunders is what'll keep you from having regrets. Regrets is something dead men don't have.'

Benjamin lowered his voice, but he knew it was too late to erase Gidley's words from the other men's ears. 'Gid. I had best not hear the word *mermaid* from your lips again.'

Gidley let out a deep breath. 'Yes, Capt'n.'

'Thessa,' Benjamin called out, leaning over the railing again. 'Can you wait for a rope?'

'Hurry,' she called back.

He realised half his crew had materialised around him. Everyone heard Gid's nonsense.

'Pull them slowly,' he commanded to the men with the hemp. His heart beat faster at the thought of Thessa boarding his ship. He turned back to the side. 'Put the loop under your arms and use your feet to keep from bumping into the side of the ship if you can.'

Half his mind and his hearing stayed on the women in the water, but he spoke to the men. 'Douse all lanterns. We don't need to be targets.'

He reached to take Thessa's rope even as he spoke and one seaman stepped away, giving up his place. Benjamin pulled, feeling the resistance as she became like dead weight, and he guided the rope to an even tug. He didn't want Thessa's skin scraping against the side of the ship.

When she rose enough, he reached out, lifting her over the railing. Water sluiced over him. He brushed his cheek against her hair, filling his nostrils with the mix of her and the salt water, and his stomach tightened and his lips parted. She smelled better than *Ascalon*.

'We need something to cover her,' he said, putting her on to her feet. He kept one arm around her waist and the other hand brushed back the dripping tendrils of her hair. He didn't have to look. He knew exactly what she wore. She'd worn it the first time he saw her. The skin under her wet garment burned into his palm. He turned her, pulling her into his arms, concealing her from the others' eyes.

He watched another man lift Bellona on to the decks.

'Coverings, now,' he snapped out. 'From the physician's bunk.' Half the men scrambled to do his bidding. The other half, he was sure, were looking at shapely legs and checking for feet.

'I cannot marry Stephanos...' Thessa pushed back from his shoulder, and ground out the words to the question he didn't ask '...and if I stay on the island, I will have to marry him. He planned to force us tonight.'

Her sister spoke. 'Mikis is evil. You must stop them.'

'We will see you safe.' Ben spoke even as the truth of what he might have to do burned in his stomach. Only Gid knew how killing affected him. Ben did what he had to do to keep his crew safe, but he would never shed blood when there was another way.

Benjamin heard footsteps pattering up and his thoughts jerked into the present. He heard a squeak befitting any able-bodied seaman whose voice was changing. He whirled and saw the cabin boy, Stubby, stumble while running with the sword.

'Mermaids?' The word whooshed out of him. His eyes were the biggest part of his body.

'Stub.' The one word, with the emphasis of Benjamin's whole body, halted the boy.

Benjamin felt Thessa tense in his arms. And she wriggled a bit, turning to looking at the men. When she moved, her wet backside slid against the exact place Benjamin would have requested in his dreams. Only one part of his body could move and that one could not think. The parts of him that could comprehend could not linger on anything else but Thessa.

Benjamin tried to pull her around again, but she twisted. He pressed his lips together and turned sideways from the men, using his body to shield her and holding her against him, concealed. He felt the heat rising in him, even with the damp clothing between them, and he stepped back. His hands remained on her waist and he was thankful for the darkness.

'Captain. We can't risk keeping her,' a voice called. 'She'll sink the ship or just get us all killed.'

'If I am a mermaid—' her voice rose when she spoke to the men '—do you really wish to anger me by tossing me overboard? How far do you think your ship would get then?' she asked. 'And the long boats would sink even faster.'

'Miss—' The seaman on his first voyage spoke up. His voice cracked. 'You surely wouldn't kill a man with a family to attend to.'

She drooped back against Benjamin. 'I would

never do such a thing—unless tossed overboard.'
Now she tensed upright again.

Benjamin bit inside his lip. The woman was
as full of nonsense as Gid.

He tightened his grip on her and moved her
forward—again increasing the distance between
them, but in doing so, his hands slipped with the
wet fabric and skin, moving to the base of her
breasts.

She grabbed his hand, grasping the smallest
finger, the one that he couldn't bend, and forced
his hand back. He firmed his hand on her waist
and she released his finger. The added elbow
jab to his midsection was more reprimand than
attempt at injury.

Touching her had not been his fault. The
woman had damn near ground her hip into his
member so that he couldn't think and when he'd
accidentally touched her breasts, she'd almost
broken his finger.

At that moment, men ran up, holding enough
coverings to wrap four women in and he helped
arrange the wool around Thessa. He'd never
smelled a woman so close who'd been doused
in sea water. If they could bottle the scent and

sell it, sailors would be lining up for it. A torturous blend to have on a long voyage.

But even after he had her wrapped, he kept his arm around the covering, holding her at his side. He'd just made the decision to sail and the true treasure would be on his ship.

'Can you not shoot at them? Now?' The younger sister interrupted his thought. 'Even just to frighten them back to the shore?'

Ben shook his head. 'In the dark, with weapons flashing, it would be easy for the two of you to get hurt. It's too hard to tell who is friend or enemy.'

'Just keep him away,' Thessa said. 'If you do not shoot him, he will board and take us.'

'The other choice is England,' Ben said. 'We can sail tonight and I can deliver you to your sister.'

The women didn't know it, but by comparison to their lives on the island, they would be wealthy. He had to let them appear to make the decision, but he was having to force himself not to tell Gid to pull anchor. They were about to sail.

Bellona said, 'I'd risk swimming to England before I'd marry Mikis. I want to leave.'

'We must,' Thessa said. 'We must leave everything in our lives behind. Everything. We do not
even have clothing.'

At that moment, Ben heard another shout from
land. He had to get the women to safety and he
did not want another dying face in his thoughts
he could never forget.

'Pull anchor.' Benjamin spoke to Gidley. 'We
have to catch the wind and leave. If we're becalmed, we risk the men gathering others from
the island and trying to board us.'

He knew he was leaving behind the sculpture
and the chance to own his ship, but he had no
other choice he could live with.

The slapping of the oars in the water came
closer. 'Stubby,' he commanded. 'Put the women
in the physician's cabin. Now.'

Stubby reached for their arms, but the sisters
didn't move.

'Go,' Ben said and realised he would have to
release Thessa for her to leave. 'He'll show you
where you'll be staying.'

The women both paused for a moment, then
turned and followed Stubby.

He moved close to his men and lowered his

voice. 'If we stay and the Greeks set the *Ascalon* alight, we lose everything. Even if we were to give the women back, there is no guarantee. We must leave.'

One woman on a ship was trouble. Two was catastrophe.

The sound of the oars slapping the water increased.

Benjamin turned back to the sea, took the flintlock from his waistband and fired into the water near the boats.

The rowing stopped.

He handed the gun to Gidley. 'Reload.'

A voice shouted out from the boat. Stephanos. 'Send the women back to us.' His English needed no translation.

Gidley took his own flintlock and handed it to Benjamin.

'You might as well ask for the ship. You're getting neither,' Benjamin shouted to Stephanos. 'We give them refuge.'

Then the man on the boat began speaking so quickly and so fast Benjamin couldn't even guess at the words.

'He said…' Thessa stood in the shadows behind him, and spoke softly '...he will trade you the treasure for us.'

Benjamin noticed how well his orders had been followed, but he would deal with that later. For now, he might need the help with the language should Stephanos speak to his men.

'No,' Benjamin shouted across the water.

Again Thessa translated the response. 'He said you will not be able to return for the treasure or steal it in the night. If you do not send us back now, you will not get us or the treasure. He says if you do not let us return, he will tell the French sailors in the harbour where the stone statue is. That you will never have her. This is your only chance.'

Stephanos started speaking rapidly again.

Benjamin heard the gentle dropping of the sails being unfurled.

'Each of our swivel cannons is loaded and we will capsize or kill them,' he told Thessa.

The command was quick and Ben knew what had been said before Thessa translated. Oars slapped the water and the men were leaving. They gave up too easily. His head darted to

Thessa. She stood still. He couldn't read her eyes and she didn't speak.

'Is there something else I should know?' he asked. 'No argument from them. They retreated as if getting water on their toes might frighten them.'

The silence was a little too long. 'I do not think he is giving up,' Thessa said and expelled a breath. 'I would say he is not giving up. I do not see Stephanos leaving so easily.'

She gripped the railing and leaned forward. 'Stephanos,' she shouted, 'I am not coming back. I am not. Do not try to get me.'

Nothing answered her call. The boats didn't slow or stop. A faint order reached Benjamin's ears, but he didn't understand the language.

'What did he say?' Benjamin asked Thessa.

'He told them to hurry.'

To hurry. Benjamin turned and shouted the same command to his own crew.

A man who had built a house for a woman would not give up quickly. A man who'd only nailed two sticks together would not turn back so easily. Ben accepted the knowledge that the battle had not ended before it had begun. It had simply not begun.

Someone moved to stand at the railing. The other sister.

Damn. Did the women not understand that orders were not invitations to be declined or accepted on a whim?

'I cannot believe we are doing this, Thessa,' Bellona said. 'We are leaving everything. We will have less than our leaking roof now.'

Benjamin frowned. He'd just traded half-interest in a ship for two women who did not follow orders and were wearing blankets and underclothes—all in front of his men.

'Gid. Take the women away.' His voice had no inflection. 'Explain to them the nature of an order.'

Gidley gasped out a 'Yes, Capt'n.' He whipped around, grasping both women's arms and taking them to the cabin.

Walking to the foremast, Ben rested a palm on the smooth wood, and inhaled deeply, letting the perfume of *Ascalon* fill his nostrils. *Ascalon.* The entire ship was coated to keep her waterproof. The mixture of oak wood and pine resin always cheered him. But now, it hardly comforted him. He felt he'd traded away his true love. He shut his eyes and rested his forehead against the wood. He hoped she'd forgive him. Being in *Ascalon's* bad graces could make for a very difficult voyage.

He heard a ripping noise and a cacophony of curses from the crewman. He didn't need to look around to know a sail had just torn.

Taking stock of the room where a demanding man had deposited them, Thessa realised the space wasn't built for two people. The lantern didn't give much light, but she could see well enough.

The bunk built into the wall could only hold one person. With cabinets under and cabinets over, even sitting in it would be near impossible. Rough brown covers rested on the mattress. She expected a bed better than the straw mattress she used, but wasn't certain this was it.

Taking the woollen wrap the sailor had given her, she folded it and placed it on the bed.

She thought of the swim and the escape. Stephanos hadn't been the only reason she'd jumped into the water. Something else had pulled at her. The captain was leaving and she'd not wanted him to go. She didn't know why she felt that way, or why the captain's face kept appearing in her thoughts. Even his voice. She'd heard the irritation and the sound of command mixed together when he'd spoken after pulling her from the water. When he'd put his hands on the underside of her breasts, something had taken over her body with the same burn of a volcano. All the warmth was pulled from the air and released into her body through his fingertips. She'd had to remove his hands to stop the rippling warmth he created.

She could still feel the imprint of his fingertips. Every place he'd touched still warmed when she remembered the moment. He might have taken his hands away, but her body retained the knowledge. The intensity had been too overpowering to trust. And too volatile to be safe.

'Are you going to tell the captain about Stephanos's sloop?' Bellona asked.

'I can't. What if the captain doesn't take us then? It will not go well if he sends us back to the island. And Stephanos—by the time he readies the sloop, we will be well on our way. And the waters are vast. He'll not find us.'

Bellona groaned. 'I hope not. But I do not think I will wager. I would have once wagered I would never be on a ship to London. And now...here I am. I want to see the town, but I fear sailing.'

Thessa listened. Through the wooden walls she could hear strong orders and muffled curses. 'I don't think you are the only one who is upset about the travel.'

'I thought we would have to... That you would wed Stephanos...' Bellona stood so close their shoulders touched. She lowered herself on to the wood beneath their feet. With knees propped up, she huddled, but let the covering the men gave her fall from her shoulders to the floor, but it rested partway under her. 'I thought perhaps you would marry him and then cause a fight between him and his men, and hope he was killed.'

'That is wrong.'

'Less wrong than what he does.'

'*Skase,*' Thessa ordered, hoping her sister would quiet.

Bellona ignored the word. 'If I had seen the captain though, I would have known what you

were planning. I would have had my satchel prepared and sent ahead to this ship.'

'I did not want this.'

'I never claimed you were much on thoughts.'

Thessa nudged Bellona's foot. '*Skase.* You talk
nonsense.'

'He left that statue to save us.' She rested her
arms across her knees so she could prop her
chin. 'Well, if you do not want him, I would like
to have him. He has already done more for us
than Father ever did.' Bellona clasped the leather
string at her neck and pulled free the gold medallion she wore. She held it for Thessa to see.
'But we do have this.'

Thessa turned away from her sister. Bellona
said so much just by mentioning their father's
name and touching the necklace.

Thessa had found one of the gold coins in the
rubble, and been so happy. She'd taken it to her
father, and he'd insisted she give it to him. He'd
traded it to one of the French sailors for brandy.

When Thessa found the second one, she gave
it to Bellona and told her never to let their father
know. To save it unless she had no food and then

trade it. Bellona had made a necklace of it and kept it hidden under her clothing.

Thessa could still remember seeing her father drink the brandy and the look of sadness in her mother's eyes. But the older woman had said nothing.

Bellona leaned back into the wall and straightened her legs after tucking the necklace away. She shrugged. 'The captain. You really did not tell me about him. I would not mind if he notices me.'

'You are not to touch him.'

'I said nothing about touching him.' She nodded. 'But if he wishes to hold me, I will let him. I expect he will want something in exchange for our passage and I'm not giving him the coin.'

Thessa's hands fisted. 'You…you should be beaten. Mother would be angry with you. Besides, the captain asked before if I would sail with him and he mentioned no price.'

Bellona frowned and drummed her fingers just below her neck. 'Very well. You kept me away from the men on the island. I could not talk to one without you or Melina appearing at my side and treating me as a child. I have never even been kissed. Be aware you cannot do that any longer. I am twenty-two and will do as I wish.'

'We had to keep you alive and safe. We did not want you taken by one of the men.'

'I still almost had to wed Mikis. I will find my own way, and learn to protect myself, rather than chance that again.'

'We escaped. Stop thinking of it.'

'If a woman is to be in a prison,' Bellona muttered, 'it is better she choose the gaoler and choose the one who is most pleasing. And I do not see anything but walls around us and water that we cannot swim through. And a captain who looks very strong.'

Thessa jabbed a finger in the air. 'I will throw you overboard if you touch him.'

Bellona smiled. 'That's what I thought...' She met her sister's eyes. 'I will promise not to bed him—if you will do the same.'

'That is insensible to talk of.'

'Promise.'

'You are evil.'

'And our sister is going to have a child if what the captain says is true. And I have figured out what causes babies.' She leaned forward and kicked her toes out, nudging her sister. 'Promise you will stay from his bed?'

'I had no thoughts of his bed.' She paused, and reached to pull the cover from under her sister, causing her to scramble to keep upright. 'Until you mentioned it.'

Chapter Ten

They'd been at sea two days and their seasickness had all but vanished, when the door to Thessa's cabin jerked open. She raised her head from the pillow. Bellona sat on the decked floor, resting on a pallet she'd made from the bedcovers. One of the crewmen stepped in, his light brown hair a tangled mess. One hand stayed on the latch and the other held a knife.

His gaze locked on Bellona. His lips twisted. The dark streaks under his eyes shone against the sallowness of his skin and Thessa knew he did not truly see Bellona, but some vision that only he would ever be able to view.

Thessa moved from the bunk, standing.

'You… You'll cause our deaths.' He took one

step into the cabin and reached for Bellona, pulling her to her feet.

Thessa jumped forward and wrenched herself between them.

He still had the knife, but his free hand reached for Thessa, clasping her neck. The pain from his grip caused a fury in her and she kicked while she pulled at his hand.

Bellona leaped on to on his back. He released Thessa, grasping behind to pull Bellona from him. When he pushed at Bellona, Thessa shoved, putting not just her arms into the motion, but her whole weight. The anger inside her controlled her more than her mind ever had.

His reaction of tossing Bellona aside when Thessa rammed forward caused him to stumble and fall backwards through the opening, his hand hitting the wood and the knife falling to the deck. Thessa landed on top of him.

She lifted herself only enough to stretch her arm to grasp the knife. She put the blade at the vein in his neck. Leaning forward, she held the knife tight. 'You will not hurt my sister.'

The clamouring of footsteps around her let her know they'd become a spectacle.

'You're a sea devil,' he gasped.

She didn't raise her voice, but applied pressure to his neck. The memory of her uncle's death had taught her that even slight strength could prove fatal. 'You could see for certain if I just moved forward.'

'You're mermaid witches,' he said. 'No mere women could steal my sleep. You've bewitched me and the seas.'

Thessa put her tongue at her teeth and hissed, mocking his words. 'If I were a witch, I would not have stolen your sleep. Why would I care about that?' she said. 'I would have stopped your heart.'

His eyes widened when she said *heart*. 'Your power might not be strong enough,' he responded. 'You need to drink our blood to be strong.'

'A man's blood?' she gasped, letting him feel the blade. 'That could not taste well, even mixed with wine. Only a fool would think any kind of woman, spirit or witch, would want blood. Wine is a much better choice.'

'Get off the man.' The voice sliced through the sailors standing around her and the crew shuffled back, eyes still affixed to the pair.

Benjamin stood, staring down.

'Off,' he commanded again.

'He touched me.' Thessa leaned back, removing her blade from his throat. 'And attacked me with this knife.' She held it up. 'And he is two times my size.'

'Now.' Ben's voice wasn't loud, but it had the authority of a gunshot.

She returned the tip of the blade to the downed man's neck. 'Before or after I check him for gills.'

'Now.' The captain's voice whipped into her ears, jarring her.

She lowered the blade and used both hands to shove herself up.

The seaman scooted backwards, using his palms as leverage. 'T'wasn't my fault, Captain. They bewitched me. I was bringing them outside and gonna toss them overboard in the daylight so they'd turn back into fish and swim away.'

'Truly?' Benjamin spoke, the inflection in his

words holding the softness a lover might use whispering in the night.

'Yes, Captain.' He looked up. 'They're in my dreams. Swimming and swimming and swimming and turning me into a fish. And I had to get them off the ship to save us all. They'll take over every man's mind, and then, then we'll all jump into the water, believing we are fishes, and drown. No storm will have to get us, Captain. They'll drown us all with their mesmerism.'

'Do you feel like a fish now?'

'No.' He gulped.

'They're not doing a very fine job of mesmerising you, then.'

'M-more'n you think.'

'Gid. Samuels. Put him in irons. Tell Cook to keep an eye on him.' His vision took in each seaman individually. 'And every man on this ship is to inspect him at the end of the watch to make sure he has not sprouted any fish parts. When he has scales, which do not wash away, or gills, I wish to be informed, immediately. Otherwise, there will be no more talk of mesmerising or mermaids. Understood?'

One of the others stepped forward, voice terse.

'We smell the rain. When you had her sister on board, you about went in the deep. You were laid up until you hit port. We don't want you to die either.'

Benjamin planted his feet wide. 'Last winter, Collins fell from the mast and went in the ocean. We never found his body. I heard nothing about mermaids then.' He stopped speaking, letting his words linger, and his gaze sharpened. 'Accidents befall us. Storms. We had waves last spring that had water pouring into the hawseholes. Water choked us while we stood on deck. Not a seaman here hasn't been in a score of storms, or many more. And if women could turn into fish and sink ships, every one of us has left a woman be hind at some time who would have turned into a mermaid and sent him to the deep. If she killed other seamen as well, I daresay she'd not shed a tear. We'd have been sunk many times over if women could sink this vessel.'

He waved a hand out, encompassing the ship. 'She is the *Ascalon*. And like the sword she is named for, she can move swift, and straight, and subdue greater beasts than a mere man can. Not a one of us could tackle a storm without her. No more talk of fish women—unless you're willing to see how well you can turn into a fish man to swim to England after I toss you overboard.'

He reached out his hand, took Thessa's and pulled her forward. His hands held her shoulders and he turned her so the men could all see her face. 'Her hair is askew and she has a scrape to her cheek. You've seen the mermaid painting in my cabin. Does this look like a mermaid to you?'

'She is right handsome,' someone muttered.

'That is not the...' He paused. 'She has toes. Ten. Count 'em.'

'Aahhhhh,' Gidley's exhalation reflected the look on the other men's faces. 'They's clean.'

'Now does any man here think she's a mermaid?' he called out.

'She's a goddess,' Gidley spouted. 'I just remembered the story of the goddess Thessalonia. She were the most powerful goddess of them all. And she could hold out her hand and catch thunderbolts and lightnin' spears and toss them back into the sky like they was dewdrops. We need her on our ship. She can protect us.'

'Anyone else mentions mermaids and they'll be praying for one to be rescued from my anger.'

Benjamin called out, making sure the men dispersed, 'Furl the royals.'

Ben met Gid's eyes, gave a silent command and saw the blink of a response. Gidley's voice rose and he turned away, half-shouting as he spoke, and pushing the errant seamen along.

'One thing I kept to myself all these years because I didn't believe no man here would think it true is the time I seen this…this fish what swam in in front of the ship and chattered like a baby learnin' its words. Let me tell yer…' He raised his voice to carry to the heavens and he moved away, the men following him like baby ducks gathered around their mother.

A wisp of air brushed Benjamin's cheek and he looked overhead. The clouds were dark. He hoped the weather took his mind from the sight of Thessa's delicate toes.

'Inside. Both of you,' Benjamin mumbled to the women.

Thessa looked at him, her brown eyes showing thoughts he wasn't sure how to decipher. But after that look—he knew if she were an artist, she would have been able to sketch his face to perfection. Though he couldn't ascertain whether she might draw a knife sticking in him.

'He's a fool,' she snapped, staring after her attacker. 'No mermaid would want to mesmerise someone as useless and ugly as he.'

Nodding, Benjamin glanced at the folded cuffs of Thessa's trousers, with the pink orbs sticking out. He wondered if the men still thought of her toes. He did. They were so delicate, and round, and he could have happily spent the rest of the night sitting at her feet, on a big bed, or a small bunk, her foot in his hand and rubbing it gently along the side of his jaw.

He shut his eyes. Never again would a woman be on his ship. Women were nothing but problems—especially the ones with…female parts. And toes.

Blast.

He'd never seen toes so perfect in his life. He gave Thessa a head start to the door by moving her shoulders in that direction and he didn't speak. He rushed them into their cabin and reached to pull the door shut and behind them, himself safely on the outside.

He'd not been able to help himself. He'd

watched her feet. His body tingled while he thought of the sight and warmth crept into him, starting at the midsection and flowing into the rest of him.

Two feet. Two feet that would fit in his hands. Toes he could kiss for hours. Blast her for having perfect feet.

He controlled himself, but he could not help raising his fist to the door.

Thessa answered the crashing knock. The captain stepped inside, shutting the door behind them, his expression dark. His anger made him seem bigger—almost overpoweringly large. His words were a growl. 'You will not cause disruption on my ship.'

'You must control your own men.'

He pulled her to face him. 'Do you wish to see more men in irons because of you? How can we stay alive at sea if everyone is locked away?'

'You could not.'

'I have done that and more.' His eyes admitted the truth of his words. 'We are at sea. My crew is human. Lives depend on my orders—every life on this ship hangs on my words. There is no gaol here to send a man should he disobey.'

'I am imprisoned.'

'No.' He bit out the word again. 'No. But you must let me handle the men. I don't want their throats slit. You only have to scream and the sound will carry. Someone will immediately aid you. I will see to that. But they will be a bit slower if they're afraid you'll stab them.'

'We did not mean…'

'This is life or death. We are far from land. A storm could come up. You *will* get the blame if that happens. I will be the only man on board not willing to toss you into the waves. And every man here will believe I am risking the lives of the entire crew on your behalf.'

She touched his arm to stop his words. The second her fingers brushed his coat, he stilled, changed. His face reacted as if he struggled to remain immovable by her presence.

And when he turned to her, something passed behind his eyes. Not anger. A longing.

Moments passed before she remembered what she'd intended to say, but he'd not appeared to notice.

The thunder returned to his face. 'If a puff of air begins ruffling the sails, I assure you, the men will not think it a coincidence. One carries a trinket some gypsy woman spewed nonsense over because he thinks it makes him manly. Gidley has to spit over the starboard side twice every morning because it somehow keeps a man from falling from the ratlines. The men are as they are. They are good seamen and better than any crew I've ever seen. But they are as they *are*. And telling them not to be superstitious works just as well as telling them to change the colour of their hair.'

'Very well,' she agreed, sighing. 'I will be very careful with what I say.'

His lips tightened briefly. Resignation entered his voice. 'I will…have Gidley take you for an… evening stroll later. The men need reminders you are a woman just like their sisters and mothers. Do not make me regret it.'

He leaned so close, his breath caused vibrations in her breasts. 'Try to act as proper as you can. No weapons. No threats to expose a man's gills. They're particular about keeping such things covered.'

The rough fabric under her hand didn't conceal the muscles and heat of his forearm. 'I *am* a woman,' she whispered.

His eyes flashed haunted before looking beaten. 'I cannot get to London soon enough.'

The captain turned, leaving, and she could hear the orders he barked out to the men.

Thessa stepped back against the wall, dazed. She rubbed her hands over her arms, not sure her skin felt the same as it had before she stepped outside. Not sure anything felt the same.

Keeping her back to Bellona, Thessa slid into the bunk. She clenched her fists, trying to stop the strange feelings in her body, making her not the calm woman she'd always been. Making her feel breathless and aware of Benjamin more than she'd ever been awakened to anything else in her life. Not a safe feeling. A feeling he could somehow change her. That he could control her, not by his own actions, but by her weakening power over her own body.

Bellona's musing voice interrupted her thoughts. 'I do not think you had to tell him you are a woman. I believe he had already noticed.'

Chapter Eleven

Benjamin let the wind run its fingers through his hair, amazed at the perfect sail after the horrendous night. The ocean hadn't been fighting them by tossing waves or winds about, but the *Ascalon* itself had seemed cantankerous, as if she knew he'd chosen the women over the ship. She would make him pay.

He stood looking out over the sea. Gidley was beside him, at the wheel of the raised deck. Now the ship slid across the water, as gracefully as a bird might catch a breeze and glide through the air. Perfection, made all the sweeter by the struggles they'd had.

He tried to push aside the knowledge that *Ascalon* would never be truly his. That thought pulsed in his head, went south to his gut and made his knee tense in pain. By the time he could buy his share of his true home, she would be too old to care. But they would be a fine match because his own teeth and hair would have fallen out by then.

This second trip to the island had garnered him nothing but becoming a passenger ship for two women. One was too many.

Granted, one had the look of a siren. And his memory of her swimming through the water kept splashing about in his mind. He almost wished she would have had those fins. Fins were safer to think about than legs. Thessa had legs, dark eyes and perfect feet. Bad luck tripled.

It had almost hurt when he'd instructed Gidley to find some spare clothing for the passengers on that first night. But it wasn't safe for the men's imagination to keep Thessa and Bellona wrapped in covers.

They'd gathered up trousers and shirts for the women on the first morning. A simple process which should have taken seconds and been no trouble at all. But the men had been quite concerned about not getting the ladies ill-fitting garments. The one who'd pulled the youngest sister from the deep had had to explain three times to the men just the size of her hips and shown just how her waist had fit in his hands and how her breasts had been.

Ben thought back about how Thessa had felt…

'Gid,' he snarled out the word, snapping himself back into reality.

'Capt'n?' his first mate answered, never acknowledging the terseness in Ben's voice.

'What are the women doing now?'

'They ain't peeped their heads out of late.'

He mumbled an acknowledgement and walked away. Gid needed no orders.

Ben looked towards the physician's cabin, thankful for the first time the man had taken ill and left the empty room. He'd not put anyone else in it, knowing jealousy would surface. So the women had privacy at least.

The crew appeared to have forgotten about the women, but he knew it wasn't possible.

The sun rose whilst Benjamin walked the deck, watching for any aberration. The men worked keeping the ropes at exactly the right length. If one rope needed tightening or loosening, then another would need changing, as well.

The intricate dance kept him on his toes, and the steps kept his interest more than any waltz or reel, but didn't take his mind from Thessa.

He'd been on deck an hour and finally put the women out of his mind when the door of the physician's cabin opened. Thessa went straight to the side of the railing and gripped. She hung her head out, so nothing stood between her and the water.

His eyes locked on her. Her clothing pulled tight as she leaned into the railing. He felt a twinge of guilt for watching her, but he didn't stop.

And then, just like a door slowly swinging open to reveal a menacing shape in the room, his eyes communicated to his brain. She was watching the seas…searching. He quietly exhaled all the air in his chest. She expected them to be followed and said not a word about it.

He stepped to the deck beside her, curious to see if she might mention her suspicions.

When he stopped at her elbow, she turned to him and straightened. She rubbed a hand across her forehead. Wisps of hair danced around her face, pointing to the different aspects of her.

'Are you having seasickness?' he asked.

'No. I am not sick. I am being chattered to death. All my sister talks of is the wondrous things she will do whilst she is in London. And I cannot swim to escape her.'

'I have two brothers. I understand. I went to sea.'

Her fingers didn't loosen on the railing. 'You did not wish to live with your family?'

He grimaced. 'I lived in London and was happy there, but I knew my heart belonged to the sea after my first sail with Gidley.'

'Is he your relation?'

He shook his head. 'Not by blood. But I didn't always feel welcome in my home. My mother had died. My father hadn't been happy with my studies before that, and with Mother gone we did not suddenly start consoling each other. He found a sweetheart and she was near my own age. I said something about her thinking of me whilst she kissed him. He overheard. And so did she, because he'd just kissed her and I'd just walked into the room. It was meant as a jest.

Almost. He sold my horse. I left, and when he found me, the next day I was apprenticed out.'

'Apprenticed?'

'Not truly. But I didn't know it at the time. I soon became used to the stench around me, I preferred it over schooling and the arguments with my father.'

'Do you get on well with your father now?'

'I never got on well with him, ever. My brothers did, but not me. He's dead now so none of it matters any more.' Benjamin leaned on to the railing. The sun shimmered and the wind blew his hair. He would have liked to have said something pleasant to the man before he died. Not that it would have changed anything. And they'd not said unpleasant things to each other in the few times they'd seen each other after he'd left home. But it had always felt like talking to a tutor when he spoke with his father.

'We could not anger our father,' she said. 'He would leave. *Mana* would cry.'

'I imagine that would not have stopped me. We just seemed to raise each other's hackles.'

'Hackles?'

'Like the fur rising on a dog's back when it

is ready to bite another dog.' He could hear the sound of his father's voice in his memory. And it was always loud and angry. 'Some people just do not get on well.'

'Would you say you would find my father a man to converse with easily?'

'Well enough.' He turned so she could see his eyes and know his words were not meant to offend. 'But we didn't find an easy accord either.' He let his eyes stay on her and didn't look back to the sea.

'I do not even wish to see him in England.'

He didn't tell her that her father would not wish to see her either. Her sister, Melina, could do that. 'You won't have to. I'll be sure you see your sister first.'

'I don't know if I want to talk with her either.'

'Now I'm beginning to think you might have your fair share of hackles yourself.'

'Melina… If she had returned as she promised, then we might not have had to be here. Perhaps together, we could have found a different way to stay away from Stephanos.'

'She's adjusted well to English life. Helped

care for my brother's children soon after she reached London.'

'English life interested her more than us. Father made her read the language so she could read his letters to Mother and write back. When we were small, he could not travel so easily among the ships. The French ships travel to Melos often, and he could speak well enough, I believe, to convince them he was a native. But still, with the war on, it was a risk to him to travel. I think, if not for the war, he would have left us sooner.'

'Your sister will be pleased to have you there. She didn't expect you to agree to leave Melos, though. She claimed you swam three times a day, if not four.'

Thessa nodded. 'Already, I am missing my mornings in the sea.'

He leaned on the rail. 'I love London, but sailing is my life. Here, on long voyages, we eat little different than the men in gaol. And the imprisoned men are not likely to drown. But instead of the bars of a prison, sailing opens my bars. It's something not everyone can do and I do it well.'

He held a hand out, feeling the breeze on his

callused fingers. 'Every day you're alive, you've beaten the ocean. And if she takes me—' He gave a one-shouldered shrug. 'It is my time. Of course, it's dangerous, though, the vast seas…' He let the silence linger, waiting…giving her an opportunity to tell him why she'd watched the water.

She let out a breath and tilted her head all the way back, but he could tell she wasn't seeing the sails above them, or the sky.

'Being in this ship—I keep wanting to reach for a rope to pull me ashore. A wall to hold me steady—motionless. And there is nothing. No trees. The morning is dead. No bird calls. How can you stand mornings with such silence in them?'

'You cannot feel it? The peace? The magic of skimming the earth quickly?' The horizon fascinated him as much now as it did the first days he set sail.

She gripped the railing. 'The greatest distance I am aware of is to the depths. There is no wonder in imagining my body sinking down into water to be eaten by creatures with teeth bigger than the sails.'

Dark smudges under her eyes didn't take from her face, but made him wonder what thoughts kept her awake at night.

'I have it on good authority that all the creatures down below only eat other fish. They think humans too salty. And the things in the depths have tiny mouths and teeth no bigger than a flea's.'

She gave a tight nod. 'I have been told that water gorgons live below. Monsters with many heads and arms and empty *stomachi*, who think human flesh such a delicacy they fight each other for the morsels.'

'Have you been talking with Gidley?' he asked.

She shook her head, smiled and leaned towards him, her voice only for his ears. 'I am a mermaid, remember. I have friends who have seen them.'

He looked at her. 'You're daft.'

Her humour bubbled out. 'To be certain.'

Benjamin took her hand and pulled her knuckles to his lips and for a moment he savoured the touch of her skin.

He linked her hand over his arm. 'Let me

take you on a stroll and show you the sights of my city.'

Her pause filled his ears. Her head ducked back and her eyes squinted. 'Water. And more water?'

'Then maybe I will see the sights—whilst you are on my arm.' He reached up to touch her hand again, noting the perfect fingers, surprisingly unmarred for someone who must have had to care for the animals and plantings as she had.

She brushed her hair back from her face. 'How long do you think until I can be back in my country? I can go to another island Stephanos does not visit.' She stepped a proper distance at his arm, not letting herself too near him.

'I would not guess. After we reach England, if you want to return to Greece, then you will probably be best to sail across the Channel, perhaps go overland, and then take a short sail back. Although I would not recommend the road travel. I do not see your sister and my brother willing to let you leave quickly. Your sister will want to make sure you are well and you will want to make sure she is well.'

Her eyes took a slow path to his face. 'I have

no relative with control over me. I am not enslaved to anyone.' She shrugged, then reached to align the shoulder of her too-big shirt and said a word he didn't know the meaning of, but was certain it wasn't proper.

He realised one of the younger men was staring at her, eyes stilled in concentration. Benjamin didn't know if the man thought her a simple woman, a siren or misfortune for the ship.

'Please do not teach my men any more words they don't already know. They're quite fluent enough in their own way,' he said.

He squired her around the ship's perimeter, trying to look at it through her eyes.

The routine of the ship was the same as any morning. The bricks rasped against the deck while men scrubbed to keep the wood from getting slippery. The contented sounds of the sails mixed with the men's low murmurs. The masts and yard-arms were, to him, bodies which held the clothing of the ship, and the oaken hull herself, tight as a cradle, hugging them close for safety.

'A ship is a miraculous thing. A world of her own.' He ducked while he walked under the ropes for the yard-arm. 'But what fascinates me the most is that she started out as trees and, when they were felled, they could have become firewood. But shipwrights took the wood and shaped her into a completely different form. They made my home instead of letting her turn into ash. And to me, she rose, much like an Aphrodite rising from the sea. I even love her pine perfume. When I sleep, she holds me, rocking gently.'

He stopped, putting a hand on one of the ropes and letting himself sway with the movement. 'And she is always demanding my attention. If one sail needs adjusted, then all the rigging must be tightened or loosened. She has to stretch her legs or relax and sometimes, just like us, she rests. This is the only true home I've ever had. My true family. My blood has salt water in it.'

Again she watched the seas. 'It's so vast. I didn't know…how we might be surrounded by so much…for such a long way.'

'Nothing to hide behind,' he said.

Her breaths came quickly. 'I suppose not. But still…we're a good distance from land, aren't we?'

He didn't interrupt the silence.

* * *

Thessa didn't know what alerted her that the ship wasn't as calm as she appeared. The captain's jaw was set at an odd angle, though, and his eyes had squint-lines at the sides of them. The men worked at their jobs. But every head was studiously turned from hers when she looked towards them and every pair of lips was grim. These men might not be openly watching her, but they certainly did not ignore her. Sometimes she saw a whisper exchanged between the men and she knew they still had their superstitions.

'I should see how my sister fares.' She meant to pull her hand from his arm, but he put a hand over hers, holding her in place.

He smiled, but she wasn't fooled. A hardness lurked behind his eyes.

'I'm sure your sister prefers moments of stillness. Perhaps she needs solitude, as well.'

She realised she had little choice in the matter of staying with the captain.

'Why?' she asked. And she could tell he knew the whole of her question. But he didn't answer and she knew he couldn't at that moment. Too many people listened.

Instead, he pointed her to the small stairway which took her up a level on the ship to the helm. Instantly, she realised why the captain's hair was trimmed. With the wind puffing the ship forward, whoever steered her would have the wind at his back. If a man didn't keep his hair cared for or pulled back, he would be fighting it from his vision.

Gidley stood at the steering and she saw the speculation in his glance and the set of his jaw.

Then Benjamin led her around the other side of the ship and she knew he walked slowly for the length of his legs. The deck inclined and she stepped into the raised bow of the ship, and he guided her there but she didn't know why.

His voice lowered. She heard him let out a breath. 'The crew needs to see you are a woman. They are watching and they see a simple conversation. A simple moment of a woman discovering the ship and the view. They've seen you walk, bend and roll up the hem of the trouser leg, and stumble when I ducked under the rigging. They need to be reassured in case the wind might change or something else might happen to concern them.'

Once she'd grasped both sides of the railing, and stood, watching nothing more than water and more water in front of it, she could see from the corner of her eye that he put one arm on the rail and leaned into it, standing almost with his back against the side of the ship. He was as close to her as he could be without touching. She turned, looking to the stern, and he moved, just a bit, and blocked the view behind them. She was trapped. And she realised it. She couldn't see anything except the captain blocking her sight. And her back was to the rails.

'I feel a bit confined,' she said.

'The nature of sailing, if one is not used to it. Don't concern yourself, though. We may be one small speck in a vast ocean, but you never know when you'll see another ship.'

He moved aside and extended his reach in a gesture of gallantry, letting her move back into the ship.

Thessa walked back into the cabin alone. Bellona was not inside and Thessa was thankful.

She had not known a man could be like the captain. He'd told her about himself and his dislike of his father. And how the man had sent him away.

She'd once waited until her father had finished painting and was washing his brush, before asking him to take them all to England. He'd said no. That they could not understand London ways. They did not have the proper knowledge of pianoforte or drawing to become true ladies in England.

Bellona had been playing with a stick, pretending it a sword. Thessa could not remember if Bellona had hit the wet canvas with the sword, or if her own elbow had nudged the art when she dived to prevent Bellona from damaging the painting. The easel fell. Sand coated the wet paint. The picture was ruined.

Her father had sworn at them, calling them *nothos*. He'd claimed no man in London would ever want them in his house.

He'd been railing at her so he'd hardly paused when little Bellona had walked up to him and slapped his leg with the stick, but he reached down and jerked the wood from Bellona's hand and attacked his picture with it.

Their mother had stepped outside and the girls

had run to her. They'd left their father to fight his painting and their mother had sent them to visit their aunt.

Days had passed before their mother came for them and said they could come home.

Even now, Thessa knew how much she loved her mother, but she'd not been able to understand why her mother hadn't just told their father never to return.

Whenever Thessa thought of Bellona hitting her father and how much bigger he'd been than the both of them, she always felt a tug at her heart, but she also worried about her sister. Slapping a twig at an angry man didn't always end well.

Bellona walked into a room. 'The men on this ship are afraid to talk to me.'

'They are scared of us.'

Bellona shrugged. 'I think they are more scared of the captain. No one would more than grunt towards me when I asked a question, so I asked the cabin boy why. He said the first mate has warned the men it would put the captain in a temper if they speak to us.'

'Perhaps it is for the best.'

'You say that because you are so busy cozening up to the captain.' She frowned and swayed her shoulders from side to side. 'Melina—Stephanos wanted her. And the other Englishman fancied her, as well. She left us and then Stephanos changed his attention to you. Now the captain walks with you and he is not afraid. But I step out and everyone turns his head away.'

'I told you—they are being careful.'

She raised an arm. 'First you and Melina try to keep me from men. And now the captain does. Mikis didn't even truly wish to marry me. Before that, I had to threaten that French sailor who kept calling me Thessa and scratching inside his trousers. Why is it that all the ones who slither like me?'

'You never told me he scratched there.'

'Yes. He scratched *everywhere*, but that one place was his most favourite.' She crossed her arms. 'All I want,' Bellona said, 'is a man who does not stink, does not scratch, does not make rude noises, does not paint, does not sail a boat, does *not* call me by my sister's name and *does* have a proper way about him. I would like his hands to be clean enough that I do not have to wash after he touches me and I would like not to know what he just ate by looking at his teeth.'

Thessa nodded. 'So a man without teeth will do for you. Good.'

Bellona put her hands over her face. 'And I will have to live with you until I find him.'

'I hope not. You are not an easy person to live with.'

Bellona let her hands fall to her sides. 'I think I will walk around the deck again and again. Perhaps it is not so unpleasant not to be spoken with.'

Benjamin commanded himself to his cabin and shut the door. He was on his ship, yet he was in an unfamiliar land. Thessa. He just wanted to stop thinking of her.

Sitting at his table, he picked up his journal, opened it in front of him, but he didn't reach for the ink. No, he wanted to think of her.

His imagination watched her slip through the sea with ease. He could see her dive beneath the surface and skim just below, and burst upwards, breaking the stillness of a calm world which contained only the two of them.

He imaged her fingers. So slender. He could see them stroking the strings of a harp, or slowly gliding across his abdomen, leaving a trail of heat which would burn into his body.

No—he should not imagine such things, and yet he could not stop. He jotted notations in his journal, hardly aware he wrote.

Benjamin tensed and shook his head, trying to clear his thoughts. If he swam with her, perhaps it would cure him of his madness. In England, his brother's estate had the stream with a pool where he'd learned to swim and he would take Thessa there if he could convince her.

He reminded himself that to swim with a woman did not mean he had to bed her. He just needed to swim with her. She could wear trousers and shirt for all he cared. Well, perhaps not trousers and shirt. She was delectable in the wet chemise. He'd held her when he brought her on board and she'd smelled nothing like the men did when they got soaked at sea.

A woman with the scent of warm skin and island spice could bring any man to his knees.

Swimming with her would be better than bathing with any mystical goddess.

Warrington must never find out, though, because after all, this was his dear wife Melina's beloved sister. There were not enough pedestals in War's opinion to place his wife above, so he certainly would take offence if Ben touched her sister.

Dane, bookish Dane, who didn't look strong enough to survive a cough, but could near pull a tree from the ground with his bare hands—would not take it well either. He had pontificated on Benjamin's heathenish mermaid paintings, even though Dane had helped select one. Dane did not understand the full view of nature. Especially bare-breasted nature. And Dane quite liked Melina as well, so he would be protective of her sister and assume the worst.

With both brothers angry it would make it more of an adventure. But still, he didn't want to hurt Thessa. He'd have to side with Dane and War in this instance, which was annoying to realise.

He wasn't their infant brother any more. He had a family now—his crew. His decisions had to be made with an eye to the future and with logic, not lust. It was one thing to bed a woman who made it her business. He could pretend it hadn't happened if he didn't even remember what she looked like.

But with Thessa, there could be no such pretensions and he wouldn't want there to be. He would want to remember every touch of her skin for the rest of his life.

Yet how much harder would it be to leave her if he could still feel the warmth of her skin on his fingertips?

A man could be on shore, swim a long way into the ocean and still turn back safely. But at a certain point, if he hadn't turned back, he wouldn't have enough strength to make it to shore. He'd have weakened himself too much. And it would be too late. He could not spend so much time with her that he could not turn back.

Benjamin wondered if he was getting some fever from the island. Some mind-numbing thing taking him over, only his mind hadn't faltered. It was banging along, ahead of his ship, thinking of Thessa. Causing his senses to erode.

He wanted to press his face against her belly. Just to lie against her, holding her, feeling her breathing with his cheek against her abdomen and pressing his lips along every part of her.

Chains. He needed a different kind of leg shackle. He needed one to chain himself to his cabin, or to the end of the ship away from Thessa. He could not let himself see her, hear her voice or get near her in any way. And he definitely could not touch her.

No female had ever before trussed his thoughts into such a tangle. He had to stop thinking of her.

Gidley walked in. 'That one been walking about the deck so many times my eyes are tired.'

'Stop watching.'

'Yer right. I did. Right after she went inside. I was just thinkin' of the ship. No chance of us not havin' a storm on this trip.' Gidley spoke barely above a whisper. 'Last time we had one woman aboard and the heavy seas nearly kilt you. This time, two women.' He made a snapping noise with his tongue. 'Yer neck be on its last leg.'

'Stubble it.' The words brooked no dissention.

As usual, Gid kept talking since they were apart from the men. He kept his voice low. 'Yer feel the same way. It's writ all over your face. I can't read much more'n my name, but I can see it. Yer best take your mind from the woman. We've worst skies ahead. They's creepin' up behind, to catch us unaware.'

'Gid.'

Gidley let out a deep breath and handed Ben the flask he sometimes kept at hand, and filled from the captain's store.

'And do you suggest I throw one of the women overboard to see if the sea lets up?' Benjamin asked between swallows. 'Or maybe I could offer up a first mate as sacrifice.'

Gid reached out and took the flask from him. 'No doubtin' yer'd throw me 'fore yer'd pitch that dark-eyed one.' He moved the flask as he spoke.

'Right now I'd heave you over before I'd toss my boots.'

'Them ain't good boots no more.'

'Precisely. And what do you think?'

'Can't say, Capt'n.'

Benjamin snorted.

'Since yer bein' so persistent.' He tilted his head to the side, firmed his lips and squinted his eyes. 'On the one side, we could die in a storm and it'd be a crime not to be enjoyin' the one afore ye' go to the depths.' Then he relaxed his face, and shrugged. 'On the other side, yer brother'll find out and, with him ownin' the *Ascalon*, yer be marryin' the wench. And on the other side, yer bed the girl and yer don't do the job right, I image she'll sink the whole ship just from spite. That's what I'm thinkin'.'

'Rubbish.'

Gid raised his chin. 'I'm thinkin' the lady be upset 'cause yer not kissin' her dainty toes, and she prob'ly be right proud of them toes, 'cause she ain't had 'em long. Yer best think to kiss her toes, Capt'n.'

He thought of Thessa's foot in his hand and how his touch could slip over her ankle and up her leg.

'Toes,' he mused, nodding.

Gidley gave a pleased growl mixed with assent. ''Specially that little high inside part of the foot just 'neath the ankle. That be the cleanest part.'

Benjamin let out a breath.

Gid continued. 'I know my woman's body parts. Has 'em ranked. One through twelve. For a woman I ain't seeing ever after, I might go straight to twelve. But if she's special, I start with one, and if you count "One Ebechenezer, two Ebechenezer, three Ebechenezer," then yer need to get to the count of five on the first one, and then yer move up to ten on the rest and count a little longer each time, until yer can't count no more and then yer go straight to twelve.' He sighed, lost in his numbers. 'Twelve.'

'Oh.'

'Just had to tell yer my secret, Capt'n.'

Ben looked to the window, seeing the sky, unable to guess if rain was in the offing.

'Gid. Are you trying to be a matchmaker?'

Gidley's cap drooped. 'Capt'n, put yer thinkin' to work,' he whined, 'if she be even one finger part-bewitched and things keep goin' the way they is—she be sinkin' us more 'n once. Prob'ly only thing savin' us now is she don't want to drown little Stubby. Women don't like to hurt young folk.'

Ben glared at Gid. He stood and waved Gid to follow him outside. Ben needed to get back on deck and let the serenity of the water slip into him. 'You are my first mate, not my mother.'

Gid didn't answer, but his lower lip poked out.

Benjamin took a deep breath and calmed his voice. 'I am not at all concerned about Thessa's actions. We have a ship to sail. That is all that matters.'

Then Gid laughed. 'I be thinkin' to ask that one walkin' around the deck to wed. Just to save the ship.'

'You can't. You're already married.'

'But yer the only one what knows it and yer'd get forgetful because I didn't leave yer danglin' from that rope twisted yer arm that one time. And I saved yer many times with my seafarin' wisdom, takin' yer under my wing when yer weren't hardly no older'n our Stubby. Besides, my woman's run off somewhere and I've not seen her in a hundr'd years. I figure two wifes who don't want to live with yer be no different than one who don't.'

Benjamin moved to the railing as Gidley re-called his wife's attributes—the main one being she always gave fair warning before she tried to stab him. The man spoke more to himself, and Benjamin appreciated that. He only listened to the rhythm of the words—his thoughts were floating in a different direction, reliving each moment with Thessa in front of him.

Gidley stopped talking long enough to stare at the sky and take a deep breath. 'I don't understand why this crew's such a superstitious lot.'

Benjamin ran his hand through his hair and looked at Gid. 'I suppose they just don't have a true understanding of the world.'

Gid shook his head. 'Me, I understand. I been all 'round the Cape and places no other livin' man ever seen. I drunk some mixture given me in a hut and by an old man what said that potion'd protect me from all kinds of evil spirits and so far it's worked.' He frowned. 'I worry that potion be wearin' thin. Bad luck ahead, Capt'n.'

Gidley's voice changed, taking on the edge that he used when times were serious. 'Them's dangerous shapes on the horizon, Capt'n,' Gidley said as they stood on the aft deck, his voice low.

Ben instantly tensed, staring even harder across the water. Then he realised Gid had his eyes overhead.

Benjamin couldn't keep his gaze from darting up. 'They are not.' He bit out the words. 'Those clouds are the kind little children lie in a field and look up at and imagine the shapes are pets and faces and such.'

Gidley cocked his head up again and looked. 'Yer right. Yer right.' He paused, his mouth contorting as he looked overhead. 'But that's a bad omen.'

'Bad omen?' Benjamin forced his words calm. It would not do for him to become angry at Gidley.

Gidley nodded, watching the clouds the same way a new reader studied words. 'See that fish's tail in that one.' He pointed up, his fingernail dirty. 'Yer other one there—an evil eye. Then the next one—'

'Gidley,' Benjamin interrupted. 'Not another word about bad luck. That's an order. And remember, the most unlucky thing that can happen on a ship is for the first mate to ignore the captain's orders. It causes ropes to fray, crews to anger and waves to roil, and first mates to be promoted to cook.'

'Yer don't have to get all lordy. I'm just tellin' yer what I see.'

'As am I.' He looked to the sky. 'See that little cloud right there. The one with the butterfly wings. It told me.'

'Capt'n. Since them women got on board yer lost all yer good humour.'

'It's right up there with that cloud with the wings. And I remember a man once telling me to keep my eyes on the sea and the ship, and to not let my mind wander.'

'Sounds like somethin' a real wise man would say.'

Ben nodded and gave Gid a thump on the back. Gid grunted acknowledgement. Ben walked away.

The thing that irritated Ben the most about Gidley's superstitions was that more than not, the man would be right. Gid had had a lifetime of sailing and whenever he felt an unease, he pulled out a reason for it. The reason might be daft, but the unease was not.

Every sense Ben could summon from his body, he kept on alert. Wind ruffled his hair and let him feel the speed of the ship. He didn't wear a hat when the sun wasn't blindingly bright, because he could tell the force of the wind by the touch of it on his face and the way it ran through his locks. He kept his hair clean and long enough to use, but not enough to obstruct his vision.

The captain who'd first made Benjamin a quartermaster had done the same. Told him the captain's body was another kind of compass and had to be kept in working order like any other tool. Said a captain's skin needed to be able to feel the air and his nose to scent the air. And if a quartermaster or first mate had two instruments telling them different directions, they'd not believe the one with the bit of grime on it. They'd believe the one looking shiny new and cared for. And a captain was the ship's main compass

Benjamin hadn't thought it possible to keep clean on a long voyage with the salt spray drying clothes into stiff shells, and little water, but he'd discovered he could easily.

Now he turned to the helm, staring into the wake they left behind. Watching and waiting, as he had been for days. He'd not been obvious enough for his crew to notice, although he wasn't certain he'd not caused Gid's unease to flourish. If something was out there, he wanted to be the first to see it.

Even the ship herself seemed to be sailing more

quietly. The seamen were not to converse over-much while they were on deck. Silence meant orders would be heard and a man couldn't risk inattention or disagreements while on watch.

But *Ascalon*. The sails were quiet and the ropes made no noise as they were tightened and loosened. Nothing creaked or groaned.

He watched the sea.

He wasn't sure if his eye had spotted the sun's reflection from a glint of metal—maybe a spyglass—or perhaps some creak from a ship had carried across the wind to his ears. But he knew something was out there and he didn't think it a myth, but something man-made.

Gidley stepped beside him, voice matching the quietness of the sails. 'I seen it, too. Don't know what it is, but I know what it has to be.'

'I saw a glint in the sun,' Ben said. 'I expect we've a spyglass trained on us right now. And a ship's coming closer. Before long, everyone will know she's there.'

Within hours, all eyes could see the ship. The sloop had one mast and her bowsprit stretched near the length of the hull. The vessel skimmed along, bow jutting out like a proud chin.

'The flag. It's white.' Benjamin could barely make out the colors, but that one glared as strongly as a skull would have.

Gidley swore and threw his cap to the deck. 'White is the colour of ambush.' He picked his cap up and slapped it against his trouser leg twice, then donned it again. 'Bet they have as many dif'rent colour flags as we do. We can't outrun 'er, but she'd have to be lucky to sink us—if we didn't have such a high dose of bad luck on board.'

'Gid,' Ben snapped out the word.

'Not sayin' nothin' particular 'bout the women, but my special braces broke this mornin'.'

Ben levelled his gaze at Gidley and the man took a step back and gave a shrug of apology.

'Yer got a point, Capt'n. If the women could sink a ship, that sloop's the one they'd choose.' He pulled out his handkerchief and wiped his forehead, then tucked the cloth away.

'It's the Greek,' Ben said. 'I knew he wouldn't just let her leave.'

Gid whispered, 'My supposin' is we should

tell them about the other good-luck pieces we carry. Swivel guns and flintlocks.'

'All hands ahoy,' Ben shouted, giving the command for everyone to be on deck. Men scurried, some with concern on their faces, others with a gleam in their eyes.

Without a doubt, the sloop was after two particular items.

Benjamin stood, eyes locked on the horizon, letting himself feel the situation and letting himself take in as much of the other ship as he could.

Every man stood listening, silent, hardly moving so that any sound from the other vessel could surround them. The sloop could easily close the distance.

Benjamin let out a breath, words quiet and controlled.

'They won't shoot straight away. They won't want to hurt the women.'

'Temptin' fer us to just start shootin' and keep sailin'.'

'True. But we could be wrong.'

'And the sun could rise from the west in the mornin'.'

'I can't blame the man for wanting her, but I

can stop him from taking her.' Benjamin wondered if he talked of himself as much as he did
of Stephanos. 'How can I fault a man for not
wanting to let someone like her go?'

'She's an eyeful—even with that pointy nose.'

Benjamin only glanced sideways. 'Her nose
isn't pointy and you should not be looking at
her so close.'

'Yer prob'ly don't want to hear my view of her
backside then, eh, Capt'n?'

Benjamin faced Gidley. Saw the lifted brow
and lifted two of his own. 'We will be letting
the sloop close—so I can stuff your carcase on
it and pay them to dispose of you as they wish.'

He turned, taking several long strides to the
physician's cabin.

Chapter Twelve

Thessa gasped at the look on the captain's face. Gone was the calm sea-look of his eyes. Instead she saw the same look of a maelstrom.

'I must speak with you now.' He summoned her to the outside of the cabin, but stopped as soon as the door closed behind her. His body shielded her from sight of anyone else and his hand moved over her shoulder, resting on the wood at her back. She could not have moved an inch if he decided to stop her.

The captain stood so close, even the pine smell of the burnished wood around her didn't completely cover the smell of shaving soap tinged with toughened male.

'Thessa,' he spoke softly, the word sounding like an endearment, but his eyes didn't soften.

His mouth opened and he started to speak, but stopped. She saw the rise and fall of his chest. She turned cold and she couldn't move, wishing him to hurry and fearing what she would hear.

Her insides churned with the same force as when her mother had warned her that sometimes people never recover from an illness, and sometimes they know they will die, and sometimes the hardest part is saying goodbye to daughters.

'The day is going to get worse for you before it gets better.' His words were direct, low—a rumble across her body. 'A ship is following us. Could it be Stephanos?'

She darted her head sideways, but couldn't see anything around his shoulder except water. He knew the location of the other boat and blocked her from seeing it.

'You know I can't let him have you,' he spoke. 'That card has already hit the table and been trumped. You played it.'

She took a sharp breath. 'Do I have no say in this?'

'You did when you swam to us. You will have another chance in England, assuming we are all alive then. You are in my protection. And if he reaches us, as he will with the faster vessel, I will not let his men board. I cannot take the risk to my men's lives. And if you decide to go, I will think it is only because you wish to prevent bloodshed, not because you wish to leave willingly. If you'd wanted Stephanos, you could have had him. You put yourself on *Ascalon* to get away from him—in the night. I must believe in your actions.'

Her arms and legs felt as if she'd swum around the island. Before either of them spoke again, he stepped back and held out his arm. She looked at it. Neither moved.

'We're going to look at a vessel and see if you recognise it,' he said.

She slowly reached her hand up and latched her fingers under and around his sleeve.

'Such enthusiasm.' The words hardly reached her ears, but the vibration of his voice trembled inside her.

She didn't answer, but looked past the rigging to see the other ship in the distance. 'I want this to be over. But I am afraid of what the end will bring.'

'We will find out soon. I will see to that. Right

now, with your help, I am requesting a meeting with him.'

She pulled her hand from his arm, facing him. 'You want him to see me with you.'

'Absolutely.' He reached out, took her fingers and placed them back on the fabric of his sleeve.

His jaw had no slack in it. His eyes changed when he searched the seas. This man could kill, but then she knew Stephanos was the same. His men had a way of boasting—just a whisper spoken too loudly, and easily denied if questioned, but pointing to deeds she didn't want to know about. Now she saw more clearly than she'd ever seen before—of a world beyond the island of Melos.

The captain leaned so close that she doubted anyone from any distance could tell their faces didn't touch.

The quiet of his words didn't soften them any. 'If you wish to return to him, Thessa, you may, after we reach England. I will know you are completely free of him then. You will be able to leave if you wish, assuming my brother and your sister agree. I will be leaving you with them.'

* * *

Benjamin led Thessa to the stern of the ship. They were too far for weapons to reach the distance.

He watched her, a different kind of unease than he'd ever felt before simmering inside him. What if she truly did wish to go with Stephanos, or what if she became hurt in a fray? He could not think of such things. Sometimes a ship was far too dangerous a place for a man. And a woman should not be exposed to such risk.

She dropped his arm and leaned forward, gazing at the other vessel.

'Look familiar?' he asked. He bent towards her, less than a finger width separating them, and cursed himself when he felt his breath catch. He clamped his hands down on the rail and stared at his fingers for a minute to clear his thoughts. He noted the bent fingers. He'd not felt the pain until the fight was well over. Danger numbed parts of him and heightened the senses he needed, and he was thankful for that.

He bent his head, shut his eyes and asked for strength, wisdom and safety for his men. And that Thessa and her sister not be hurt. When he raised his face, he thought perhaps he should have also asked for patience, but that was one thing he didn't particularly want.

Thessa's fingers skittered at the rail, never stilling.

He waited, not speaking. She had too much explosiveness in her movements to keep quiet. Her shoulders leaned forward, head moving as she squinted towards the ship. She wore a braid down her back and oversized shirt and trousers. At a distance, she could be mistaken for a male, but standing this close, no man with blood in his veins would think her anything but female.

'Stephanos,' Thessa said, confirming his suspicions. She turned, meeting the captain's eyes, and shrugged. 'Thinks himself a pirate.'

He calmed himself before speaking. 'You would see no need to tell me of this earlier, certainly, because I would have no reason to be informed of such an unimportant detail.'

She didn't turn her face his way. 'I thought— He might not have followed us. He didn't in the small boats that first night. I escaped him.'

'We had swivel guns. Doubtful those small

fishing boats had anything more deadly than a hook or a net on them.'

'Why would a man want a woman who leaves him in front of everyone?'

'To show *everyone* he could keep her? To best the woman? Because he has nothing better to occupy him? Because she swims like a fish and has a face mesmerising enough to be put on a figurehead carving?'

Her eyes widened at his words, but she didn't address them. 'I could have thought he might follow. But I wished to be wrong. The sea is big and how can two ships find each other in such a place?'

'Pirates do it all the time.' He put his hand up to shade his eyes. 'It's how they fill their bellies. If a ship is leaving one port, going to another one, using the wind to puff the sails—no mountains hide her.'

'I thought Stephanos did not tell the truth about having the fastest ship. He's boastful.' He heard the pique in her voice. 'I had hopes a man who sailed all his days might be able to best him.'

Lips in a thin line, Benjamin turned to her. 'I appreciate you informing me of all the matters

I need to be aware of. Perhaps there is something else you might have in mind that you do not think I need to know, but I could consider of some interest. You might find it interesting that a sloop is built for speed and a merchant ship is built for cargo.'

Benjamin could see her individual eye lashes and the darkness of her eyes. He didn't need to be feeling compassion for a woman who'd neglected to mention that her betrothed was capable of piracy and had a fully outfitted ship. Not that it would have mattered, but still, she should have told him.

She nodded, her tongue just brushing the inside corner of her lip. 'I cannot think of anything else you need to know.'

'Why did you become betrothed to a *pirate*?'

'He *thinks* himself a pirate. He spends too much time on Melos to be at sea overlong.' She stared at him. 'And how could a woman, who has no weapons and no one but her sisters, tell a pirate she does not wish to marry him?' She leaned a breath closer to Benjamin. 'At least he offered marriage. The other men did not and he kept them from us.'

Benjamin flinched the smallest movement. Her teeth were clenched and she dared him with her eyes to challenge her words.

When she realised he did not disagree with her, she spoke. 'I do not see how he could be a true pirate, although I know he is not a kind man. He rarely sails from the island. In his mind, it is his kingdom.'

Then her shoulders fell. 'I feared asking too many questions. The island is not an easy place to live. And one cannot live peacefully there if Stephanos is enraged. No one can. He might not be the true ruler as the dragoman is who lives away, but Stephanos does as he pleases and all on the island does as Stephanos pleases. He doesn't often fight. But, when Stephanos fights, he believes the only way to win is if the enemy is destroyed. He does not fight to win—he fights to wash away all signs his enemy ever lived.'

'I will keep what is on my ship and I have no concern with fighting to the death if it is his choice. A captain's word on his ship is law and so is his sword when a thief tries to take from the ship. They're going to get close. We're going to let them. It's our only choice other than shooting the first shot.' He took his hands from the rails and heard the quiet behind him. He would make one last check and see that the men had not forgotten their earlier training.

He'd been in a fight with pirates once before. Twice if you counted the tavern skirmish.

One man stayed in Benjamin's memory. The man had charged with a knife, but Ben hadn't been easy prey. The man had a fistful of Benjamin's hair and they'd been body to body when Ben's knife had ended the pirate's life. While sliding to the floor, the dead man's fingers had trailed the side of Benjamin's face. He could still feel them.

His words were as soft as he could make them. 'Stay in your cabin and, whatever you do, do not get close to Stephanos or to me. That is the most dangerous place to be in a sea battle—by either captain.' He let his lips turn up. 'And tell your sister the same. Though don't throw yourself in front of her if she doesn't listen. Foolishness in a fight is not rewarded with victory.'

Thessa frowned and turned to stare at the other ship, squinting as if trying to locate the face of the man she'd left behind.

Ben looked at the other vessel. After she closed the distance, the sloop would turn her sails into the wind to come alongside them.

And without his will, his hand cupped Thessa's cheek, pulling her to face him. 'I am baiting the trap,' he said and knew the words were merely appeasement for what he was going to do.

The feel of her cheek against his palm took him from being a captain to being a man looking into the eyes of his beloved. Every time he gazed into her face, he saw something that made him forget how a man was supposed to act and start thinking of those treacle-laden words that made a woman smile.

Touching her, he realised he'd completely erred thinking Thessa had any resemblance to the stone statue. She was far more appealing. Thessa's image truly should be put on a ship's figurehead.

She watched him just as intently as he looked at her.

His lips closed over hers, tasting, letting her femininity caress into every part of him. The kiss fired up his spirit. Erased the memory of what she'd forgotten to tell him. The touch of her lips cloaked him in armour and told him such beautiful things.

He didn't know if the wind kicked up or the waters exploded in movement, or if all the changes were just inside him.

He moved back, his fingertips still touching the underside of her jaw, and her eyes watched him as if she'd been in the same tumult he'd experienced.

Gidley's cough reached Benjamin's ears and brought him back to his senses.

Benjamin remembered he had not just the eyes of the other ship on him, but his own men. Then he cursed himself and backed away from her lips. He could have merely moved his face close enough so the other ship would think them entwined. He could have made it obvious to his crew that he'd not truly kissed her, only acted.

Instead, he'd told his men even more than he told the other crew.

A captain had to almost appear immortal to his men. He had to command them to take actions which would risk their lives. And whatever else, he could not appear to be under the spell of someone they thought a powerful creature who might wish to see them dead.

A romp with a woman would not hurt a captain's authority, but being under her spell could destroy it.

He was a bloody fool.

Benjamin grasped Thessa's upper arm. 'Now he's seen you. If this is Stephanos, he will not be able to put off his attack any longer. He will strike. We know what he wants.'

He watched Thessa's face and saw her trying to sort out her own reaction and her own feelings. He knew what to say to bring her mind back to the ship. She would recognise the face of every man on that ship. 'If she fires on us, we will sink her.'

Only a flicker of her lashes told him she'd heard his words. She stepped back from him.

He felt the movement all the way to his midsection, but had to concentrate on keeping everyone on board the ship alive.

'I understand that you must try to sink him,' she said. 'He is not a coward. He will do the same.'

'Except you are here to keep us afloat. He wants you.'

'I don't think it will matter to him—that he will want to keep this ship afloat because I am here.'

'I do.'

He watched as she considered the words.

'I…I do not want to see people die because Stephanos wishes to marry me,' she said.

'I do not wish for him to be killed, but I'm not risking my men. Or my ship. Or anything. I know what he wants and what he will not get.' Benjamin bit out the words. He would not give a pirate a thread from his ship. Nothing. The *Ascalon* was his mistress and another man could not have anything from her except her gunpowder.

But all his armaments would be worthless if he could not keep Thessa.

Some of his men were untried in battle, but not most. In some form or another his crew had proven themselves tough. Either being waylaid in a port, or against Boney or during a fight on another ship. Two of the men had even sailed on a ship with a letter of marque.

In a fight, when the sound of volleys began and the gunpowder burned into the air, he knew of only three types of men—cowards, ones with duty and ones with a desire to kill. And his men were not cowards. They didn't have blood lust either. But if they saw one of their own fall, duty changed. Blood lust it would be.

He'd made sacrifices early on, adding more swivel guns on the railing. Five men had been given the sole task in a skirmish of going for the other ship's leader. He and Gid had selected them on the ship's first voyage and moved through all the possibilities they could think of—including how to act when the unexpected happened—as it would.

Powder could be unreliable with so much moisture and shooting from one moving object to another did not have much success with small arms. Flintlocks worked best in close quarters. And swivel guns sprayed canister rounds across the decks.

His men knew their duties so well he needed give only two commands. Commence and then cease. He wanted the battle to carry on even if he died. None but he or his men should ever sail the *Ascalon*.

'Stand your posts,' Benjamin commanded. The white flag on the other ship moved closer.

Ben waved his hand, summoning Gidley. The first mate appeared at Ben's side in response.

'See that she gets to the cabin,' Ben said, 'and explain to them both what can happen if they do not keep from the deck.'

Gid nodded, and took Thessa's arm, half pulling her away. Her eyes lingered on Ben while she stumbled backwards with Gidley.

Thessa stopped just inside the cabin. Bellona slept in the bunk. Thessa wouldn't wake her—Bellona didn't need to know about the other ship. And if Thessa had to return with Stephanos perhaps it would be best if her sister didn't know until it was too late. Perhaps it was best if Bellona didn't know any of it until it was over.

Thessa crossed her arms over herself and tried to sort her thoughts.

The captain had kissed her and when he pulled away he'd had an innocence in his eyes she'd never seen on any man's face.

She was surprised she could recollect so much of the moment, but it hadn't seemed like only an instant. She had no idea how long the touch had lasted because it had grown in her mind, rising up to take over her whole being.

Nor had she known a kiss could be anything but another duty.

Now she felt pulled to him as if some invisible rope bound him to her thoughts and her body.

And he'd only touched his lips to hers.

She'd heard the myths and lore of the past, but she'd never heard of the magic a man could hold in his body. And the captain was filled with it. Of that she was certain.

She pressed her bare feet against the wood beneath her, willing herself to not move from the room. She was lured to him by some unseen force.

If mermaids could lure ships to their doom, then sea captains could pull women into another kind of ruin. She could resist an arm pulling her close, but this thing she couldn't see—she didn't know how to fight. And the treacherous part of it was how the magic made her not want to resist.

She'd been caught in waves before and had to fight the water to stay alive. And she'd learned from the moments and taken care. Her body had chilled at the memory, but this was the power without the fear.

Now she knew why her mother had accepted her father's lies.

Her mother could till the ground to make their garden and could nail the wood back on to the steps to the house when their father was gone. But when her father returned, she became lost in his presence. She could still care for her daughters, but she could no longer care for herself. If her father grumbled—*Mana* grovelled. She became helpless.

Thessa and Melina had whispered about the oddness of it.

And now Thessa believed in magic and it wasn't a myth or something of spirits and nymphs.

Perhaps it would be better to return with Stephanos. She would save the lives of the people on the ship and keep herself from becoming helpless, and make sure the captain was not hurt.

She could always hate Stephanos, but she couldn't always hate herself. And if—in the captain's presence—she became the helpless creature she feared, she would despise every bone in her traitorous body.

Ben tore away the thoughts of Thessa from his mind. His job was to keep her and the men alive. Nothing else concerned him. He clasped the rigging. One hand on the ropes, the other touched the flintlock in his waistband.

He heard Gid's footsteps beside him, but they didn't speak. Both watched the other ship.

Benjamin noted when the sloop put its sails to catching up with them. The wind cooperated, bringing the vessel right to their side.

Stephanos stood at the rails and the medallion he wore around his neck glinted in the sunlight. Benjamin surmised the jewellery a good-luck charm of some kind.

'I wish to talk with the women,' Stephanos called.

'Only you board, Stephanos,' Benjamin shouted out. The men on the sloop were armed, but they didn't have the weapons pointed to his ship. Still, he could take no chances. 'But you waste your time. The women are staying with us. They are mine.'

He heard a gasp behind him, of the feminine variety. He'd really not expected Thessa to follow his orders.

Benjamin let the ship toss a hook over their side, and pull the two close enough for Stephanos to climb aboard. All crewmen were armed and trained. The men at *Ascalon*'s swivel guns stood ready to ignite the powder.

Stephanos pulled his head wrap from his head. His hair fell about his shoulders in a tangled mass. Shoving one of his men aside, he climbed on board.

He wore a rough-woven tawny shirt and a coat with huge cuffs. Gold braid embellished the shoulders. His doeskin trousers did nothing to hide his muscled legs. Two pistols were tucked into his belt and a sword hung at his side. He hurled himself forward, his boots landing with a thump on the deck.

Stubby's high-pitched voice broke through the air. 'Bleedin' pirate's big.'

So much for a well-trained crew. He'd forgotten one person who held a sword bigger than he was.

Stephanos stayed at the railing, staring across.

Benjamin looked him in the eyes. Their weapons matched.

Stephanos spoke first. 'I know two words—Latin—I often say when I board a vessel, *Carpe navis*. On long voyages, I try to have someone of a different language. Learning words makes the travel well.' He pointed the sword tip towards Benjamin. 'I recommend.'

Benjamin slapped the other blade away with his own tip. The ring of metal against metal caused everything but Stephanos to fade from his sight. 'Seize the ship, or seize the navy, I'm not sure which you say. But you're not taking my ship, or anyone on her.'

The pirate's black eyes showed feigned nonchalance. He gave a sniff. 'You also spend little time on your attire. It is no sin to look the part of a ship captain. But perhaps it is best you do not wear good clothing. It will be ruined.' He smiled. 'By me.'

Ben's grip tightened on the sword hilt and he flicked his brows up in acknowledgement of the first thrust. The coat had been made to match the Wedgwood buttons and was a fine garment. He'd spent too damn much on it.

'I was not expecting an uninvited guest.'

'I hope you were not expecting me to bring the stone woman.' He shrugged. 'While my men readied for us to find you, I visit the French vessels in the harbour. I told them of the rocks.' He sighed and shrugged. 'I lied to them all. I told them the armless woman was a goddess who would bring them fortune should they take her to their homeland. I told them she is a treasure worth much gold to their museum.' Stephanos put his sword blade slanted across his own chest. 'They believed.' His smiled deepened, but his gaze narrowed and became dark. Stephanos stood straight. His eyes followed movement behind Benjamin. Benjamin could watch the other man's face and see where Thessa stood. 'Now I am here for my treasure that you wished to steal.'

Again movement from behind Benjamin's shoulder.

'Go to the cabin.' Benjamin turned his head only slightly, directing Thessa.

Thessa had one of the deck scrubbing stones in her hands. She did the exact opposite of the command. She stepped in front of Stubby, but the lad quietly took a step to the side.

Ben's throat tensed. He couldn't take his eyes from the Greek. But Thessa stood too near and she also had a green lad with a blade almost at her back. The boy could easily swing wide, not understanding the length of the weapon. She could be slashed from either side.

If Ben lunged in front of Thessa, three blades would be much too close to her. Yet if he moved away, attempting to draw Stephanos's attention, Ben would leave an opening Stephanos could use to capture Thessa.

He had one option. Forward. He made two small, quick thrusts, meaningless—except Stephanos had no choice but to raise his weapon to defend himself.

Stephanos rebuffed the movement easily. His eyes gleamed. 'Ah, English, you can surely do better.'

Just as the man moved his arm the slightest bit, Ben pushed forward again and the Greek had to take two steps back.

Thessa still stood too near. She didn't move. Her eyes were locked. Her face pale.

'She stays,' Stephanos said. 'I want her to see you die.'

One side of his lips turned up and his teeth reminded Ben of a stallion before he took a nip from a mare.

'Thessa,' Stephanos asked, voice calm, 'would you like the fingers from his right hand, or from his left?'

She flung the rock with all her might towards the Greek. He hopped aside. The rock clattered from the railing to land on the deck. His eyes changed. The pupils could not be discerned from the iris and even the white seemed to diminish. 'Thessa, my sweet, remember you will birth my sons just as well if you have only nine fingers.' His voice lowered as if he were speaking to himself. 'If I am generous.'

He looked at Benjamin. 'Before you die, you will have to *beg* me for *her* life. We will see how much you truly care.'

Thessa's heartbeats jarred her. She could not speak. The world around her turned the colour of the blood she'd seen before, but she could not fall. She forced herself to stand and kept her eyes on Stephanos, even through the haze in her vision.

'Stephanos—' Ben's voice, sounding no different from when he'd asked her to step from the cabin. 'Do you wish to fight with the woman or with me?'

Ben's words flooded into Thessa's body, bringing her sight back to her and her mind into alertness.

The cabin boy, Stubby, stood at her side, holding the hilt of the sword with both hands.

'I will…' She'd thought to say she would leave with Stephanos, to stop what she was about to see, but she could not. The words wouldn't form. 'I will stay with the captain,' she said. 'And I will let no man beg for my life.'

'Thessa—' Benjamin's words bit into the air '—go into the cabin.'

The hardness of his words jolted her again. He'd spoken easily to Stephanos, but to her—he sounded as if he spit poison from his mouth.

She didn't move, afraid to set off a bloodletting. She could not see compassion in either man. Benjamin's face had no humanness in it. Stone. More cold than the statue.

The two men took the measure of each other and the perusal left no room for weakness.

Stephanos's eyes didn't leave the captain. 'She needs to stay. To see what she has caused.' His hand reached towards Thessa. 'Look at the Englishman quickly, Thessa. You will need to remember his face to tell my sons how he looked before he died and I will insist you tell them the story every night, especially the end. His end.'

The captain's blade appeared just at the tip of Stephanos's fingers.

'*Meno.*' Benjamin spoke the Greek word, a harsh command. Benjamin took a step forward and his sword, lying as a wall between Thessa and Stephanos, moved closer to Stephanos's chest.

'I believe she wishes for you to go,' Benjamin rasped. Then he softly added, the sound no less the command for its muted strength, 'As do I.'

'I care not for your words.' Stephanos's eyelids dropped a hair. 'Thessa leaves with me. Now. If you care for her, you will tell her to go to my sloop. For her life.' He snapped his head back and the men from the other ship moved closer, ready to board.

'She does not wish to go.'

Thessa opened her mouth to disagree, but at the intake of her breath the captain's stance tightened, a predator waiting to pound on his prey. She didn't know how she knew, but she could sense his blood rushing in his veins, feel the heat in his eyes and the hunger to overcome Stephanos. His blade edge remained still, but he was poised for an opening to lunge at the Greek.

'She stays.' Benjamin's voice matched his eyes.

And she saw the change in the men around them, heard it and felt it, although she truly saw nothing—heard nothing different. But each man standing was within an eyelash of fighting to the death.

Thessa did not close her mouth, or speak. If she voiced a wish, one of the men would take it as a signal to fight. The cabin boy would rush forward, most likely into the tip of a sword.

She didn't move. Even the raising of her hand, one way or the other, would commit one of the men to battle and the other would have no choice. And Stephanos had no heart. She'd seen that. He'd kicked the face of a dying man and laughed.

'Exodos,' Benjamin whispered. Only his eyes spoke loudly.

Weapons were shifting on the sloop, almost as if by the slow movements no crew member would notice the barrel of a pistol being pointed at his midsection.

She imagined the outbreak of blood fury and could not bear it on her conscience. She did not want bodies wrapped in shrouds and tossed overboard because of her. And the crewmen had no reason to die. To a man, the crews would fight at the smallest commands from their leaders. And the little cabin boy—the memories, if he lived, would be with him the rest of his life. A boy should not see life dripping red from a dying man's body.

Stephanos stepped back, just a finger width, she supposed, but enough to lessen the greater danger.

'My love.' His words were quiet, backing from the fury, but not releasing her completely.

She couldn't speak. He moved back, almost to the rail. The tip of the Benjamin's blade followed him. No one relaxed enough to take in a full breath.

And she knew the promise of death still floated against them all.

Stubby stood near—an almost child, ready to protect her with his life.

This time it would not be one man who did not breathe again, or two. But more. And the boy was so young. The same age as she'd been when she'd seen her uncle killed.

'Thessa, you know my men are strong.' Stephanos's voice curled like smoke. 'I will not die. We will take you from the ship. Tell your captain you are leaving and I will go easier on you.'

Her head jerked the smallest bit sideways, saying no. Stephanos took in the movement. He looked up at the sun and shook his head in a gesture that made his hair flare.

Then his chin lowered and his lips parted, and he stepped back. His eyes flashed weariness from deep within while he looked at Thessa. 'When the ship took your sister Melina, I didn't chase. I had you to take her place. I will not lose again.'

Stephanos turned to Benjamin. 'Captain. Fortunate for you—the weather is too warm to fight long.' He swirled the blade tip. 'I will kill you quickly.'

'It won't be your choice how I die or when I die.'

Stephanos took a step sideways and the metal glinted closer to Benjamin's face. 'I wish to be on my way with my bride.'

'But she wishes to stay.' Benjamin could see nothing but Stephanos. He looked at the pirate's eyes. They were no different than the ones of the last man he'd killed. The one he'd seen in his dreams and wished to erase the memory of. And now he saw the man's face again—on Stephanos's body. He would have to kill him again. A second time—and the first had haunted him.

He stepped back.

Stephanos's laugh crackled in the air and he reached his arm towards Thessa.

Ben's blade slashed forward, stopping the movement. 'You should not have given the French the marble. Now you will not even have the stone woman to hold.'

Stephanos pulled the sword nearer his own body, in the same manner of a viper about to strike. He lunged and Benjamin raised his arm, blocking the thrust.

'So you have held a sword before,' Stephanos said. 'I feared I might have to tell you which is the sharp end.'

Stephanos dived forward again, but not with enough force that he lost his balance or his chance to protect himself when Benjamin countered with a quick move that had Stephanos stepping backwards.

The pirate's mouth formed a straight line and his eyes darkened.

Then he jumped forward, his blade slashing to dislodge the other weapon. Ben stepped aside, lowering his sword enough to miss the main force of the thrust and deflect the metal, but keeping his tip pointed towards Stephanos.

He brought his blade up, swinging to the underside of Stephanos's weapon, pushing up while he dived forward. He shook with the strength he expelled to keep Stephanos off balance. Then he twisted, bent his knee and dropped his shoulder.

Stephanos stumbled back two steps, against the railing and near the ratlines, which worked in his favour to balance him. Ben lunged forward too quickly. Stephanos used the ropes to hold himself steady against the side of the ship and he kicked Benjamin backwards.

Benjamin kept his balance and the pirate rushed at him again, hair flying like dark flames around his face.

Benjamin braced, but he didn't have enough time to raise his arm into a swing. He backed and opened his arms, dodging the blade that whipped across his chest. Stephanos twisted, gripping the sword with both hands and swinging up, hard enough for his blade to connect with Ben's and flip it upwards and from Ben's fingertips.

Stephanos stood, ready to pounce. His eyebrows twitched up. 'You take no care for your clothing.'

Air rushed across Benjamin's chest. He put his hand up and felt the slice. His coat sagged open horizontally across his chest and his fingers felt wetness.

Stephanos took the moment to hurl himself towards Benjamin, ready to deliver the final blow. But Ben kicked the stone that Thessa had tossed and, in his rush forward, Stephanos's foot landed on the rock. The stone rolled and Stephanos moved with it, thumping down on to the deck.

Ben swept forward and kicked hard at Stephanos's hand, causing his sword to skitter away.

Just as Stephanos rose, Benjamin's fist connected with Stephanos's jaw, sending him reeling. The second punch doubled him over at his knees and the third backward sweep threw Stephanos against the rail causing him to lose his balance, tumbling overboard into the sea.

Ben stood at the side and called to the sloop's crew, 'If you fire on us, we will sweep your deck with the canister rounds in our swivel guns. Many of you will die and for nothing.'

One of the men on the pirate crew tilted his head at Benjamin, a salute of sorts, and then the same man called for the ship to sail. Almost as an afterthought, the man shouted out to another and they made efforts to retrieve Stephanos.

For the first time in his life, Benjamin could not move. He was aware of Gidley shouting orders to the quartermaster, but he didn't attend the words until he heard quiet ones repeated.

'Livers or hearts?' Gidley asked at his side.

Forcing himself back into his body, Benjamin looked at the first mate. 'What?'

'Livers or hearts? Which is it them savages cuts out of their enemies to eat? That's what I'm thinkin' yer was wantin' to feast on of that Stephanos.'

'I...' He could not take his eyes from the departing pirate ship, or his mind from how Thessa might have chosen the other man.

'Capt'n.' Gidley's voice held a father's firmness. 'Yer a bit drippy.' Gid put the sword back in Benjamin's hand.

Benjamin looked at his hand, surprised to see the weapon. 'Perhaps the fencing master wasn't just another tutor...'

'What?'

Ben shut his eyes and shook his head. 'My fencing master...I hated him. And he would taunt me. Always. And by the end I wanted to kill him. I'd try and he knew it. He would not let up. Relentless...' Ben continued. 'He said some day I would thank him.'

'Well, yer goin' to thank him?'

'No. I'm just angry he was right.'

Benjamin slipped the sword in the sheath and reached to unbuckle the belt, then looked around the deck, expecting to see Thessa. 'Where'd she—?'

'I had to get Stubby to take the woman to her cabin. I had to hold her up to keep her from sliding to the deck. I know a shavin' cut when I see it. She don't. That women was starin' after yer like yer the last drop of ale and she's been days without a drop.' He looked at Ben's chest. 'I wouldn't have even bled.'

'You might still. Today,' Ben insisted.

'We had us two ships of men ready to slice and shoot themselves into nothing. 'Cause of a woman. Storms can be on the water, or inside the ship. And this tempest was about to bust open the ship from the inside. Yer know what calls up storms…and we just had one.'

Benjamin gave a sharp shake of his head.

'She had two choosin's. Stay or go. And *was* yer goin' to let her leave?'

Benjamin shrugged. 'If she truly wished for it.'

'And yer can just start callin' me the prince

regent...' Gidley walked away, still muttering. 'We'd be swimmin' in blood now if that woman had 'ave took a step to that other man. She's like that goddess Thessalonia...that one yer don't hear much about, but I think the Good Book has a whole chapter about not worshippin' her.'

'Gid,' he called out, unfastening the remains of his coat. He'd never wear it again. Sea life had already harmed the buttons.

He used the edges of his shirt to daub at the cut. 'Stop your yarns or you will be hurt worse than I am.'

'Capt'n.' Gid nodded and moved away, but his words continued. 'I was hurtin' worse than yer when I left my bunk this mornin' 'cause my bones always hurts before any sort of a storm. And that woman be all sorts of bad weather.'

Benjamin took the ewer and poured water into the washbowl. He dipped his hands in the liquid and used both palms to wet his face. He had to get the ship to England. And to avoid Thessa.

First he removed the coat, folded it and put it on the chair. Taking his shirt off and bunching it, he tossed it against the closed door. Next he carefully cleaned the wound, noting Gid was right about the superficial nature of the cut. Only one side had any depth and the edges of the skin didn't separate enough to need a bandage.

Leaning over the basin, palms flat on the wood of the table, he watched drops of water from his face splash. She had some power that made even his skin breathe in the scent of her. He could hold out his palm if she stood near and it tingled, wanting to touch her.

He was like some besotted youth. He had some madness. *Foolish madness.* He jabbed the cut clean with so much force he winced. But the pain didn't help clear his mind.

He needed someone to talk some sense into him. Perhaps there was some ritual to remove the curse of a woman.

He'd seen the curse resting on his eldest brother twice and knew how it addled a man.

Warrington's first wife had been evil wrapped up in angelic form and eyes dripping with innocence. No one could have been more endearing than Cassandra, and no one had been more heartless. Benjamin's eldest brother had experienced a woman controlling his thoughts.

Warrington would understand.

But Thessa wasn't Cassandra. She wasn't.

Thessa was bursts of warmth and stoked needs burning within him that he had not imagined existed, much less felt.

He had the *Ascalon*. He needed nothing else. He had his mermaids in the paintings. He had coin—to buy all he needed from a woman.

He didn't need a woman with legs. They were tentacles to snap around a man and drag him from the sea to the hard earth and the depths of despair. He had to breathe the sea air to live. He would suffocate on land.

But how could he stay away from her for days when she was so close? He needed an ocean between them. Even that might not be enough.

He'd had the misfortune to meet the woman who could mesmerise him—a woman of his dreams. A woman he thought unreal. Safely stored in his imagination. Out of his reach, impossible to touch.

But now she rested only footsteps from him, and she called to him with a strength stronger than any siren's.

Thessa controlled the secret corners of his

thoughts. She rested in his mind where no one else had been before.

But again he'd been ready to kill, and if she'd chosen Stephanos Ben would not have let her go. He'd not lied to her. But perhaps he'd lied to himself. Perhaps he'd not killed Stephanos only because he didn't want Thessa to see such an act. In those moments, he had no conscience. Perhaps he was no better than the pirate.

And now he had a woman on his ship who called to him like a siren and she had no idea.

He did not know if he could stay from her only hours, so how could he finish the journey without touching her?

He dipped his hands in the water again, wrung out the cloth and put it aside. Using his wet hands, he pushed his hair back from his face, trying to be cleansed of his thoughts.

And his mind would not obey its own command. He kept thinking of Thessa and the walls seemed to whisper how desirable she'd look naked before him. It even filled in the curves of her body.

He would go to the helm and he would sail

Ascalon better than she'd ever sailed before, and they'd get to England.

And he'd see the women to Warrington—no, he'd send them with Gid to Warrington's estate. Gid could give the message to War that they'd failed on getting the treasure. After all, Benjamin needed to get the ship loaded quickly and leave the dock.

Thessa would be gone, and he would sail to the other end of the earth. The women were his brother's family—not his. And he would deliver them to the earl and tell himself Thessa was a dream.

He had to make up for the losses. The lost time because he'd gone haring off to the island. And the loss of funds because he'd chosen a woman he could not touch, over a treasure which would have brought him the ship which cradled him at night.

He'd betrayed his true love.

Fool.

Chapter Thirteen

Thessa sat in the cabin, on the planks, letting the gentle glide of the ship soothe her. Bellona walked around the deck again.

Thessa could hear the captain shouting orders through the wall. People in Greece could hear those commands.

She had been surprised when the captain had bested Stephanos. She thought no one could. And when she saw the sword slice through Benjamin, she'd known how her own death would feel.

Wrapping her arms around herself, she relived the kiss again. His eyes had changed. He'd looked at her—into her. She'd been able to see his thoughts, only they didn't speak words she knew. They'd connected her to him in a way she didn't understand.

When he backed away after the kiss, crinkles had formed at his eyes and around his mouth. But he'd been affected, she'd thought. And now she wondered. She should not be thinking of him. It had been days since Stephanos had boarded the ship. Since then, the captain had never looked her way once.

He could not have kept any more distance from her, yet he was no further away than her elbow, almost. He seemed unaware of her. But something told her he ignored her too well. She could not be as invisible to him as it appeared. A man who had no concern of her would have spoken at least a bit. Would not have managed to stay at the other side of the ship whenever she stepped outside.

Bellona mentioned she'd spoken with him several times and he'd told her the cut was nothing. A sword had slashed across his chest and he thought it nothing…

And it had almost knocked her to her knees.

She moved to the window, hoping for a glimpse of the captain, but she couldn't see anything but shadows and shapes.

Thinking of the captain made her feel the same

as when she walked into water, seaweed brushing her legs. She could move her toes and bubbles from the earth rose up and tickled over her body.

Once they reached shore, the captain intended to sail again. Gidley told her the voyage would be two years, if they came back at all. She had no illusions that Stephanos was the only man at sea who would attack a ship. The captain might never return.

The *Ascalon* was going to deposit her in London. The ship would dock and she would be with her sister and the captain would be gone. For ever.

She could not become like her mother and be waiting and longing for a man who did not want to stay with her. She could not, and would not, because as soon as the captain reached London they would go their different ways. He would sail and she would be with her sister, and the captain would be gone.

She only thought of him because he'd been willing to die for her.

Leaning her forehead against the windowpane, she tried to see more of the ship.

He'd been willing to die for her.
She wondered how a mermaid would proceed.

Benjamin kept himself too busy to think. He worked to exhaust himself. He wondered if the ship had reached the point where the only one not consumed by Thessa's presence was Gidley.

But Ben had adjusted. Kept himself busy and hadn't gone to her cabin. He had to be thankful she shared the room with her sister. And he was. That had saved him.

Now he had himself completely under control. The cut on his chest was healing nicely. He reached up and pressed against it. Tender, but no pain. And some day, somewhere, a woman would see the scar and he would not have to embellish a word of the tale. He would not mention Thessa, but he would mention Stephanos.

And his secret would be that he relished the scar. Was pleased that he had received it for Thessa. He would always have that reminder of her.

He could almost feel pleased as he turned the last watch of the night over to Gidley. Benjamin admired the perfect sea and the shimmering stars overhead. He wished for a taste of the brandy he had stored snug and tight in the bottom of his sea chest.

He stepped into his cabin and lit the lantern. He would put Thessa from his mind. He would not think of her.

After turning to his wash basin, he heard rustling behind him. He jolted around, his hand clasping the hilt of the knife in his belt. A shape half rolled, half fell from his bunk.

Thessa perched herself at the side of his bed, her eyes nearly asleep. 'I waited until after darkness fell and I crept very carefully. I don't think any of your men saw me. I didn't mean to sleep,' she said, her hands smoothing the tendrils which had escaped from her braid. 'Bellona is in our bunk and the floor is hard.' She sighed. 'And I thought, just for a moment, I'd rest while I waited for you.' She yawned, her fingertips sliding along the covers.

Benjamin nodded, thoughts crashing into his mind so quickly he couldn't speak. He put his hand on the table to keep from falling off the edge of the earth. Her tousled hair called for his fingers and her sleep-filled eyes slammed thoughts of pleasures into his body. He steadied his voice. 'No harm done.'

Her trouser legs dragged the floor. He could not see her feet. Thank goodness.

'I have not told you how pleased I am you sent Stephanos away,' she said.

'My job. For my crew.'

'I will never forget it.'

He shrugged. 'I have put it from my mind.'

He wanted to shout at her to leave and he could no more do that than he could turn into Poseidon. Awareness of her rippled throughout his body. This woman could have walked into the cabin—a room which now felt smaller than it ever had before—with horns on her head, put a trident tip to his neck and he would have been thinking of how warm she made him feel. He suspected nothing, ever, would completely dull his awareness of her when he saw her.

Her siren's smile hit his stomach, causing an eruption of desire to take his breath. Her lips moved again, speaking. He wasn't sure if she spoke English or Greek. He didn't hear what she said.

'Thessa…' This called for blunt talk—talk so

clear it had images attached. He had to frighten her away, because he knew he wouldn't be able to push her out the door. Once his hands touched her, he'd not be in control of them.

She took a step closer.

He sneaked a look at her toes. Perfect.

But he had to get her away. She had to run from the room. Now. He had to frighten her to safety. He was experienced at getting women to leave without upsetting them.

He undid the ties of his shirt. He pulled the garment over his head and let the sleeves slide off and catch at his wrists.

The air now touching his chest must have brushed over her first, because he could feel every current of it, like embers floating in the air, but not hot enough to burn, just warm enough to feel.

But—she didn't seem to mind that he'd removed his shirt.

'Oh.' Her lips parted and she moved to him. Her fingers touched the slightest part of the wound. 'You are so fortunate to have survived.'

He could not move. He swallowed so he would be able to form words.

'I am not injured.'

'But you are.' Her eyes didn't move from his chest and her fingers brushed the edges of the cut, leaving volcanic heat in their wake.

'Thessa. You must leave.' He kept his shirt so it covered the front of his trousers. She didn't need to see the truth. And she really needed to take her fingers from his chest, but he couldn't move her to the door. He had his shirt gripped in both hands. If he reached to push her away—he would not push her away.

She stood, her hand at his chest, and he looked at the wall beyond her shoulder. 'I am not unaffected by you.'

'I hoped…you were not.'

'I think of you occasionally.'

'As do I you.'

But he was honourable. 'And I would like to bed you, but if I did, then I must offer something in exchange. Money, love or marriage. One or all three. I can offer you none of those, Thessa.'

She shrugged away his words. 'You will be pleased. I will ask for no love or ties.'

He shut his eyes. 'Thessa. What in blazes are you thinking?'

His eyes couldn't stay away from her. He threw the shirt to the floor.

'I don't know. But you are so beautiful—' She sighed and her voice held a hint of sadness. 'And I look at you… What if I die? What if the ship sinks? What if you die? I feel that we should not…avoid each other.'

'No.' He pulled out the chair, and pointed to it, mentally commanding her to sit. She didn't move and her lips were now in a firm line.

'Have you forgotten I am from the same land as your father?' he asked.

'You are not anything like the other men. The water has washed your blood clean.'

Benjamin shook his head. 'No. I am as unclean as can be. I am not a…man to be with you, Thessa. I've…I'm not a—'

'Perhaps.'

The little shrug of her shoulders, the tilt of her head, the turn of her chin—she didn't look convincingly upset.

He put a palm flat on the table and leaned towards her, trying to ignore the screaming inside his head which called him all kinds of a fool for still speaking and not moving towards her.

She stared at him. 'You could have died.'

'It's not uncommon.'

She shrugged. 'I understand, I suppose.'

Benjamin closed his mouth and dried his palms on his trousers. 'Thessa, I would very much like to take you to bed.'

She glanced at the bunk. 'I know. I understand. The bed...' She inhaled. 'It smells of the sea, the ship...'

When her face turned back to him and he read her thoughts, he could not move.

'It is like being wrapped in the scent of pine and leather and warmth,' she said. 'I do not know how you ever leave this bed. It's almost the same as being held in the arms of the sea and gives the feeling of wine even when none has been tasted.' She stepped back and sat on the side of his bed. 'I have never felt a bed like this before.'

'You have to leave.' The words made his throat hoarse. 'I think of you night and day, and have since the moment I first saw you. No other woman has moved me so.'

When he spoke she moved and closed the distance between them.

He traced her mouth with his fingertip. Her

lips parted. Grasping her shoulders, he pulled her to him. The kiss was more than he could ever have imagined.

He reached to her bottom, picking her up and sitting her on the table, sliding his hands down her hips as she sat, and he stood between her legs, letting their kiss blot out everything from their minds.

When he ran his hands back up her thighs, she wore no skirt to flutter up, and, instead of silks or even the soft feel of a chemise, he felt rough wool.

He'd rarely undressed a woman. The ones he'd touched were able to give a twist and lose their shyness, stockings and corsets in less time than it took him to undo his fall. He'd always been impressed.

But the difference in clothing reminded him this wasn't just any woman. This was Thessa.

He reached under her shirt, stopping at the gentle slope of her waist, and ended the kiss.

He took a half step back, ready to remove their clothing, but she gave a tug and pulled him against her. Her hand found the side of his head and pulled him back into another kiss.

He went forward, one hand bracing, palm flat on the table, the other almost pulling her up his body.

He tried to lever himself back enough to work her shirt buttons and she relaxed her grasp. He wanted to feel her breasts pressed against him and her skin sliding against his.

'I'll take care.' He spoke the words against her lips.

Her hands danced over his back. 'I knew I waited for you.'

He fell into her kiss again, but then he the words she said began to turn into a sentence. He buried his face in the crook of her neck, savouring. 'Waited?'

'Yes.'

'Waited?'

'Yes.'

He struggled for air. 'As in, not done before?'

'No.'

His mind slowly chugged into a semblance of thinking and he did not move, except to speak. 'One does not *take* a virgin on a table.'

She just looked at him, her eyes unfocused.

He shook his head several times.

He moved back, still holding her. He mentally talked himself step by step through what he must do. He kept his voice calm. 'One does not take a virgin on a table.'

Her voice barely reached his ears. 'You have a bed.'

'No. A *bunk…*'

And I am going to hate myself in the morning either way.

'I need to leave.' He grasped the door. He had to leave. He remembered his shirt and swooped his hand to pick it up. Then he touched the door latch and kept his back to her. 'Thessa, your first time—it should be in a soft bed and one you do not have to leave in the night. It should be with a man who doesn't have to pull himself from you, but can hold you close as he finishes and can make you feel the same pleasure he feels. You should spend the night skin to skin, heart to heart, knowing when you wake, he'll be there.' He turned back. 'Please promise me you will not settle for less.'

'I offer myself to you and you say no.' Her voice rose. 'Stephanos had to threaten the men on Melos to keep them away. And the French seamen asked for me many times.'

'Thessa, you know it is for the best.'

'If we only did what is for the best, would you be on this ship?'

'Yes.'

'You lie to yourself. You tell yourself that, but it is not the truth.'

The dowry. He still hadn't told her about the dowry. But that would not be a problem. He would let the earl handle it. Thessa need never know the funds were on his ship. One thing he knew for certain, now was not the time to tell her.

'I know,' he said, 'that my brother will find a man for you in London.'

She crossed her arms and looked at him. Stephanos had received a gentler stare.

He stepped out the door, moving to the side of the ship distant from the cabin door, and into an area where he could not be viewed from the cabin.

Damn. He went to the railing and, for the first time in his memory, a wave of seasickness rushed over his body. He'd done the most foolish thing of his life, turning away from the one woman in the world who could surpass any mermaid in his mind.

Gidley whistled low when he stepped beside Benjamin. 'Yer sure pulled yerself back together quick,' he whispered. 'Me, I takes my time so they don't be slammin' a door.'

Benjamin kept his voice low, calling Gid words the older man had taught him.

'Ah, my wife called me worse than that afore she woke good in the morning. And I can tell yer not quite happy. Damn near rolled the ship to its side when she slammed the door. Don't think any of the crew realised she was in yer cabin, though—I been singin' out orders right and left to keep 'em hoppin'. When I seen her goin' in, I was expectin' yer to stay a little longer.'

'I did the right thing.'

'Yer sure?'

'No. I did the wrong thing. I just don't want to think about it.' He used his shirt to wipe his forehead and then pulled it over his head.

'Many's the time I told yer, lad, don't ever admit to wrongness. Doesn't look right fer a capt'n.'

'I just thought…' He shook his head. 'Once I get to England and we get on a real voyage, not this waste of time, then I'll be thinking straight again. First port we stop at out of England, we'll take an extra day and I'll make sure I never think of her again.'

'Yer has yer plan. Now all yer has to do is follow it,' he said, nodding. 'I see that workin' out real well.'

Chapter Fourteen

Benjamin had not gnawed his fingers off or any other parts of his body to keep himself from going to Thessa and he had not spoken to her or asked of her.

He'd had no need.

The air on the ship carried words of Thessa and he only had to breathe to feel her presence. Whispered voices carried through his open window. Montgomery told Wilson that when Stubby took her breakfast plate, she'd thanked him 'like she was a real lady.'

And then they'd entered on to a discourse of their first time under a woman's skirts.

And Gidley snapped at one of the other seaman about bringing more bad luck on to the ship with such coarse talk of women. 'What if them women in the cabin could hear through the walls?' Gid had asked.

And then a man had remembered a woman who had ears so big she could have heard through the walls and that wasn't the only thing of note about her. Then the men had discussed the best pleasuring they'd ever had and Benjamin had left the cabin and shouted out more orders than two ships of men could handle—obviously no one would draw conclusions from that. They'd all been given enough direct commands to keep them angry enough at him they'd be hating him instead of thinking of Thessa.

He'd returned to his cabin, resting his forehead against the wood. He breathed out, and in, and squeezed his eyes shut so hard they hurt.

And if he spent one second alone in her company, he would be not be able to do the right thing. He could not abandon Gid, Stubby and the rest of the crew. He'd turned his back on his father and brothers and their world had continued without him. He didn't know that the men's world would go on if he wasn't there to guide them.

He only had to live out the rest of the voyage and then she would be in his brother's care and he would *not* be visiting his brother who had started all this by listening to Thessa's sister and having the misfortune to get besotted by some woman who if not for bad luck they'd have never seen or heard of or known of the rest of their lives.

If his brother hadn't been on some foolish diplomatic mission to try to keep the Turks and Greeks from dissolving into bloodshed because a Turkish leader had it into his head that the English would side with the Greeks, then Benjamin wouldn't have been having the dreams he was having and the feeling that his skin boiled on his body because it was so feverish with need.

He could not hide in his cabin and he could not continue to snarl at the men every time he heard mention of Thessa. They seemed to have forgotten completely about their superstitions and now he wished their fear of the women to return.

Thessa, with her dark-velvet eyes, and her sea legs, had lodged into the men's thoughts as well as she had his. Again the image of her stepping from her water in daylight, her chemise hugging her body, slipped into his mind.

He could only be thankful his men hadn't seen that.

'I can see land.' Bellona closed the door and stood just inside the cabin. Her eyes sparkled. 'We are almost there.'

Thessa nodded and put her hand at her stomach. She would be leaving the captain. Even if she had not seen him in days, she'd listened for his voice every waking moment.

'Perhaps now you will recover from this illness which has kept you from leaving the room,' Bellona said.

'I feel so much better.' And she did. She truly did. The captain had done the right thing. They'd both done the right thing. She knew, because it did not feel good at all.

'I cannot wait to see the captain's home.'

'What?' Thessa asked, trying to make certain she'd heard what she thought.

'Gidley says that is where we must wait for our sister to collect us. He said her husband will be certain to have suitable clothing.'

'But? Can we not wait for them here?'

Bellona shook her head. 'Why would we want to do that? We have had to take turns making pallets on the floor to sleep and the bed is no softer than the wood. Besides, they have to get the ship ready to sail and Gidley says the docks are no place for us.' She raised her brows. 'He claims the sailors all have to go see their mothers the first night the ship is in port.'

'The captain, too?'

'His mother has passed and his father, too, because after Gidley told me we would be staying at the captain's house, I asked him if his family would be there. He said, no, but because we are dressed as his crew, no one will notice us. We'll only be there a short while because he will send word to his brother that we've arrived.'

'I meant will the captain be at his home?'

'I asked the captain to take us there. He said he had a lot of duties to attend to once we'd reached shore.' She shrugged, smiling. 'But he did not say no.'

Seeing the other boats in port didn't give Benjamin the feeling of comfort he'd expected.

The last of the voyage had been calm. The only rough sailing had been inside his own skin and the waves in his mind were just as choppy as they'd been on the night he didn't bed Thessa.

He stared at the familiar sights of the dockyards and smelled a cargo of cinnamon or some spices, a short while later tobacco, and then perhaps odours from animal hides and horns.

Plain lodgings housed dock workers, and provision agents were everywhere. This world touched a part of his soul no Almack's assembly could find. No part of London felt as alive to him as the docks. This world was flavoured by the waters.

But now, seeing the port gave him the sense of death. The memories of working at the warehouse and feeling the aloneness twisted inside him with the knowledge that he was sending Thessa to her new world, whilst he was staying in his old one. Air kept wanting to clog inside him. He had to keep telling himself to breathe and to move and to think—that she was going to be with her sister—in a world of finery where she belonged.

He would be with his ship and taking care of

the men and making sure they stayed alive—where he belonged and where he was necessary to keep the people around him safe.

Stubby stepped beside him. 'Capt'n, you takin' Thessa home with you?'

The words put a sensual image into Benjamin's mind. Thessa in his home. Examining the mementos he'd collected from the sea. Curled among his bedcovers, enticing views of skin for only him. 'I'll get her settled. At the family town house.'

If he put a cap on her, since she was already dressed as a male, no one would notice him bringing a seafaring man to the town house. And the man and woman who tended his home were not of the *ton*. They'd seen so many different people with unfamiliar manners of life, they accepted more than Benjamin did.

Ben gripped the rails and looked down at Stubby. The boy would need clothing before they left the dock. He couldn't count on Gid to think of it on his own. He'd have to mention it and make sure Stubby had something better than rags to wear. The lad should start dressing better. Some day he would be using himself as a compass to guide his crew. Ben knew he could give the boy all he needed to grow into a captain, just as Gid had done for him.

'Stub, make sure my gear is ready,' he commanded, 'and see to Gid's and your own. You're to stay with Gidley and make sure to keep him from trouble.

The boy skipped away and Benjamin saw him catch up to Gidley. Gid reached out and tugged Stubby's hair, as a grandfather might, and Stubby's laughter rang in the air.

At that moment, the door of the physician's cabin opened and the women stepped out. Thessa's eyes stopped on him and his stomach tumbled. He had to force a pleasant look to his face when he walked to her. The thought of leaving her churned his insides.

She turned her eyes to him. Neither looked away while he spoke. 'I've made plans for you to stay at the town house. Even though my brothers and I share it, we're hardly ever there at the same time and it's a simple place. I'll get you caps to hide your hair. We'll arrive at dusk or after. No one will even notice.'

He put a hand to the ropes to steady himself.

'The country estate my brother has is very different, though. That's where your sister lives. With all the servants there and it truly being an earl's household,' he continued, 'you shouldn't arrive at an earl's house wearing trousers, but as ladies. We don't want to cause any talk which might reflect badly on Melina, or her future children. I have to present myself there much better than wearing a seaman's rough sailing wear.

'Will you be there?' Thessa asked.

He held out his arm to her. 'I will leave Gidley in charge of *Ascalon*.'

Chapter Fifteen

Thessa sat in the hired coach, gripping the bundled chemise in her lap. She glanced at the clothing, while she picked at the threads coming unsewn on the garment's shoulder seam.

Her stomach flip-flopped. The captain was taking them to his home. On the *Ascalon* every time she'd heard his voice though the wall, mostly shouts, she'd stilled to listen.

Now Thessa rode in a carriage, something she'd never expected, and looked at a world her father had mentioned many times, yet she hadn't been prepared for.

So many carriages. People. And houses. Houses and people. If she had thought of how a goddess lived, she would not have imagined such lodgings even for the highest spirit.

When the hackney stopped, she and Bellona stepped out. They waited for the second carriage to deposit the captain and his chest. The captain promptly paid the coachman and the driver helped him with the trunk. None of this was new to anyone else around them and the others accepted the grandeur as commonplace.

Benjamin whistled as he walked up the steps to the entrance and a manservant opened the door—a mountain disguised as a man. She wondered if the giant had to bend his knees and turn sideways to go through doorways. His appearance would have been overpowering, if not for the happiness bursting in his eyes.

The barest hint of something baked touched her nose, something she'd never smelled before. And the other foreign scents must have had something to do with the cleanliness of the house. How did people sleep in such a cavernous place?

'Captain. Was almost worried about you.' The servant bowed to Benjamin, her and Bellona, an elaborate movement.

'Never concern yourself about me, Broomer.' Benjamin's face lightened.

'Was almost—almost worried. Not quite,' Broomer repeated, his voice sounding like a chuckle rippled beneath it.

The servant led them up the stairs, near walking backwards so he could hold the lamp, shining the way for them. She held tightly to the railing and then she realised it held fast, without swaying.

She saw nothing rotted or worn. Broomer took them to a room without a bed in it. It lacked a table for eating. Just sitting furniture filled it. Even the walls had a well-cared-for look, with feathery-wispy shapes painted just below the edge of the ceiling and running around the whole of the room. A weapon leaned against one corner of the wall—a harpoon. She smelled mixed pigments and looked to the painting over the fireplace.

It hadn't been finished long. *Ascalon*.

Broomer spoke to Benjamin, 'Dolly said you'd be home any day now. Tried to catch me in a wager but I've learned better than any games of chance with her. Sometimes I think she is part gypsy. She has some treats made so you'd have a bite of her fine apricot tarts soon as you get settled.' He swept an arm to the rendition of the ship. 'And your painting arrived. The earl took the one of the three children by the sea to his home.'

Benjamin's lips turned up, but sadness took over his face and he took a step towards it. 'The painting is exactly as I'd hoped.'

'Delivered just yesterday.'

'He captured her beautifully.' He stared at the ship again, unmoving.

Thessa saw nothing about the painting to bring such a look in the captain's eyes. But again, the ship was painted like some majestic vessel. The artist had lied.

When he turned back to them he gave a half smile.

'Tell Dolly to prepare meals fit for goddesses.' He paused. 'Is Dane about?'

'No. He's been at the earl's house, making sure the gardener knows his duties, though I expect him back when he gets tired of digging around the dirt. So, I'm not planning on seeing him soon…'

'Then Bellona will have the room with the garden-like fripperies and Thessa can take the red-and-golden chamber. Tell Dolly to help you. I want the ladies to be comfortable.'

'Ladies?' Broomer asked and then turned to Thessa. His eyes widened and he took a step back. His arm knocked a vase askew and, without fully taking his eyes from Thessa, he caught the porcelain. 'Didn't realise you weren't the captain's crew mates.'

Thessa pulled at the shirt, indicating her male clothing. 'We had to swim to the ship and were rescued in the water. They had no extra dresses.'

The captain turned and she saw the look he gave her. In a brief second, something from his gaze burst heat into her body. Her heartbeats tumbled into a rhythm she could feel to her fingertips. She could not look at him directly because she must continue to breathe.

'I'll need a hackney in the morning...' Benjamin ran his fingers through his hair. 'The women need clothing so they will be able to leave the house.'

The servant closed his mouth, turned his view from them and gave a nod to Benjamin. 'They're both a head taller than Dolly and a stone lighter so they couldn't borrow from her.' He scratched his chin. 'But my sister can round up some female wear soon enough. When she's not sewing, she buys clothes sometimes and mends 'em well and sorts 'em out and sells them.'

'That sounds perfect. They would be able to travel to my brother's house and surely his wife has enough dresses now that she could share until they have their own.'

Broomer gave a respectful nod to Thessa and Bellona. He backed to the doorway to leave, but Thessa didn't think it was so much subservience as hero worship of Benjamin. 'I'll get Dolly started on helping me and it'll only take us a whisker shake to get the pitchers filled for the washbasins. Dolly's making the tea now. If the ladies would like, I can show them a room to settle in.'

In moments, Broomer had shown them each to a room, but Bellona hadn't stayed in hers. She hurried back to speak with Thessa in the red-and-gold room.

Thessa imagined the tester bed grand enough for any goddess and she had never seen so much cloth in any one room. Even the window coverings were more elaborate than any dress she'd ever had.

'Did you notice the harpoon in the corner of the grand room?' Bellona asked.

'I saw,' Thessa said. That room had many reminders of the sea, filling her with realisation that the captain's heart and mind stayed at sea even when he was on land.

'It would make a fine weapon. If I had a weapon, then I could protect us. No man could force us to marry, or keep other men away from us just because he wants no one but himself to touch us.' She frowned. 'I would have liked to have seen Stephanos defeated. I thought we had escaped, but he could have taken you before I knew it. I still imagine all the things I could have awoken to find.'

'We must put our other life behind us,' Thessa said. But she knew it wouldn't be easy for either of them. Everything she'd seen was so different than her home. She couldn't have imagined so many people moving about. Even the water was different—without catacombs nearby and the rocks jutting from the sea.

She'd looked through her father's sketches

once and seen drawings of houses and people who did look as if they'd spent the day playing the pianoforte. And now she was standing in a home with servants, and even though she wore men's clothing, Broomer hadn't looked at her as if he'd thought her beneath him. He'd treated her just as grandly as he treated the captain.

When she looked around the room, she could see she'd left behind the world of pirates and quick death. On the ship, she'd known all along that a storm could come and take them all.

And if this was the simple house, she could not imagine how her sister's home must look. Nor where her father might live, but she didn't care about him, except to let him see she was no longer a child who could be ignored and disparaged. She could toss away the seafaring garb and wear the clothing of a lady. She was not some vermin crawling in the corners of life.

'This is a safe world with people who are seemly. We won't need weapons. We must be proper. We are ladies.' Thessa said. 'Our sister is here. The people are different than on Melos. Look at this house. There is no straw, no barn and the carriages… So many of them…'

* * *

Benjamin sat with them during the evening meal. Thessa hadn't been hungry. The cook hadn't used any thyme or basil and nothing tasted familiar.

It was a simple meal with simple conversation, yet, she knew Benjamin was just as aware of her every movement as she was his. Neither of them spoke more than a few times and not once to each other.

Bellona did not pause for more than a few words during the entire evening, even after they'd moved to the library, asking questions of everything from the royal family to how one found a hackney cab.

Finally, Bellona had taken herself off to her bedchamber. But Thessa couldn't force herself to leave Benjamin's presence.

When Bellona left, the captain turned to Thessa. 'I've always been fascinated with the way mermaids are imagined by artists and I've amassed as many paintings as I can. My bothers have moved the artwork out from time to time but I've always had them returned. I'd like to show them to you.'

Benjamin stood and held out his arm. Thessa took it, but something of his house, and all the collections she could tell he'd amassed, made her think of her father's ways. Her father had been driven by painting and she wasn't certain Benjamin didn't favour the sea just as her father favoured art.

She walked the hallway to his room and his voice was quiet, companionable as he spoke.

'The tale of women who could call up storms to sink vessels, having the power over wind, caught my attention. I suppose to an able-bodied seaman, to feel at the mercy of the seas, sometimes he might like to think it's not merely a storm or a tempest, but something he might be able to control. If he can keep the mermaids happy, then he can continue to sail. And that an earthly being could direct winds…that lore catches a sailor's ears.'

She speared him with her glare. 'Women bring less bad fortune to a ship than men. Men have been on every ship that has ever gone to the depths. Few women.'

Ben didn't answer, but opened the door to his chamber and let her step inside.

He felt like a little boy who was going to show a princess his favourite toy soldiers and he stilled, watching her examine the things which had once meant so much to him.

To stand in his room, at her side, feelings covered him as strong as an enormous wave washing over him, but, instead of feeling that he couldn't breathe, he felt he could take in all the best parts of the world with just a gentle inhalation.

Even in the duck trousers, her womanliness showed in the delicate line of her neck and the way the shirt pulled against her as she moved. Her hair needed about a score more of pins to hold it in place and each tendril framed her face.

His heart pounded and he could hear the rustle of fabric when she turned to look at the walls.

He raised his hand, letting only his fingers brush her stiff shirt, and ran his fingertips up her back, and he didn't move elsewhere, just watched the slow upward slide of his hand until he reached her shoulder and stopped. He'd never felt he could spend years fascinated by nothing else but gazing at a woman, but with Thessa he could.

'That's rather—odd.' He knew she'd spotted the huge painting of the mermaid barely wrapped in seaweed. His brothers had surprised him by having the picture commissioned as a jest. But he liked the painting, jest or no. He'd fallen asleep many nights in the town house, staring into the dark shape of the painting.

The only art in the room not dealing with a sea creature was the quite plain larger one—nothing more than a rendition of the ocean's horizon—he'd bought after seeing the painter's work at Somerset House.

Had he not been so captured by the sea, he might have been an artist. The life-like images they could create with a pencil and a scrap of paper fascinated him. His proof of that was the quick sketch, about five inches by eight, that Thomas Rowlandson had managed for him of a plump, leering mermaid. He'd found the artist at a gaming table and had wagered and wagered until Rowlandson lost, then asked for a drawing instead of coin. Rowlandson had thought Benjamin quite foxed, but Benjamin had carefully planned the moment.

Thessa stepped sideways and turned to Benjamin, but she didn't increase the distance between them. 'Are all captains searching for mermaids?' she interrupted his thoughts.

He shook his head.

Thessa spoke. 'You have more of a fascination with the creatures than I realised.'

'I did.' He touched her cheek.

'Do you wish for me to be a mermaid?'

'After I met you, I realised imaginary women aren't quite as lovely as I thought. You surpass them all.'

He memorised the shape of her lips, never wanting to forget them. The red bow: perfect. Taking her cheeks in his hand, he brushed a kiss against her lips and, this time, another thought jarred him. 'The problem with mermaids is they disappear back into their world. In a flash they're gone. Only to remain a memory.'

'Much like a sea captain.' She pulled from his hands.

Chapter Sixteen

'The paintings...' She looked at them. She didn't like even one of them. Not even the one with only the waves in it. It didn't look like her sea. 'Art...'

'I would like to pack these away and only have a portrait of you. Will you let me introduce you to an artist tomorrow?'

She shook her head. 'My father has painted me before. I cannot bear the thought of posing again.'

In front of her she could see more about the captain than he understood. Women who weren't real stared back at her from the walls.

One of the women had dark hair and eyes. Just like Thessa's own. She couldn't keep from examining it closer. She stepped to it, touching the frame and letting her fingers trail the wood. 'I think she…almost resembles me.'

'No. She looks nothing like you. Nothing.'

'Can't you see it?' she asked. 'The hair and eyes, both the same shade as mine.'

'Brown. That's all the closeness you share.'

She shook her head, unable to take her eyes from the painting. She supposed it truly didn't resemble her. The woman in the art was too perfect. Her hair too dark. Her lips too full.

Another image of what someone wanted rather than what was true. But she wondered if that was why the captain noticed her. Because Thessa had the same look of the woman's face, even if the features were shaped differently.

Thessa thought back to the many paintings her father had finished. 'I could never pose again,' she said. 'I don't want to be…something that isn't real.'

His lips pressed up, but the smile didn't reach his eyes. 'You could never be.'

She reached out, touching his sleeve again, unable to explain to him that he didn't see her as she truly was, but as a part of the imagined world he'd created on the long voyages.

'It wouldn't be you, anyway.' Benjamin shut his eyes, moving towards her, and let his temple rest against hers.

His hands clasped her waist. Even through the bunched layers of the shirt, she could feel the firmness of his grasp. He still had the faint scent of the boat and the sea around him and she suspected it would never leave.

'Captain.'

'Thessa...' His head still rested against hers. 'I don't mind that you call me Captain. You may call me whatever you wish. But it wouldn't hurt to call me by my name.'

'It might,' she said. 'You're leaving... You're going away.'

'Yes. And all I can think of is how I will hate to leave you.'

She put her hands at his chest, but she didn't push. She stood, letting the moment linger in her memory. For the rest of her life, she would be able to shut her eyes and remember this moment and the feel of standing alone with him. With all the rest of the world further away than an ocean.

And the captain's chest, moving with his

breaths, and the silence, more quiet than could truly be real, surrounding them.

He held her in his arms and the air around them was different than when they'd been on the *Ascalon*.

And she knew how a goddess would feel to be revered. She could feel it in Benjamin's touch and see it in his eyes.

He moved back from her enough to lead her to the bed, stopping at the edge to stand so close she could feel the warmth of his breath on her lips. He closed the distance, gently, and touched his mouth against hers.

The pine scent of the ship still clung to him and his lips guided her into somewhere she'd never been before.

When he breathed the smallest exhalation, she took it inside herself, and the air created more intensity in her than lightning flashing across the sky, snapping its power into the ground or sea.

His arms banded around her, enclosing her, and they didn't just surround her body. His touch delved deep into her spirit.

When he pulled back, she saw his eyes and they'd changed. Softened and dazed. The blue had faded and the centre darkened and he looked at her more deeply than anyone else ever had.

He pressed the side of his face against hers and his roughened skin changed her. In that instant she understood the true difference between a man and a woman, and a man's magic, and how a simple touch could transform a person for ever.

Pulling away, she reached up and brushed his cheek lightly, and it was as if she had put her hands over his whole body. She could feel that much of him. If she stepped back—and only looked—it would be as if they still embraced.

But she wasn't about to release him. She couldn't have. This moment had been gifted her and she could not stop it. It would be like trying to stop rain.

And for all she knew the world could have been flooding outside and the water swirling up against the door, but it wouldn't have mattered. They were safe, completely at harbour in each other's arms.

Ben nuzzled his face against her, feeling the warmth. Thessa had taken him into her realm.

'I do not know how a goddess would feel,' he whispered, 'but I know that she could not possibly be better than you.' Or perhaps he just thought it, he wasn't sure. But it was true. Thessa was beyond a mermaid. She was a woman created for him.

Forget the legs, the lashes, the siren's smile and the most perfect feet. Thessa. For this moment she was *his* Thessa.

He kept his face against her neck, tasting the salty skin, then he turned her so he could feel her lips.

Her flattened palms danced over his chest and traced downwards, feeling his stomach. His voice—it was gone.

Stopping, he pulled back, gauging her response, hoping his mind hadn't lied to him. Her eyes mirrored his feelings.

He grasped her waist and pulled her closer, against his body, pressing himself against her. His fingers tensed against her and the slightness of her amazed him. He'd seen her powerful strokes when she sliced through the water and noted the strength in her legs when he'd pulled her on to *Ascalon*. But his arms surrounded her so completely he worried that he might crush her.

Reaching

Ben lightened his touch, but she tightened hers.

Reaching her back, he felt for hooks or ties or something that might be unfastened, but he only felt the smoothness of fabric covering her back. He slid his hand downwards, finding the end of her shirt, and slipped the garment up.

Thessa shivered when his fingertips brushed over her nipples. His fingers were long, tapered, but not smooth. They were hands of strength.

He slipped his hands to her waist and backwards, to the swell of her bottom, and pulled her even closer against himself.

Her mouth parted and she looked at him. She wanted to hear his voice again—to hear him speak.

'Benjamin...'

He stilled, but he didn't answer, his lips still brushing along her skin like petals of a heated flower.

'Ben...'

He responded, little more than a murmur or a groan, filled with strength and weakness, all combined into one sound—but that was all she needed to hear.

The coarse fabric of the trousers slid from

her hips and he swept her on to the bed. Now the only clothing between them was his and he pulled back enough to work loose his fastenings, but their bodies only separated the barest amount while he freed himself from his trousers.

Running his hand down to the triangle of her legs, he traced her cleft, while his tongue explored her mouth.

The pulses he created in her grew, moving to enclose her in his touch, and she felt the same maelstrom she'd felt when the waves pulled her under, only this time life burst into her body, swirling her into another realm and then pushing her back to the surface whether she wanted to go or not. She no longer needed to breathe or move. She existed and that was all she could manage. She didn't think she even breathed, but the air still flowed into her lungs and life returned to her body.

Benjamin rose above her, sliding his hand along her thigh until he could lift her leg and wrap it around him.

He joined himself to her and she heard him whisper her name, slowly, reverently. His eyes were closed. Water on his forehead turned his hair into wet tendrils. She held him, locking every moment into her memory.

He shuddered and gasped, and no longer said her name, but he didn't need to.

When he pulled from her, his head dropped into the curve of her neck and she listened as he struggled to control his breathing.

His husky whisper touched her ear as he struggled to speak. 'I…love you, Thessa. And I always will.'

One kiss, softer, delicate, fluttered at her cheek and he turned as if he would leave the bed, but he bent to take her foot.

His hand stilled when he saw the mark. The darkened birthmark she shared with her sisters. The smudged form that neared the shape of a heart. And he kissed it.

Ben had held Thessa for hours, asking about her life. He'd wanted to know the answers, but mainly he'd wanted to keep her awake so he could hold her and hear her voice. When he woke, he slipped free of the covers, knowing he should wake Thessa so she could move to her room, but when he looked at her face, he couldn't disturb the vision. Morning sunlight fell across her face and the rumpled bedclothes only added a white purity to the scene. He didn't need this sight painted. He'd never forget it.

But he had to turn away, thoughts of the future tearing into him.

The water from his morning ablutions chilled his skin, but revived him. He needed to take his mind from her. But his eyes caught the mirror and he saw her reflection in the bed. His movements stilled and he was locked in a trance.

He shook himself from his imaginings and forced himself into the day, changing from a captain into a gentleman. He frowned as he held out his buff pantaloons, but he had no time to visit a tailor. The white shirt appeared more yellow than white to him and he vowed to get Broomer to take it to someone and get them to make a replacement. At least the garment would not show after he tied the cravat and dressed.

Before he added his blue waistcoat, he paused, looking at the fastenings. They matched the larger ones on his sea coat. The quality of the old buttons couldn't be topped. Cut steel by Wedgwood, they sported a cameo-styled centre with a family surrounded by the blue background. A simple family. A father, mother and child from the sea. The father carried a trident and all were the half fish, half people of his imagination. He'd had the coat and waistcoat made after he'd seen the buttons.

Still standing at the mirror, he touched the gold ring on his left hand. His father had taken pieces of their grandmother's jewellery after she'd died and had the gold melted and made into rings for his sons, and one for himself. And when Benjamin returned from the voyage after his father's death, Warrington had insisted Benjamin take the fourth ring. War said it hadn't fit his own finger. So Ben sported matching rings on each little finger.

He'd wanted the ring and yet he really hadn't. He'd been surprised it fit and felt compelled to keep it. But sometimes when he looked at it, he could remember seeing the ring on his father's hand when his father pulled him from the floor after the slap.

He didn't think his father had noticed the oil or the cut on his son's back. Ben hadn't been aware of the cut either at that moment, although even now sometimes the scent of oil would bring back the memories.

His father's face had been flushed. His lips jerked out words faster than Ben could listen and nothing Ben saw looked like the man Ben knew.

Ben didn't want to have those thoughts and his father wouldn't want to be remembered that way and yet that was the moment he'd begun to change. He'd shouted out his plans to leave again and his father had said he'd do all could to help, and later Ben had ended up as an apprentice, or so he'd thought. And really, he was thankful for it.

He'd never treat a son that way. He'd never treat Stubby that way and Stubby was as nearly a son as he would ever have.

Ben shrugged the memories aside.

He only had such a short amount of time with Thessa—he didn't want to waste any of it. He wanted to get her clothing he was sure would be waiting in her bedchamber, so he could have an excuse to wake her and touch her.

He went to the red-and-gold chamber and he saw a dress lying on the bed where Dolly had placed it, along with a pair of slippers nearby and some stockings and various dressing needs. He opened a small fabric bag. Hairpins.

Glancing over the bed which hadn't been slept in, he knew both Dolly and Broomer would be aware Thessa had shared his bed, but it didn't concern him. He gathered the garments, draping the dress over his arm.

He turned, leaving the room, and stopped cold. His brother, the Earl of Warrington, stood in the hallway, arms crossed, one shoulder leaning on the wall, lips grim and a brow raised.

'Welcome home, infant.' War moved from the wall. 'Lovely brown frock, but it doesn't go with your eyes. After you deposit it in your room, where I am sure there is a woman to wear it, will you join me for breakfast?'

Benjamin turned. 'Certainly. We have a lot to discuss.'

'I'm sure,' Warrington said, 'and I do want to see the statue.'

Ben turned quickly. He didn't really want to discuss the statue. But if he had it to do over, he still would have chosen Thessa.

He tossed the clothing on to a chair and every bit of the wondrous feeling inside him turned into a charred mass.

Chapter Seventeen

In the breakfast room, Warrington sat at the table, making a meal out of buttered bread, tea and a rasher of bacon that Ben was certain had been prepared just for him. Broomer gave Ben a nod and left, and Ben knew platters of food would arrive presently.

Ben stepped to the chair, putting his hands on the top rung, and leaned into it.

'How did you get here so quickly?' Benjamin asked. 'Broomer said his message would not leave until, um, about now?'

'Aunt Ida asked me if I would find our dear cousin William and pull him out of the taverns so I had already planned to arrive today. She thinks because I have lost a wife that I can talk some sense into him. Our sotted cousin was not, however, receptive to anything but the contents of a bottle.'

'You can understand his feelings.'

'I can.' He picked up his bread, but didn't put it into his mouth. Instead he returned it to his plate. 'If I'd lost my children at the same time, and blamed myself, I doubt I would have been able to stay alive as long as he has. I asked him if he needed anything and left. I could not stand the look in his eyes.'

Warrington looked up, eyes narrow, and spoke. 'So forgive me if I appear tired, I set out early this morning. And when I got here, I saw Broomer's sister leaving and saying she hoped the clothing fit, and that she would be pleased to take the women's trousers later. I suppose this is something I cannot mention to my wife.'

'It might be best to keep the details a bit fogged.'

'Which sister?' Warrington asked. 'The next oldest or the younger one.'

Benjamin sat, shaking his head briefly, not touching the food in front of him. 'If you knew the other two at all, you'd know it's Thessa…' He looked at his brother, and let out a breath. 'You would not believe the sight of her in the water. She swims like a mermaid.'

War put the bread down and pushed his plate back. 'Blast. You and your fish women.' He rolled back his head before looking again at his brother. 'Your nursemaid addled you with some story after she dropped you on your head and made you believe in sea creatures. Or you've caught that Gidley fellow's madness.' He raised his hands while ducking his chin.

Benjamin gave a hard blink. 'I know she's not a mermaid. She just…I've never seen a woman like her. I mean, if she were a regular woman I would have seen a woman like her. It's not like I haven't…seen a few women.'

War shook his head and put his hand to his temple. 'What of those rocks Melina wants?'

'Couldn't get them. That half-mad Stephanos said the French were taking them. The carving wasn't particularly bad, but broken, chipped—half-destroyed. And the statue's close to naked.' Benjamin shook his head. 'You would have hated it. Even in the garden as Melina planned.'

War shrugged. 'Probably met a sea captain before she posed. I heard that can cause a woman to lose her clothing.'

Benjamin raised his chin. 'I have noticed that before.'

Warrington waved Benjamin's words away and straightened in his chair. 'Broken rocks, already dismantled for travelling, and you still didn't bring them.' He waited a moment while he looked at Benjamin. 'But you're not getting *Ascalon* now. You had quite enough reward I suspect on your voyage.'

'I had to choose between leaving with Thessa or the marble.' He shrugged. 'Anyone would have done the same. Even an earl with many years of life experience.' He glanced at his brother. 'Many long years…'

'I've enough experience I could knock out your teeth.'

Benjamin interlaced his fingers, put them behind his head and scooted his chair back. 'Even toothless, I'd be a hell of a lot younger, and better looking, than you.'

'Pick a tooth.'

Ben smiled and pointed a finger at his brother's mouth. 'That one.'

Warrington shook his head and put force into his words. 'If you've bedded Thessa, you will marry her.'

Ben continued, not addressing the statement. 'I had to leave the island immediately and had to either take Thessa or the stones. Stephanos wanted her and I couldn't leave her with that man. According to Bellona, he wants to start a rebellion against the Turks, wears gaudy clothing and smells worse than a nightsoil man.'

'Gaudy clothing?'

Benjamin nodded. 'He's a pompous oaf who thinks himself a pirate because he has a ship. Melina would not want her sister marrying him.'

'Some men think they're a captain because they have a ship.'

'And some men are an earl because they're born first. Doesn't make 'em a hair smarter or more handsome than the next brothers—just older. And arrogant.'

'...and rich.'

'Blast the luck.'

War smiled, shrugging one shoulder. 'I know. I curse it all the time. You know I would have preferred you or Dane to be the eldest.'

'And we both feel the same.'

'So, have you bedded the sister?'

'I can't marry her.'

'If she has a babe you most certainly will. You'll have to stay on land long enough to discover the truth of that. The *Ascalon* is docked until I say she can leave. I'll make sure you have a living somewhere. In fact, you can pick whatever you wish…on land.'

'No,' Benjamin said, knowing his brother had half ownership in the vessel, but knowing he could sail her out of the port no matter what. 'I can't leave the men. I can't sacrifice those men's lives for…even for her.'

'Think of it. What you're doing. To her. To yourself. With the dowry she has, it won't take long for her to marry if she wishes.'

Thessa walked into the room, wearing the trousers and the shirt she'd worn for days and which had spent the night in a crumpled heap on the floor. Her hair was braided and she didn't smile at either man. Ben had never seen anyone more lovely, but then he noted the scowl in her eyes.

'Dowry?' Thessa asked. 'There is a dowry?'

Ben rose from his chair so quickly it clattered back on to the floor.

Warrington gasped. 'You did not tell her?'

Thessa paused, staring at Benjamin. 'Is it true?'

Ben watched Thessa and answered her question by a quick upward movement of his head.

'How much?' she asked.

Before Benjamin could think of calming words to put with his answer, Warrington spoke. His words were smooth. 'Enough, I think, to make even a woman who'd just killed a sea captain have appeal to an unmarried man.' He flicked a crumb from his waistcoat.

Thessa didn't take her eyes from Benjamin. Men in the tower had looked more pleasantly at their executioner. 'A small sum?'

Warrington shook his head. 'Quite a large amount.'

Benjamin spoke each word slowly. 'Thessa, I was waiting until Warrington could tell you. You will be his...ward until you...' The next word he forced into the air, ignoring the ache in his chest. 'Marry.'

Her braid twirled with the toss of her head. 'I

am not *any* man's ward. You knew of this dowry all those days we sailed and you did not tell me. You lied.'

He stepped towards her and reached out a hand. 'Let us discuss it in private.'

She jerked her hand from his. 'Do not touch me, *Englishman*.'

Bellona stepped into the room. 'Sister. The harpoon is in the room with the large fireplace. I don't remember where I saw the axe and I am sure there are knives near this room if you would like me to get them for you. Just remember…do not kill him. We are proper ladies.'

Thessa spoke to her sister, but Ben knew the words were directed at him. 'We will take our dowries and find men we can trust.'

'Thessa…' Bellona spoke, voice soothing, but the smile in her eyes was directed at Benjamin. 'I am not so particular. I will find a man here in England to marry.'

Warrington addressed Thessa, but he jerked his head towards his brother. 'He must wed you. Neither of you has a choice now. Besides, your staying will make Melina happy.'

Thessa stared at Warrington. 'You know my sister?'

He raised his chin. 'Yes. She is my countess.'

Thessa shook her head as if she didn't believe her ears. She looked at Benjamin, her mouth ready to form her next words as soon as she could find them.

Warrington turned to Bellona. 'Perhaps we can leave them alone and you and I can discuss what type of man I might search out for you.'

Bellona turned to the door 'We should leave, but do not think of finding me a husband. Right now, I would much rather collect dust than suitors.'

They left and Benjamin waited. This time the storm was in Thessa's eyes.

Chapter Eighteen

Her lids fluttered. 'Dowry? Who would do that?' Thessa asked, her voice a bit too companionable to ease him.

'A friend of your father's.'

'A woman?' The words had jagged breaths attached.

'His wife.'

'And this woman sent a purse for my marriage?'

'I believe you should talk with him about that.'

'I am asking you.' She spoke with the assuredness of a well-trained archer looking at a carefully selected target. 'And you had it with you on the ship?'

He didn't speak, but he knew she could see the answer in his face.

'And while I was in my homeland, you knew of this dowry and did not tell me.' Her words were not a question. 'And,' her voice rose in volume and speed '—you did not tell me when you...before you kissed me. Before you held me in your arms—'

Then she reverted to the language of her homeland.

At least she spoke in Greek and the servants two houses past wouldn't be able to understand. Her hands moved in the air. He had no knowledge of what the gesture she gave him meant, but he could guess.

'*You,*' Thessa's voice shook, 'should have told us of the dowry when we first met.'

'You already had marriage plans. Your decision had been made and if I were to discuss it with anyone, it would have been Stephanos. I did not know when I first met you that you did not wish to wed him.'

Her eyes flashed raven dark. '*Stephanos.* At least I suspected the secrets he carried,' she ground out. 'But yours I did not. With a dowry I could have chosen anyone on the island, or any of the nearby ones.' She stopped, her chest heaving.

Something ripped at Ben.

'I can tell the truth in two languages, but you cannot in one.' Thessa said each word slowly. The fight left her body. She had no reason to shout any more. It would not matter.

'Men come to our island,' she continued, 'and they say words and they make promises, and they are very convincing. After all, they have practised the same words to the women in their country.'

She paced two steps to the left and two steps to the right. He still did not speak.

'You must have forgotten completely about the funds when you bedded me,' she said. 'Were you planning to ask me for my hand this morning? Decide now that you had taken me to your bed that you must do the right thing, marry me, get the funds and sail away?'

Thessa controlled herself. This was not her home. She could not throw things.

'I could have...touched you—on the ship,' Ben said, taking a step to her, his hand outstretched. 'You know that.'

Her body clenched. She wished to be in the room with the harpoon. He would not step close to her then. 'Oh, but the bed was not soft enough. You waited for the soft bed. So kind.'

'You know—you have to know there was more to it than that.'

'Pillows, too? Yes, the pillows here are much better.' She lowered her chin. 'But the men are not. And I let you touch me.'

'It meant as much to me as it did to you. More, even.'

She took a breath. 'I believe you. I do. I am sure it meant more to you than it did to me. Because it meant very little to me.'

The captain's mouth firmed.

'True.' She shrugged. 'My betrothed had a ship. You have a ship. I note the ships and then I forget to pay close attention to the man at the helm. It is merely my love of the sea—and ships.'

'If I hadn't brought you, and had chosen the rocks, I could own my vessel outright. Do you remember that?'

What he said was true. But it didn't change that he hadn't told her of the funds. Or that he had taken her to bed and kissed the mark on her foot and still not told her.

Her father had spoken lies days after he'd spoken the harsh words, trying to please *Mana*. *Some day I'll take all my sweet ones to London,* he'd said. *We'll have ices and we'll go to soirées and my daughters will be the most beautiful in the* ton.

He'd put his arm around *Mana* and she'd looked at him as if he were all her dreams wound into one. Thessa had continued whatever she'd been doing. His promises meant nothing. A flower to be picked and handed to *Mana*. It would wilt, but no matter, he would have received a smile and devotion.

'And my father's wife,' Thessa continued. 'Why would she give us this? She doesn't know us.'

His eyes gave nothing away.

She waited as long as she could for him to answer, but when he didn't speak, she continued. 'Tell me the truth. Why would the woman help me? I am the offspring of her husband and another woman?'

Benjamin's voice was so low she had to attend his words carefully. 'Because you favour her own children. He was married to her first. Not second, but first. Her children are not much different in age than you and your sisters. She suspected that he had another wife, and when she saw a picture he'd painted of your sister, she knew she saw his daughter and it was not her own child. So for years, when he left England, he would go to your mother, leaving his London family.'

'He allowed her to give us funds for a dowry now—after letting us be hungry? And feeding another family?'

'It's his wife's funds. He doesn't know. He treated you the same as her children, only worse. His wife didn't like that he abandoned both families. She gave you the same dowry she would give her own daughter.'

Her father didn't know and his wife had provided a dowry. Oh, he would not like that. 'I will tell him.'

Benjamin held out his hand in a stopping motion. 'No, you will not. She asked it to be a secret. I should not have even mentioned it.'

'Well, it would not be like you to keep something from me.'

'Thessa.' He snapped the word out.

'Captain?' She opened her eyes wide.

'I am leaving soon. I will never see you again. Can we not have peace between us so the memories will not be so sharp?'

She didn't know how he thought the recollections would be any easier. 'I would so dislike your recall not being laden with soft pillows and soft beds and gentle thoughts. I assure you, though, mine will not have those things. So perhaps it is for the best that I finally learned what sort of man captains a ship. I did not learn it easily. Now I will not forget it. So I must thank you for making our parting easier.'

'I would never choose it to be like this.'

Sadness flowed from his eyes. She wanted to hold him. To have him comfort her and take away the knowledge that he'd deceived her. That he'd be leaving. But he could not hand her any kind of flowers and remove the truth.

'Is the dowry enough to…take it from another man's mind that I have lain with you?'

'Your eyes are enough for that.' He walked

around, straightened the earl's chair, kept his hands on the back of it and faced the table. 'With my brother's support, and the funds, and the fact that you will be seen as a rarity, you will not be short of suitors. You could be betrothed very soon. It's already been whispered about that Melina is of the highest lineage. It's assumed she received the good bloodlines from the Greek heritage. But you are related to a duke on your English side.'

She could tell he expected some response from his saying she was related to a peer, but she didn't care who her ancestors were on her father's side.

She looked at the way his shoulders bunched while he held the rungs and remembered that he had kissed her longing mark. She could still feel the kiss, only now it knifed into her stomach and made her very bones ache. 'I could possibly find another man who owns a ship.'

His neck tensed. 'I'm sure.'

'I will be in my room until I leave to see Melina. I will stay with her. So have a safe voyage, Captain, and do not catch any mermaids. I hear they very much like to sink ships.'

* * *

Benjamin stood at the window in his captain's cabin, staring at the broken curve of his little finger and the gold ring that adorned it.

The man he'd killed in the tavern skirmish had broken Benjamin's fingers, but Ben hadn't felt it until later. He'd expected to die before the fight ended—was fairly certain of it. He'd only cared that he inflict enough wounds on the other man to make him die later.

None of it would ever go away. Not the bent fingers. The dying face he often saw. Or the latest scar he'd added to his body. The deepest one.

Thessa was at Warrington's country home and Ben hadn't wanted to be at the town house with the big bed and empty pillow. Besides, he was needed on the ship.

Gid opened the door. 'I'm supposin' she took it real well 'bout the dowry and all.'

Benjamin nodded, eyes still on his hands.

'Women always do,' Gidley continued. 'They ruffle their feathers, but they's not so good with loadin' arms or throwin' knives. If they was serious, they'd practise.'

'Yes.'

'Well, did yer brother tell her in that real gentle way he has?'

Ben shot Gidley a glare.

'I'd say it be time to throw a few coins to buy something a lady thinks more of than a man ever will,' Gid continued. 'Hothouse flowers or something of that ilk. Don't know why things that yer spent coin on, but don't mean nothin' 'cept they're eye-catchin', can take the growl out of a woman.'

Benjamin nodded.

'Ever note how a woman can be salved with fripperies? Shiny things?' He looked around. 'Yer could throw some her way.'

Benjamin shook his head.

'Paper and ink. Yer have plenty of that. Tear a page from that book yer keep yer records in and write her something. Draw a picture of a rose.' He looked at Benjamin. 'Yer don't draw good, do yer?'

Ben just looked at Gidley.

'Poem. Yer remember any them kind that makes women swoon—all about fair hearts and yon lights in windows, and bein' noble?'

Benjamin turned to stare at the sky outside the

window, not answering Gidley. Trying to calm the turbulent seas inside himself.

He'd made a momentous mistake when he'd touched Thessa—not to mention the smaller one of not telling her about the dowry. Or perhaps it was the other way, but he didn't understand it. He braced his arm on the wall, but leaned to look at his boots.

He'd been lied to many times by women and he'd not taken it so hard. *I've never seen such a stallion. I'll never forget you, Benjamin. No, you don't look a day over twenty-five.*

And, *I love all my sons the same.*

Chapter Nineteen

Melina's voice interrupted the silence. 'Send for the captain.'

Thessa and Melina were alone in the sitting room, the cups of steaming tea untouched and the scent of the second plate of biscuits Melina had requested scenting the room. Bellona was in the gardens, playing with Warrington's children from his first marriage.

'I will not.' Thessa kept ripping the letter she'd written to Benjamin. She'd forgotten to say a few things to him that morning on the ship and she'd not been able to sleep for thinking of what she should have said.

'Then go to him. You should tell him goodbye,' Melina suggested.

'I did. And I was very kind and pleasant.'

'You shouldn't have been.'

Thessa's loud breath was loud enough to show her opinion. What the captain did to her was no different than being a pirate. Hiding the dowry. Taking her body.

She concentrated on the paper in her hands. She'd not known enough of English writing to make sure the words were right and she'd refused to ask her sister for help. And the picture she drew of the demon tearing the heart from a woman's body did not please her either.

Thessa worked to make the smallest bits of the paper that she could, imagining this was just what a man did whenever he neared a woman's heart.

'He doesn't tell the truth.' Thessa tore another piece of the paper smaller.

'The captain didn't steal the funds. They have all been given to Warrington for your dowry.' Melina broke a biscuit in half and ate part of it. 'I know he should have told you, but…'

'He kissed my foot,' Thessa confessed. 'That was a lie.'

She hated him most of all because he'd kissed her foot. The part of her that was different than any other person. Even now—thinking of it— her breasts warmed and her toes would not be still.

'Did he see the mark?' Melina asked.

'He kissed it.'

'You know what *Mana* said…' Melina leaned back, hands on her ever-increasing stomach.

'Yes. But she's not here now and I won't marry him and besides, that only counted for you and Bellona. My spot is on my foot.'

Melina touched the line of her bodice where the mark peeked out. 'Warrington kisses it every morning.'

Thessa coughed. 'Don't make me ill.'

'He is a kind husband.'

'I don't like him either.'

'What harm will it do to visit the captain on the ship? You can be pleasant to him. Ask him why he didn't tell you. Then push him over-board.'

'What harm?' She looked at her sister's girth. 'I am fortunate now if I am not already *harmed*.'

'You do not have to repeat what must have been such an unpleasant moment for you. But I promise, you can get quite used to it.'

She leaned towards her sister. 'He asked me…' she paused '…to swim with him.'

'Did you?'

'No. I am a good woman. I was betrothed. We were on Melos.'

'But you were in his bed.'

'You know what the beds are like here.'

'Sinful.'

Thessa nodded three times. 'The ones on the ship are much…safer.'

'Talk with him on the *Ascalon* then, where it is safe.'

'No. I will not go to him.'

'What if you never again meet someone like him?'

'If I am fortunate, I won't.'

'I don't like him either.'

Thessa stilled. 'You don't like him?'

'His language. He is vulgar.'

'No, he isn't.'

'Yes,' Melina insisted, crossing her arms over her stomach. 'When I was on the ship, during a storm he was dashed into the wood whilst saving the cabin boy. The captain had laudanum for pain.' She let out a sharp breath through her nose. 'He talked of Warrington's first wife and called her all sorts of names. Some I recognised. Many I didn't. I have never heard a man with such strong language.' She put her hand to her cheek.

'If he was hurting…'

'Now that I remember I can imagine why you do not wish to return to him. I gave him brandy after the laudanum. He was sotted so easily. And the rest of the time he was unkind to Warrington, trying to keep him from me. I don't like him at all.'

'Perhaps he was doing you a boon to keep Warrington from you. The earl's…so…I don't know. He grumbled all the way here in the carriage.'

Melina frowned. 'Warrington is the best of the three brothers. Warrington said Ben has always been difficult. Worse since their mother died, even though War said his brother was no angel before.'

She patted her stomach. 'The parents always coddled Ben because he was the youngest. He ran away from home and their father would bring him home time and again. Ben didn't want to go to university as he should and their father let him stay at the docks. Warrington gave him the simple task of returning with the stone woman and you see how that turned out.'

Thessa kept her voice quiet. 'Yes. He chose me over a pile of rocks. Broken ones.'

'If he'd planned properly, surely he could have brought you both back. I wanted that statue and Warrington was to pay well for it.'

'The captain did not want to leave me with Stephanos. You know how the Greek is.'

'Yes. Not a wise man at all, and he almost out-smarted the captain. I am surprised the captain was able to keep you and Bellona on the ship. It's wondrous he didn't leave you both—and the sculpture—with Stephanos.'

'I don't like you either.'

Melina smiled. 'I can have the carriage ready if you wish to leave my home.'

'I will do that because I do not wish to listen to your nonsense.' She stood, looked at the two biscuit plates beside her sister and took the empty one. She held the plate just lower than the edge of the table and scooped the torn pieces of paper into it.

She didn't say anything as she tried to get every last scrap of paper.

Melina made a ticking noise with her tongue. 'I do understand why you are upset. It is a shame to let the captain get away with so much. I thought him a most irritating man.'

Thessa stood straight and gripped the plate in both hands. 'I know why you are saying this. I know what you are doing and I am still angry at you for it. Only because I am a guest in your house am I not shouting at you.' She paused. 'Never—ever—talk badly about the captain.'

When she left the room, she held the plate very carefully so the torn paper would not fly about the room.

Chapter Twenty

Thessa had her new reticule on her wrist and her new half boots which were quite fashionable, but felt like what she imagined a tight saddle would feel on a horse who'd eaten too much. The doeskin gloves she wore reached to her capped sleeves and she particularly liked the large ring she wore over the gloves.

The maid had insisted to add some powder on her face and a bit of smudge at her eyes, which Bellona claimed made Thessa look entirely unlike herself and almost appealing.

Thessa walked up the plank connecting the ship to the dock. Gidley saw her and met her. His eyes widened and he took in the bonnet with blue ribbons fluttering in the wind. Her dress matched perfectly and the bodice was exactly as one would wish when visiting a man who had not been truthful.

'Miss Thessa?' Gidley asked, eyes wide.

'Where is the captain?'

'He be in his cabin. Plannin' our journey.' Gidley's sigh could have puffed the sails had they been unfurled. 'After spendin' his mornin' hours tryin' to think of ways to tell yer of his everlastin' sorrow for one sad misstep.' He put his hand to his heart. 'He's mournful. I near had to wipe the tears from his eyes.'

'I can't sink the ship unless someone leaves a cannon lying about so you do not have to worry.'

Gidley stiffened his spine. 'I know yer can't, but I thought Capt'n might need some help with his flowery words. The lad's never had to use 'em before and he's not good at sayin' he's wrong.' His eyes narrowed. 'Yer can trust I know what I'm talkin' about on that.'

'I don't need any sweet words.'

She turned to the captain's cabin, but just at the door her feet stopped, then she took a stroll around the deck and, as each crewman took her in, she smiled. She saw the confused stares, heard the whispers in her wake and held her head even higher as the men speculated on whether she truly was that woman who'd just sailed with them.

Then she went to the captain's cabin and opened the door. He looked up from the desk, eyes a bit smudged underneath—even without a maid's help. The room was dark and she knew the sun was bright behind her. His glance narrowed and his head tilted as he tried to place her.

She stepped inside and used her strength to shut the door.

One side of his mouth turned up. 'Thessa.'

'I wrote you a letter,' she said. 'And I brought it to you.' She reached into the reticule and pulled out the scraps, letting them flutter over his desk. 'I don't write well, but you can understand that, I'm sure.'

He examined the top of his desk as he put down his pen. 'I'm not having any trouble at all reading it.'

'Do you have anything to say?'

'I should beg your pardon, but I don't regret what I did.'

She reached back into her purse, pulled out

more paper and tossed it towards his face. 'That is the second page.' Scraps littered his hair.

He blew a puff of paper from his lips and dusted across his head, removing a few scraps. 'Is there a page three?'

She reached in and, with a flick of her wrist, more paper flew into the air.

'I don't know who you are in that clothing,' he said to her. 'But I love you anyway.'

'It is too late. I came to tell you again to have a safe trip. I hope you find a thousand mermaids—kind ones. That does not mean I have forgiven you. And I don't like your brother—he frowns until my sister walks into the room—then they make me seasick to watch them. And I hate your paintings.'

He flicked a piece of the letter from the desk. 'Is there anything else you hate?'

'I am not fond of either of my sisters right now. And I am not fond of you.'

'But you do not hate me?'

'No.' She shrugged. 'In the letter it says I hate you so if you read that, I changed my mind in the carriage ride. It is a long journey. I had time to think.'

'I am pleased you do not hate me.' He stood.

'And I do not care that you love me because—' She touched her bonnet, adjusting it. 'I can tell in your face it changes nothing.'

His sea-blue eyes took her in. 'It doesn't change that I'm sailing and you are staying.'

She took her reticule, turned it up and dumped the remaining fragments on his desk. 'This is the next letter. It says the same as the first, though.'

He leaned across the desk, took her face in his hands and gave her the smallest kiss on her lips. 'I thank you for again giving me a chance to tell you I love you, and for not saying you hate me.'

She dropped the reticule and clasped both his wrists as he pulled away. 'You do not say you love me and then show that it means nothing to you. I am worth much more than that. And you are the one who misled me.'

His hands circled hers and he held her fingers, letting their grasps fall to just above the desk. 'Thessa. I don't know what I would have done that morning on Melos concerning the dowry if I had collected the statue. Stephanos might have been right. I wondered after we sailed if I'd intended to take you with us when we left. I'm not certain. It would have been wrong, but I already knew I wanted you with us. I'm no better than Stephanos. I told Gid we'd get the stone, and before I went to the cabin that night I told him we weren't going to sail immediately, but that he should be ready to leave quickly at any time. I could not abandon you and Bellona.' He put his eyes down. 'Even if, perhaps, you did not want to leave.'

'You wouldn't have forced me to marry you as Stephanos did. That I know. You have not tried to persuade me one—one time to marry you. You have not even asked nicely.'

'No.'

'If I told you I was going to have a child, would it matter?'

His shoulders sagged a bit, but he looked at her. 'You simply cannot know. And it will not matter in that I will still sail if you are having a child. We will just have to wed first and I will get a special licence and speak the words for you if I have to. My brother will certainly let you live in the town house, or with the dowry you can live wherever you wish. I will see that you always have your needs cared for and the child will be cared for. But I cannot risk your life at sea.'

'That is not as endearing as the proposal I had from a sailor who described how I could earn his coins. Gid was right in that you do not know sweet words.'

'You have been discussing this with him?'

'Not truly. But I can see I should have. Perhaps he could have taught you some of his grace.'

He didn't release her hands as he walked around the desk. When he got to her side, he pulled her fist up and first kissed one hand and then the other.

'The sea is too dangerous. Especially for a woman who should be protected and cherished.'

'Yes, I should be cherished,' she said. 'But what of you? Is that not true?'

'The *Ascalon* cherishes me.'

'She's wooden.'

'I am fine with that.'

'I am not.'

'Thessa. Gidley has been like a father to me. The cook worries over us. Stubby is near a son to me. They are my life. They have no other family, and if the men on this ship had other family they could have stayed with—they would not be here. They need me.'

She let his words flow through her body. She heard them—truly heard them. 'You do not feel close to your brothers.'

His chest moved in and out. 'To be with Warrington on the last voyage was pleasant, but we were nearly strangers. I had not been near him for more than a few days every year or so since I…well, most of my life. He was at school; I was in the nursery. He was in London; I was in the country. Or I was in London and he was in the country. I have seen Dane less, I suppose. At our father's funeral, we were all three in the same room, and my sister. But looking back I am not sure if I remember another time that happened except right after my mother died.'

'You hardly know them.' She saw the truth in his face. He didn't have to say it, but she wanted to be certain.

'In my nursery, sometimes when I was to be asleep, I would sneak into the hallway and I would hear them laughing and talking in the sitting room. I was too young to join them. I could not sit still.'

He shrugged his words away, but continued. 'I would look out the window and see Dane, War and my father riding, and sometimes my mother and sister, but I never finished my lessons correctly and I was not allowed to join them until I did. I never, ever completed the lessons correctly. The stable master taught me to ride. Mother was most likely sick then. I can't remember.'

Thessa had slept in the same room with her sisters all of her life. Other than when she swam, hardly a one of them had been further away than a shout. She could have turned her head at any time during most of her life and seen a sister or her mother. 'I wish you could have grown up with a family.'

He shook his head. 'My men need me. If I had close ties on land, the men would have to sail on other ships and other ships are not like mine.' He smiled. 'I'm a damn good captain and we are all a part of the ship.' He gave an apologetic grin. 'Sometimes I do get a bad sailor aboard, like the one you took the knife to, but they leave at the next port.'

'My sisters and I...' She didn't look at his face. 'It is almost as if we were born on the same day and the same year. I didn't realise how much we needed each other until Melina left. Our lives without her... A part of us had sailed away. You should have that closeness.'

'I have that. Here. I have been sailing with Gid and most of the other men for the past ten years. And then we found Stubby living where his mother worked, in a brothel, and she wanted him to have something more. He chattered so much at first and I kept telling him to *Stubble it*, and then we were calling him that and one day we realised none of us could remember his name.' He shook his head. 'That was unforgivable, but I've told him he can pick whatever name he wants and he said he would have Forrester as his surname, same as mine, and I agreed.'

'You can't leave them.' She said the words as a statement, not a question.

'No. It was too hard to find them. And I could not live if the ship sank and they died. I would feel it is my fault for leaving them.'

'You would give up me for them?'

'A man should do the right thing. And he does not leave his family to fend for themselves.'

Chapter Twenty-One

Something tickled Thessa's nose and she opened her eyes. The covers were pulled up to her shoulders and she was naked except for the half boots and stockings. The captain had claimed there just wasn't time after she'd thrown her body into his arms. But when he'd said those words about family…

Ben was lying beside her and she half lay across him, his arm the only thing keeping her in the bunk. His body was not a bad pillow, though it might not be possible to sleep in such a way. He held a lock of her hair in his fingertips and was trailing it over her face.

'Did I ever tell you I like pointy noses?' he asked.

'What does that have to do with me?'

'Your nose. It's a fine one.' His leg rubbed along her stocking. 'But I don't like your boots. Not at all. If there were time I would like a miniature painted of your feet to take with me. With the longing mark. But there's no time.'

'Ben...'

He clasped both arms tight around her, holding her. She could feel his heart beating and the roughness of his skin against hers.

'I saw a man die once,' she said, holding him as close as she could. 'One moment we were all laughing, and then someone screamed out and I ran towards the noise. I didn't know why I ran there, but we all did. And my uncle lay on the ground bleeding and then he was dead. My aunt was crying and crying. Stephanos turned and slit the throat of the man who had killed my uncle. I could do nothing but watch in those moments. I could not move. Both men were buried quickly and my aunt married again soon, and it was as if my mother's brother had never lived. Bellona and Melina didn't see it.' She took in a deep breath. 'I'm thankful.'

'You shouldn't have seen it.'

'I tried not to think of it. And when the man

reached for Bellona on your ship, I was not inside my own body.' She'd meant the man no harm, but yet she'd had a knife in her hand just as Stephanos did. 'When I thought back later, I was sick. I knew the blood I would have felt. I had seen it before. I didn't care.'

He kissed her forehead. 'I know. At sea. In ports. It's not unheard of to be attacked. That is why we have the extra guns. Because we have been attacked. Because *Ascalon* is not as big as most and they feel it will be simple to take her and her goods. Stephanos was not my first pirate and I don't think he'll be the last. I can't even think of you going with us. Danger comes from below, above and the sides.'

'Benjamin, I don't want you to die.'

'Sweet. I would like to stay alive. But you can't wait on me. It isn't fair to you and I can't return thinking you'll be there and find you with someone else. You have to have a family. I don't want you to watch your sisters have their children whilst you are looking towards the sea.'

'Ben, I might love you for ever.'

'I will love you twice as long. But you have

the family you were born with and you will have more. You'll be safe with them and loved.'

'I'll never let you see my feet again,' she said, hugging him with all her strength.

But the words were a lie. Before the next morning, he'd kissed her toes, and the little heart again, and helped her dress and fix the pins in her hair, and he'd helped her with the half boots. And then he helped her get a carriage to leave.

Thessa stood at the fireplace in the town house, endlessly running her hand over the carved leaves in the mantel.

The door opened and closed in the distance. The rumble of voices told her that Warrington and Melina had arrived. Broomer had arranged to send for them while Dolly had cooked as if her very happiness depended on Thessa enjoying her meals.

Having servants was better than she expected. Dolly and Broomer didn't feel like staff, but more like two people who only cared that everything be done to make her happy.

Melina walked into the room and took Thessa

in her arms. 'We've come to take you back to Whitegate,' Melina said, hugging her sister.

Thessa ended the moment by pushing away. She'd spent many hours thinking while she was in the town house. 'You planned for Bellona and me to come to England, didn't you? When you sent the ship?'

'Of course I'd hoped.' Melina stepped back, the fabric of her dress tight and her corset long since discarded to make way for her changing form. 'I wanted my babe to have aunts nearby and I wanted the older two children to get to know my sisters. And I knew you would like London once you arrived. Englishmen,' her eyes softened as she looked at her husband '—are not like our father.'

'Why did you not send a message asking?' Thessa said.

'Asking means you are willing to accept an answer that you might not like. I did ask Warrington's brother to get you to England if he could at all. But…' she frowned '…he said the choice had to be yours. With the dowry you could have a comfortable life and I could visit you as soon as the babe was old enough for us to leave it for the journey.'

Bellona walked in, lagging behind the others, one glove on and the other in her hand. 'I am so pleased we came to London.' She twirled around. 'This dress is the same colour green that the archery club uses and I have a bow and arrow now.'

'I hope it will be safer than fencing,' Melina said. 'You must never touch that sword again near the children. And you must promise not to get killed in front of them.'

She shuddered. 'It was because of that beast of a horse called Nero. I will never ride him again. He is a monster with four legs. And he jumps like a rabbit.'

Warrington's voice rumbled into the room. 'Perhaps if you hadn't been waving a sword about and nearly took off his ear.'

Bellona removed her remaining glove and glanced askance at Warrington. 'Jacob did not see it properly. Nero turned his head suddenly.'

'I'm sure,' he said and turned, waving an arm

for the ladies to sit. 'Now let us get settled and decide how you and Thessa will proceed with your futures.'

Benjamin sat at his desk on the *Ascalon*, hurting from his forehead to his boots, and yet, he felt numb. It would be less than an hour before they sailed. He'd visited his sister and their batty aunt the night before and taken his leave. Warrington and Dane had arrived to wish him well and had left a few hours earlier.

For a moment, Benjamin considered delaying his departure and asking Thessa to marry him, but he could not. A woman deserved a husband if she married, not a memory. Two to three years was too long to wonder if someone still lived.

And he would be at sea, wondering if they'd had a child. Claws of apprehension raked through him. And if they married and she didn't conceive in the short time he was in England, then he could be robbing her of the chance to have a child. A marriage without either a husband or children was nothing but wasted words on paper. Wasted vows.

And how could he keep his mind in the direction he needed for his ship to stay afloat and his men alive if he could not take his mind from concern for her? Men often returned from sea to find grass grown over a loved one's grave.

Nor could he truly give her a place to live. He didn't even own the town house outright, but in union with his brothers.

He loved his life, but now he wished he'd been content to live in England as Dane and Warrington did. He'd left his family behind the first time, and when he returned it was as if they'd not even noticed him gone.

Gid opened the cabin door and walked in, the small box in his hands. He put it on the table, to the side of Benjamin's papers. 'He won't take 'em. Says he took a belly ache and don't want no food might make it worse. Then he says our new physician don't even know a belly ache from an earache, and he be wonderin' if that Broomer could 'ave found a man what didn't smell like camphor and didn't have so much hair stickin' out his nose.'

'Broomer is adept at finding good seamen for us.'

'The quartermaster said the other one Broomer sent didn't even know to bring his own plate and cup.'

'Leave it be, Gid.'

Benjamin didn't look up, still scribbling on a page he'd torn from his journal, thankful Gid couldn't read the list he couldn't seem to complete without writing Thessa's name. She was what he wanted most, not barrels of peas. 'Send Stubby to me.'

Gid stood, just staring ahead, lips in a thin line.

'Get Stub. Now.' Benjamin kept the pen moving.

Gidley stepped to leave. 'Whatever the Capt'n wants. I am just here to do your commands.'

Benjamin's hand stilled. He lowered his voice. 'I didn't mean to hurt anyone's feelings.'

Gid didn't move from the doorway and didn't turn back. 'Yer near shouted my ears deaf and say one little hard word to the boy and then yer send...' His voice rose to a shrillness best left to adolescent lads. He turned, his forefinger thumping his own chest. He faced Benjamin. 'Yer send *me* to get the little critter treats.'

'Didn't mean to shout at you so, Gid.' Benjamin nudged the box to the edge of the table without looking up. He didn't want the pain on his face to be obvious to Gid. 'You can have the treats.'

'No.' Gid hurled the word out and his nose went up. 'Them is not to my taste. They is the kind *Stubby* likes.'

Gid left and Benjamin restrained himself from throwing the box at the wall.

Stubby walked in so fast Benjamin knew he'd been just outside the door and brushed past Gid on the way in.

'I made up my mind. I won't be able to sail with you again, Captain. Ain't no ladies on this ship no more and I be thinking it's time for me to find me work on land. My talents is not appreciated here.' His jaw worked sideways.

'Stubby,' Benjamin put down the pen. 'I did not mean to hurt your feelings.'

'You did not hurt my feelin's, Cap'n Benjamin. I…' he sniffed '…be tough as leather.' He sniffed again.

Benjamin looked at the cabin boy's trembling

lips. Blast. If Stub cried they'd both be blubbering like little chits.

Benjamin swallowed. 'I just wanted to tell you that I want you to do the cabin-boy duties because no one could ever do them as well as you, but I'm thinking I...' He stood, reached to his seaman's chest and pulled out the spyglass still wrapped in the shopkeeper's paper. 'You have sharp eyes and I'm thinking you might need a spyglass to help us look for pirates, so I wanted to give you this if you stay on.'

Now Stubby's lip trembled more. He raised his hand, fingers outstretched, and then stopped movement. Benjamin put the package down on the table and turned his back.

He heard scrabbling noises, turned around and saw Stub holding the box of confectionaries and the spyglass, eyes downcast.

Slowly the lad put the items down. 'Capt'n. I be honoured beyond honour to sail with you, but I been thinkin' and thinkin' a lot, and not just today, and I decided that I be leavin' the ship. That anchor's about to be lifted and I...I'm not wantin' to leave London.'

Ben could hardly make his mouth work to

speak. 'You can't…. You're like…you are my family.'

Stubby nodded. 'But I be missin' my ma. And I be thinkin' I'd like to know if I can find her again.' He looked at Benjamin. 'And I be listenin' to all them men talk about the apple dumplin's and tarts they leave behind and I be thinkin' I…' His cheeks reddened. 'I think I'm plannin' to like confectionaries a lot.'

Benjamin paused. He didn't want Stubby leaving, but perhaps the boy had a point. Ben knew what it was like to feel abandoned by his mother.

When she was ill and would never leave her bed again, she'd called his brothers into the room. She'd spoken her last words to them. And he'd waited in his bedchamber for his turn to speak with her, not really knowing what was happening, but wanting to see her, and she'd never sent for him. She'd never asked for him to come to her side. He told himself she'd meant to, and hadn't had the chance, but he didn't believe it. She could have called him in with Warrington and Dane.

The next day, servants were covering all the mirrors in the house. No one told him what had happened, but he knew quite well when he saw the first shrouded mirror.

He didn't want Stubby to lose his mother some day and feel he never had the chance to know her. The lad could already have brothers he didn't know about. Brothers who would return home and his mother would reach out to muss their hair and tell them how pleased she was to see them again.

Stubby's mother had told Benjamin she didn't know what she was going to do with the boy. The same words he'd heard about himself from his own mother's lips.

Convincing the lightskirt to let her son sail hadn't been difficult. Relief had shown in her eyes and Stubby's belongings had been gathered before Benjamin had a chance to change his mind.

He would *never* have changed his mind.

'Broomer told me your mother is still in London,' Ben said to the lad. 'He can take you to visit her. He'll see to your needs and he'll find work for you at Warrington's town house. Tell him to treat you as my son.'

Stubby raised his eyes. 'I be thankin' you,

Capt'n.' He smiled. 'I be wantin' to work on the docks. Some day I might sail with you again.'

'I wish you all the good fortune in the world. And take the confectionaries and spyglass. You might need the eyepiece later.'

Stubby's lips firmed and he took them both. 'I be keeping the spyglass for ever, Capt'n, and I'll share the other with Gid before I leave. He's goin' to miss me.'

'Yes.'

Benjamin flopped back in the chair, but then moved forward, putting his elbows on the table. He steepled his hands and put his temple to them.

What he wouldn't give to speak with his father. And yet he'd spent so little time with the man. He tried to pull the image of the older man's face into his mind, but couldn't. He could remember his father's portrait—the one of him as a young man. Even with the feeling of anger gone, he still couldn't remember the man as clearly as he wished.

Gid's head poked in the door. 'And yer give the cabin boy yer new spyglass.' Gid just stood there and blast if his bottom lip didn't tremble, too. 'And he just told me he's leavin'. If that don't cause me to turn into a waterin' pot, nothing will. Don't know how we'll make it without the little fellow.'

Ben jerked his brows up in a quick acknowledgement.

'Since everyone's back, we'll leave with the tide,' Benjamin said. 'We don't want to give Stubby a chance to change his mind.'

'Yer doin' the right thing, Capt'n.' He took off his cap and used it to wipe his eyes. 'The boy don't need to be washed overboard. Yer givin' him a chance to ruin his life right proper instead of bein' swept out to sea like the rest of us.'

'You should have had your own ship, Gid.'

He shook his head. 'No. Swore I'd never take on that chore. When storms hit, I start seeing death and worryin' over my ever' thought. Can't think if I don't have someone to give me a answer if my mind gets concerned. Couldn't keep a journal. Don't like snarlin' at the men as much as yer do.' He pulled at the sides of his cap as if he could put it in shape. His eyes stayed on the cloth. "Sides, seein' you grow into a captain is better'n bein' one myself.'

He took a deep breath. 'Yer just like I would

have wanted in a boy of my own.' Then he raised his eyes and grinned at Ben, even though his eyes were moist. 'Worthless as they come.'

Ben looked at Gid. 'I learned from the master.'

Gid nodded. 'Have to agree.'

Gid turned and left the room, and Ben followed. In what seemed to be the mix of a lifetime and just a second, he gave Stubby a gentle shove from the ship and watched as the ship left the docks behind.

The sea called him, but for the first time, he regretted his choices in life. And he knew he was no longer the infant son.

The jagged edges he had inside were scars only a man could have.

Chapter Twenty-Two

Thessa touched the back of her neck, feeling the blunt ends of her hair. The straggling locks tickled, poking from her cap. Broomer should never again be let near a pair of scissors. As soon as she'd agreed he could cut her hair, he'd pulled out rickety shears and she'd not had time to open her mouth to stop him. She'd nearly cried. Never again.

But the sailors had all seen her dressed in trousers. If she'd only tucked her hair under a cap, they might have recognised her.

She gave a tug to the waistcoat and ran her fingers over the roughened texture, pleased with the contrast of the coarseness, and the softness of the shirt and crisp trousers. Broomer's sister had fitted her well and these clothes were so different than the cast-offs she'd worn on the first voyage. She almost looked like a gentleman. Even the scrap of a cap was her own.

The boots were feeling much better now. The sailors often went barefoot at sea, making it easier to feel the ropes under their feet when they climbed, but she'd insisted she wear the boots with the new clothing. She had fond memories of the footwear.

Ducking her head, she walked past Gidley as he swore at one of the other men. Without even looking her way, he commanded, 'Take in a sail.'

She hardly knew what to do, but she watched one of the other seamen and followed his lead. She inhaled when the breeze brushed her cheeks—and for the first time ever out of the water, she felt the same freedom as she did when she swam.

She gripped the rope, pulling, when something slammed into her shoulder. She'd stepped into another sailor without realising it. Hands still on the ropes, she stumbled to keep her footing. 'Watch yourself,' the sailor at her elbow said, his voice a harsh rasp.

Planting her feet firm, she concentrated on her

duties, but a wisp of her thoughts kept watching for the captain.

She heard him before she saw him, the tight orders he gave little more than snaps in the wind, but easily heard from the bow to the stern.

And Thessa couldn't help herself, her eyes turned to him, and she could not move. Her whole body unfurled with warmth, spreading from the deepest part inside of her to heat the rope she held and to warm her to her boots.

'Holy—' His words were said with the same strength as his orders, yet with more emotion than could be packed into trinkets in a thousand sea trunks. Every man on the ship stopped moving. The captain's eyes locked on her face.

When she blinked, she became aware that all the sailors had followed the captain's gaze and were staring at her.

'Who brought her on board?' the captain shouted, voice grinding.

'Her?' Gidley asked, eyes squinting.

'Thessa.' Benjamin took one step forward. 'Thessa.'

'Well, yer could slap me with an anchor.' Gid stared and his cheeks plumped into a smile.

'That man what yer brother's servant had me hire don't look like no Albert after all.'

'No. She does not look like an Albert. She never did look like an Albert, and...' Benjamin put his palm out flat. '...how? How could you not see that?'

'Never looked real close as yer have, I s'pose. 'Cept she does have that pointy little nose.' Gid smiled at her and tugged his cap. 'Welcome back, miss.'

'Gid. Take over.' He spoke softly, keeping his eyes on her. 'And you, Albert, will have a word with me in my cabin.'

'It is the captain's cabin, is it not?' she asked, meeting his eyes and keeping her feet still.

'Yes.'

'And you own half the ship, do you not?'

'Yes.'

'Then I suppose I will take part of the cabin as I own the other half.' She dropped the rope and turned to his quarters. 'Your brother gave me his share of *Ascalon* in exchange for my dowry.' She shrugged. 'I think it a good investment.' She shrugged. 'Assuming I keep the captain.'

By the time she'd moved a step, he was at her

side. 'You will be returning to England,' he said. 'I don't care if you own all of the seas.'

When the door closed behind him, she took her cap off and put it on a peg, then dusted the hat a bit.

'Your brother. I might like him—eventually.' She slowly perused the room, noting the empty spot where the little artwork of a mermaid was once nailed.

She smiled. 'He did not even make me agree not to replace the captain.'

'You, however, will not be allowed to sail with the ship.'

She walked over and picked up the compass, examined it and put in back in place, then she looked at him and shook her head.

'You have to go back, Thessa.' His words were quiet. Unwavering.

She saw the small mirror affixed to the wall, stepped in front of it and for a moment didn't recognise herself. She'd expected the sight of her mop of hair, but had forgotten about the smudges of soot from the fireplace they'd added to increase her brows. How the captain recognised her, she had no idea. She brushed at the smudges of blackness where they'd tried to give her a moustache, but she only smeared the markings.

'It's a two-year voyage—at least.' He put his hands behind his back, but otherwise he stood perfectly still.

'I am not used to a gentle life.' She examined her now sooty fingertips. 'I realised when I talked to you that I have seen two men killed, have been chased by a pirate and bedded a sea captain. I am not the gentle miss I thought myself.' She smiled. 'I also know gestures I learned from the men on Melos.'

'Could you not talk my brother out of a decent cap?' Benjamin asked, his voice softening.

She again looked in the mirror. 'I like the one I found. A boy was selling them and I asked your brother to stop the carriage and he purchased it for me. He said I might need it for cold weather because he didn't want my head any more muddled. He said I am already as daft as a certain captain he knows.'

'You are.'

'Careful,' she cautioned. 'You would not want to anger me. I might sink the ship.'

He shrugged. 'Thessa. You are daft.'

'I know. Your brother told me. My sister Melina told me. And Bellona asked if she could come with us. That convinced me I was not thinking as other people do. But Warrington wished me well and told Melina you could take care of me, not that it is needed.'

'He did?'

'Yes.'

'So he gave you half the ship.'

'For my dowry.' She took a step forward and brushed a lock of Benjamin's hair behind his ear. 'I suppose you can choose whether you wish to stay as captain or not. But you cannot tell me not to sail on my own ship.'

'It doesn't matter, Thessa.' He took her fingers from his hair and held them. 'I can't risk your life. You will not sail with us. No person in a right mind would sail—and to a man this crew would agree with you. It's like Newgate without the comforts or chance of escape. I started when I was too young to understand death. I was fortunate just to stay alive.' His hand tensed into a grasp. 'I don't care if you truly did own every stick of this ship, I will be depositing you at the first harbour we see. This ship is no place for you.'

'Then Gidley will have to sail her because I will relieve you of your command.'

'You cannot.'

She could feel every inch of him without moving. 'You cannot leave me at a harbour.'

'Gidley will leave with you and transport you back to London.'

She grimaced and didn't know if he moved or she did, but there was no longer any space between them.

'No.' She put arms around him and rested her face on his shoulder, feeling the texture of skin roughened by the elements, and softness, created for her touch. 'If I cannot relieve you of command, then you cannot remove me from the ship.'

His tone changed, almost pleading. He pushed her away. 'Thessa... You can't. You're going back where you'll be safe if I have to put you in the longboat and row you there myself.'

Her fingers latched around his waist. 'I'm not leaving you. You might find a mermaid and need me to send her on her way. I will.'

He grasped her hips, pulling her close. She felt her knees weaken, but her heart beat even stronger.

'Thessa…please…'

'If you're asking me to stay, I agree.'

'I'm asking you to leave.'

'Not unless you leave with me.'

'You can't.'

'Captain Benjamin. I have caught you.' She tiptoed, putting her lips closer to his. 'You just have not accepted it yet.'

His head bent so close she could feel his breath. His hands tightened, pulling her into him. 'You have caught me, or *I* have caught you?'

'Do you really wish, Captain, to toss me back?' She brushed her lips against his, feeling the tingle.

His voice roughened. 'I will deposit you at the *second* harbour we reach.'

She kissed him again, letting her lips linger, and she only pulled back enough to speak. 'Not even the third.'

Another kiss. Another explosion of sensations.

'The tenth?' he asked against her lips.

She shook her head slightly.

'Well,' he whispered, 'we will decide upon a number we can agree on eventually.'

She felt herself laugh on the inside, but knew she didn't make a sound.

His lips were at her cheek, her ear and his face pressed against hers. 'Do you truly think you can live on a ship, Thessa? Because as soon as this voyage is over you will not sail on a second one.'

'Perhaps I won't sail again. Perhaps I will,' she said. 'I am at home here now more than anywhere else. More than on Melos. This is closer to the sea. And to you. Your being here makes it a home for me.'

'Can a mermaid marry a sea captain?'

'I do not know.'

'We can find out at the first harbour we reach,' he said. 'If you would like to.'

'Perhaps...I mentioned to your brother that I might wish to marry you. He is not happy because away from England, he is not sure if it will be a proper marriage unless we marry by the laws. But my sisters and I have decided it is proper enough for us.'

'Then I will see how persuasive I can be.' The

last words were spoken against her lips, and he only left her enough strength to say yes.

Two-and-a-half years later

Thessa locked herself in the cabin with her son, Albert, and put him on his pallet on the floor. She'd hardly seen him in days and he needed a nap.

'Thessa,' Ben rapped on the door. 'Let me in.'

She expelled a breath and unlatched the lock she'd had put on the door so the baby couldn't get out without her knowing. Benjamin walked in and put his arm around her. 'You can't blame them for being attached to Albert. To Gid, he is a grandson. To the others, he's like a son.'

'But they are always taking him and walking him, and playing with him. I do not know why you let them shirk their duties so.'

'They do their work. I can't blame them for being fond of Albert.' He looked at his son, pleased that Albert had inherited the dark eyes of his mother.

'I am quite fond of him, too.' Thessa buried herself in her husband's arms. 'But when we get to London, I am wondering if we should look for a bigger ship.'

Ben held her close. 'I think we should stay with the *Ascalon*. If we take on a larger ship, we'll need to double our crew. And I hardly have enough time to spend with my family as it is.'

But no matter how little time he had, if they docked in a place where the water was clear and he could find a secluded place to swim with Thessa, he always did. Those moments were too precious to miss.

He rocked Thessa in his arms, still amazed she'd never had more than a few moments of seasickness at the beginning, and no illness during the whole of her…he could not exactly say confinement, as they'd all been confined together in some way of every day. The only problem had been that if he'd so much as sniffed wrong to either her or Gidley, he would see her whispering to Gidley and giving terse little snaps of her shoulders and shakes of her head, and glaring his direction while she tried to look as if she couldn't see him.

And occasionally she called him Captain and

if she pretended she couldn't see him for too long a time he called her Captain Thessa.

And his son—he feared the boy would have to learn to walk twice. Once on the ship with ease and then on unmoving ground.

Albert—the boy was too young to swim, but at the last port Thessa had put him in the water and he'd moved like a fish. He swam better than he walked. Thessa claimed her mother had done the same with all her daughters.

And his son had a little mark on his shoulder. Thessa called it another splash of mud. Ben kept jesting with her that it was a trident.

* * * * *

MILLS & BOON®

Why shop at millsandboon.co.uk?

Each year, thousands of romance readers find their perfect read at millsandboon.co.uk. That's because we're passionate about bringing you the very best romantic fiction. Here are some of the advantages of shopping at www.millsandboon.co.uk:

* **Get new books first**—you'll be able to buy your favourite books one month before they hit the shops

* **Get exclusive discounts**—you'll also be able to buy our specially created monthly collections, with up to 50% off the RRP

* **Find your favourite authors**—latest news, interviews and new releases for all your favourite authors and series on our website, plus ideas for what to try next

* **Join in**—once you've bought your favourite books, don't forget to register with us to rate, review and join in the discussions

Visit **www.millsandboon.co.uk**
for all this and more today!